THE UNSUNG SONG OF A WREN

Erin Forget

AOS Publishing, 2025

Copyright © 2025

Erin Forget

All rights reserved under International

and Pan-American copyright conventions

ISBN: 978-1-998662-44-9

Cover Artist: Meredith Lindsay

Visit AOS Publishing's website:

www.aospublishing.com

For the handsome coffee agent who made me a latte every morning while I wrote these words

Chapter 1

2023

The stench of wasted youth fills her Honda Civic. Greasy fries and burgers remind her of high school, even if she graduated almost eighteen years ago. "I fuckin' hate it when they request that the food be hand delivered," she complains to herself. Ninety-nine-point-nine percent of the time customers prefer the food to be left at the door with a text notifying them that their meal has arrived—no human interaction required. But judging by the chipped paint on the stucco walls and half-lit neon vacancy sign of the motel, food left unattended would most definitely get snatched by the sticky fingers of some malnourished and shifty tenant.

She eyes the door with the tarnished chrome number seven screwed into the faded red façade and raises a brow. It's rare for someone from these parts to have a credit card to order food from Door Dash, let alone twenty-five bucks to spend on a single burger and fries from a fair trade, organic bougie eatery. However, the idea that the restaurant this person ordered from serves healthier food is pure marketing garbage, as these fries will clog your arteries just the same as the ones from Rotten Ronnie's. The assault on her nostrils never seems to fade in spite of delivering food for every damn restaurant in town.

She rolls down her windows to air out the stink. The air

tingles with a crispness she's not yet ready or dressed for. She's not worried about leaving the windows down as she delivers the food. Her car is creeping in on fourteen years old and it's a five-speed. Today's thieves are too lazy to learn manual. Plus, shifting from first to second takes skill, as one millimeter to the right makes the gears screech like a wounded cat and would make any unsuspecting driver jump out of their skin and stall the engine.

Parked as close to unit seven as possible, minding the out-of-place shiny black BMW, she secures a black latex glove over her palm. Someone is having an affair, she thinks as she exits her car, the rolled-up rim of the bag gripped by her latex-clad fingers. Small yellow leaves pepper the parking lot. The smell of summer is gone.

With her free hand, she raps two swift knocks on door number seven and looks around, including over her shoulder. Force of habit. No one is watching.

A slender woman with tight black curls opens the door and tightens the knit belt of her long burgundy sweater while eyeing the delivery person through a narrow gaze. "You're Birdie?" Her dark eyes are sunken, like sleep has eluded her for the past decade, aging her brown complexion.

The name Birdie never sounds right, but it doesn't matter what strangers call her. It was the only name she could think of when she didn't want to use her real name. She places the woman around the same age as herself. And the thought crosses her mind that her own experiences have aged her past her years as well. "Yep, here's your food. *Bon appétit.*" She extends her hand with the bag containing one burger and a side of shoestring fries. No smile required.

The stranger keeps her eyes on her and reaches for the bag. The woman's finger grazes her knuckle.

She doesn't flinch. The gloves protect her skin. A side effect of living through a pandemic: wearing latex gloves everywhere you go doesn't seem out of the ordinary. If anything, she blends in better than she once did.

"Do you ever go by the name Wren?" The woman grabs on to the door with her free hand and transfers her weight to her other leg.

Her fingers tingle with numbness. She hasn't heard that name in quite some time. No one's called her Wren since she dropped out of police college almost fifteen years ago. All she can do is stand there and let the thought of spinning, running, and jumping into her car dissolve into nothing. The irony of calling herself Birdie and having the name Wren when she can't fly away isn't lost on her.

"Birdie isn't exactly the stealthiest alias if your real name is Wren," the woman adds.

Why did I choose Birdie? It's because it's what she thought she deserved. Growing up, she hated when people would call her 'little bird'. It wasn't cute or endearing. And there was always pity in their tone on account of her absent, runaway mother. *Why did she have to name me Wren?* The little bird symbolized being small, prey for larger animals with sharp teeth. She didn't like who she was born to be, an image of what everyone assumed she was—weak and weird. Instead of soaring effortlessly on a gust of wind, she hopped from city to city on her short, thin legs, running, hoping to lose her past.

"It's funny, with a name like Birdie I'd expect you'd be like a hundred years old." The woman sets the bag of food on a round table sitting inside the door. "Don't just stand there catching flies. Come on in." She waves Wren in. "Sorry, no pun intended."

Wren snaps her lips shut and her muscles catch up to her mind. She turns and bolts to her car. She doesn't care who this woman is or how she knows her name. It's time to go.

"Wait," the woman shouts. "Sorry, I didn't mean to insult you."

The crunch of the gravel behind her tells her the woman is following. Wren doesn't care, she just wants to get into her smelly, cold car and leave.

"A man sent me. He said a woman named Wren could help. Said you delivered food around here."

The only man she could imagine telling a stranger she could help them would be AJ. *Why would he think I could help her?* Her nose crinkles, trying to figure out how he knew where to find her. She rolls her eyes at the thought of this: his idea of a joke. With a blink of an eye, AJ is now on her shit list. *Fuckin' AJ. This is something he would do.* AJ once made her act like some psychic gypsy on the beach to get money for train tickets. He thought it was hilarious when wrinkly American women on vacation wanted Wren to touch them, to tell them who they were in a past life. In retrospect, she wonders why she didn't just walk away or say no. Heat rises in her ears. She climbs in her car and shouts out the window, "Tell AJ we're not married in this life and I'm not his little puppet." With her foot on the clutch, she turns her key in the ignition and the four cylinders awaken. Latex squeaks against the worn leather steering wheel.

"Wait, please. I need you to tell me what you see. You're the only person who can help." Her hands touch the car, hoping to prevent Wren from driving away, but she snatches them back quickly when the vehicle rolls backwards.

"I know about Hilary Clarke," she says in a last-ditch effort to make Wren stay.

Wren slams on the brakes and stares at the woman through gritted teeth. *How dare she mention that name?* How dare AJ share her deepest, most guarded secret?

The woman tightens her sweater and wraps her arms around herself to stay warm. She treads lightly to Wren's stopped car. "I know what you're capable of, and I believe in what you can do."

All Wren can do is stare into the women's eyes and see her deep-rooted desperation. She's seen desperate people before, but nothing like this.

"I get the sense that all you want to do is run away—get as far enough away from whatever's troubling you. Hilary

Clarke..."

"Don't you say that name." Wren pounds the steering wheel with her fist. "You know nothing. Whatever AJ told you was a lie, and I can't help you." Quick breathes heave her chest.

A wave of confusion hits the woman's face, but it dissipates quickly when she licks her lips. She steps closer to Wren's car. "Who cares what anyone said? I can help you if you help me."

Wren's eyes flicker to the black BMW. It clicks that this car doesn't belong to a well-off businessman taking part in an extra-marital affair in the seedy part of town where no one will catch him, but to this woman who knows Wren's secret. She regrets telling her once-best friend and former spouse from a past life. *Fuckin' AJ.*

"Please, just give me ten minutes." The woman puts her hands together in front of her chin like she's about to pray. "I'll pay you five hundred dollars. I can be stubbornly persistent. I just want to know what you see."

Thoughts bounce in Wren's mind. *What exactly does she know about Hilary Clarke? I bet that asshole blabbed everything.* Saying the name Hilary Clarke, even only to herself, sends a shiver across her skin. *How can someone I barely know forever ruin my existence?* And she's not talking about the strange woman asking for help. Wren's talking about Hilary Clarke. The little girl who is the reincarnation of her deadbeat, deceased mother, Heather Roussel.

Wren shifts into first and slowly lets her car roll forward into the parking spot. She glances around the motel to see if anyone has witnessed this situation, but no eyes follow. No curious stares peek from behind curtains. "Ten minutes." In her thirty-six years living as Wren Roussel, she's come to learn that maybe it's better to complete unpleasant tasks as they arise as opposed to the alternative. Plus, her lip curls at the thought of this woman, whoever she is, constantly stalking her. Hiring her to bring food to random motel rooms. She could move again, but she's getting tired.

"Thank you," the woman says. "Really, thank you." Her eyes soften.

Wren turns off her car and stares at her hands gripping the steering wheel. Her fingers itch under their thin protective layer of latex. It's been a while since she last touched human flesh.

Chapter 2

"Come, have a seat. I'm Scarlett..." The woman closes the door after Wren enters.

Wren raises a hand. "Stop. I don't want to know anything more about you. Frankly, knowing your first name is more than I care to know." The scent of bleach and artificial fragrance hit her nose. Not even the greasy fries can overpower this motel. The room is neat, most likely neater than the motel's cleaning staff keeps it. The television, lamps, even a book, are all placed in line with the surfaces they're sitting on. No sign of a suitcase or bag. Either Scarlett has put everything away or she has no intention of staying in this economy lodging. With an invisible label, Wren marks Scarlett as someone with possible OCD. After taking in the room, she turns to Scarlett and is reminded of the woman's desperation. The cracks around her eyes and the sunken stare signal to Wren she that is about to witness something disturbing.

"How do you want to do this?" Scarlett asks.

Wren eyes the small round table and two chairs in front of the window. "Here will do."

Scarlett snatches the bag of food and places it on the bureau next to the dated television.

Finger by finger, Wren loosens the latex from her sweaty

hands, a hint of hesitation in pulling the gloves completely off, as if the air is acid and can burn her skin. "Take a seat and put both of your palms down on the table." Wren finally removes her gloves and dries her hands on her jeans. She positions the chair to sit directly across from Scarlett. "I'm going to place my hands on top of yours. And I'll remove my hands when I'm finished." Wren floats her hands over Scarlett's, preparing herself for the worst. Blood, death, murder. If Scarlett went to all the trouble to find Wren, what she's about to see isn't going to be a nice girl playing with her pony.

"Wren," Scarlett says, "sorry, Birdie. Is something wrong?" She asks with genuine concern. "Sorry, I should have asked, what name do you prefer?"

Wren continues to focus on her hands. "No, and it doesn't matter to me, because once we're done here, we're never going to see each other again."

"Fair enough, Wren. Sounds prettier than Birdie." Scarlett offers a stiff smile.

Wren is done with this chit chat. She wants this to be over and reminds herself that this time tomorrow, it *will* be over, and she'll be alone. Most likely driving. It's calming to think about not-so-far-away times in the future. She inhales deeply and lowers her hands, like a boot crunching an unsuspecting bug on the sidewalk.

Florescent lights hum overhead. It's harsh to my eyes, but I adjust quickly. It's not a tall ceiling and there are no windows.

Within seconds, I know we're in a basement. Looking down at our clothes, they seem worn and dirty. The high waist of the jeans and baggy fleece sweater with a high collar makes me think we're not that far in the past. Mid-eighties to early nineties, maybe. There is a scent of ripe onions and sweat, with a familiar undertone like that of being in an old library with a chemical stink. The cement floor is cold. On the other side of the twenty-by-twenty room, there is a table and a double bed in the corner. Either she's being held captive here or they are very poor. A voice calls from behind us, "I want to go home," with some sort of European accent. Polish, Russian, or maybe Ukrainian, it's hard to tell. We twist our neck to see who is speaking. A blonde young woman clutches her protruding belly. A soon-to-be teen mom wearing grey sweatpants and a sweatshirt that says 'Club Monaco' a few sizes too large, even with her belly. These conditions are no place for a pregnant teen, no matter how promiscuous her parents think she is. "It's going to be okay, Bojana, I'll help us. I just need to come up with a plan." I feel my foreign lips move and the voice of a stranger speaks to the teen in trouble. I watch the girl named Bojana stand there with a pained expression. We get up and help her to the bed. "Just lay down and rest." Closer to the table, I can see a pitcher of water and small white bottles that look like vitamins, but can't be sure until I'm offered a closer look. With no windows, it's hard to look for any clues to place them—where they could be. We look back to the wall and see another girl, around the age of fifteen maybe, curled under a blanket like she is hiding from the boogie man at sleep-away camp in a bad horror movie.

On a shelf I see games, books, and puzzles. If I had to wager a guess, these girls are being held here against their will, a place where young girls are sent who have found themselves in an unfortunate situation.

A heavy door, probably steel, opens and closes in the distance. The girls eye each other and stir as if looking for a place to hide, but this barren space offers them nothing. Whistling draws closer. We stay where we are and hold Bojana's hand.

"How are all my pretty ladies feelin' today?" A gruff voice calls. "Bojana, my prize pig, how's that lil' baby doin' inside ya belly?" A stocky man with hairy arms and knuckles comes into view. Average height, dark brown feathered short hair, and more rings than I've ever seen on a man. "I brought a nutritious lunch for ya today, gotta keep ya nice and healthy."

We see Bojana pretending to be asleep and continue to hold her hand. Fear grows inside my borrowed body as our chest tightens. Our eyes turn back to the man. It's a face I'll remember. Dark eyes, thick black eyebrows, round cheeks, and puffy lips.

"Hey, my African princess, this is for you." The man tosses a box in our direction, and it lands at our feet.

We don't make any attempt at catching what he tossed our way. We look down at the box. Clearblue Pregnancy Test. Our lips part as our stomach turns from what I pray is not a fetus.

"Take it in the morning, and ya better ace it this time. The lovely clients can't wait forever." The man laughs at his own stupid joke. "Remember what I told ya. If ya can't provide me with a baby, I can't save ya life."

Chapter 3

Wren remembers a time when she would have sold her soul for a vision like this. For an unsolved mystery that she could solve on her own. A mystery with clues and answers only she could bring to light. But that tingle to explore the unknown is gone. The only thing on her mind is collecting the five hundred dollars. However, there is a sliver of curiosity in knowing how Scarlett is aware of her own past life. She opens her eyes and shutters at Scarlett's heavy gaze. *Has she been staring at me like this the whole time?*

"What's his name? Wren, tell me, what do you see?"

Wren fumbles with her gloves in her lap, eager to put them back on. "Before I tell you anything, tell me how you know."

Scarlett's shoulders deflate, and she rubs one of her eyes. "Why does it matter?"

"It doesn't, I guess." Wren sits straight and squares her shoulders. "I've just never met anyone who actually knew something that happened to them in a past life." Wren finishes pulling the latex over her hand.

"Well," Scarlett leans back in her seat and keeps her eyes fixated on Wren. "The nightmares started after my twelfth birthday. The doctors guess they were triggered by puberty." She licks her lips. Her eyes avert to the yellowed floral curtains, hanging stagnant in the unfiltered air of the cheap room. "They're always the same. Either someone is having their way with me from behind, or I see an ugly man's face lurking in the distance, or I am in excruciating pain from the waist down. I've never given birth, but I imagine that's what having a vaginal birth feels like. Having your insides clawed and ripped apart, then dragged out of your body to be on display."

Wren swallows the excess moisture that's gathered under her tongue. "I guess you aced that test," she mutters to herself.

"Pardon?" Scarlett asks.

"I saw a man, probably the ugly man you mentioned. He threw a pregnancy test at you and told you to ace it, and I said it sounds like you did." Wren keeps her face stiff. A tingle in her fingers forces her to tap the beige melamine tabletop. Scarlett's nightmare fits with what she just witnessed. The corner of her mouth twitches. There is a tiny bite of satisfaction.

Scarlett leans forward with demanding eyes. "Did you get his name?"

Falling back on the little police training she had, she knew she couldn't say for certain this was the man that raped or impregnated the woman who Scarlett was in a past life. She only could confirm that he was an accomplice that kept the woman locked away and told her to take a pregnancy test. "No name, but he was stocky with dark hair, and hairy knuckles and arms, and wore too many rings."

Scarlett's complexion grows pale, and it looks like she is going to throw up. "Yes, he's the ugly man, but not the one who rapes me. What else did you see?"

Wren clears her throat. "There was a pregnant teen. Her name was Bojana. You were trying to help her. And another teen girl whose name was not mentioned. In a basement. There were no windows. The smell was unshowered teens with undertones of musty books, or paper and glue, maybe."

"You don't seem fazed by what you saw."

"That's because I've seen worse," Wren answers.

Scarlett thrusts her arms forward and slaps her hands back down on the table. "I need names. Do it again."

"It doesn't work like that. I can only see life through their eyes. I see moments of their life. I can't ask them questions. I don't float above as if I'm some sort of angel. I can only know what they show me. If it's any consolation, from my experience, most people have mundane or happy moments from past lives. Yours is rare." Wren's eyebrows bounce.

"What kind of consolation is that?" Scarlett balks. "I don't want to have a rare past life. I don't want to have nightmares. I don't want to lie awake every night with fear that if I fall asleep, I'm going to be awakened by someone else's tragedy." Scarlett's eyes water and her voice strains. "I need help, and all the doctors in the world can't help me. All their fancy medicine does is turn me into a vegetable. And self-medicating…" Scarlet averts her eyes from Wren. "It's no way to live."

"How did you know your nightmares were fragments of a past life?" Wren leans forward.

Scarlett's eyes fall to her lap. She takes a few moments to find her words. "I was in this group therapy, and there was this guy that told me sometimes our dreams were windows into our lives once lived. Good and bad memories were buried deep inside." She looks back to Wren. "That's what gave me hope. I thought if I could find out who did this to me, to her…"

"And that's when AJ told you to track me down?"

With hesitation, Scarlett nods.

"AJ was in therapy with you?" Wren asks through squinted eyes.

Scarlett nods again.

Maybe AJ turned over a new leaf, going to therapy and dealing with whatever shit he's keeping locked up. Then it hits Wren. She is no better than him. Not dealing with her own shit, trying to pretend she's living someone else's life. She takes a deep breath. But there is no way she can go to group therapy and tell people what she's seen, what she can do. People will think she's crazy. Maybe even a doctor would recommend she be medicated. No one would believe her truth. Wren laces her fingers under the table and the latex squeaks.

"So, I'm just supposed to live with this?" Scarlett searches Wren's hazel eyes for an answer. "Exhaustion doesn't begin to explain how I feel. I'm at the end. Those men haunt me. There has to be a way to make it stop." She wraps her arms around herself.

Wren studies Scarlett: the action of a woman hugging herself, trying to comfort the child inside, to no avail. And no one has ever been able to throw this person or the person she used to be a lifeline. That is, until this day. She knows she can lay her hands over Scarlett's again and see something different, but most likely it'll only be more sights of neglect and disgust caused by another human; but with time, answers may be revealed. The ideals Wren once chased come full circle. She used to search for someone with a past that was a mystery in need of solving, and that's what got her into trouble before. But here, now, sitting in front of her is a case that would have made her younger self feel alive. A genuine case of kidnapping, abuse, rape, and who knows what else landed right in her lap, handed to her by AJ as a bizarre gift. She smiles to herself and wonders if she and AJ were still living their previous lives, what wedding anniversary they would be celebrating. *Married ninety-something years and the traditional gift is a puzzle. A sick and twisted puzzle.* The bag of takeout food lands on Wren's periphery. Her eyes bounce from the bag of greasy food to Scarlett. A restlessness causes her leg to bounce.

"Why are you smiling?" Scarlett asks, unamused. "I hardly think..."

Wren interjects, "How much are you offering me to help you?"

"Fifty thousand." Scarlett's voice doesn't waiver.

Wren has never fathomed having that amount of cash at once, but she knows there is an art to negotiation. "Make it sixty." *If you never ask, you'll never know.* Her Nan's wise words echo in her head.

"Fifty-five."

Wren twists her lips. "Fifty-five and you take me to AJ once we've figured out your mess." Surprised by her own words, her body freezes. "And you forget everything AJ told you about me and my past."

Scarlett lets a few seconds of silence settle around them before she answers. "Okay, that's fair."

That kind of money could get Wren a new stress-free life in the Caribbean. One where she could rent boogie boards to tourists on the beach and forget all about who she once was, and what she's seen. No more eating ramen in the dark watching mind numbing videos online. Nothing but sunshine and a warm salty breeze to fill the days. The sound of squawking birds soaring over the ocean on the hunt for fish. Maybe find someone with a brand-new soul. Take a stab at a relationship with the opposite sex. *Here's to hoping it doesn't take long to get names and a location from whoever Scarlett used to be so I can collect my money and get the hell outta this shithole.*

Chapter 4

"This case isn't going to be solved by me touching you. I'm going to have to do research, too." Wren stands and bites her lower lip. "We're going to have to set up how this is going to work. Boundaries, a contract. And the police can never know I am involved." She turns her back to Scarlett. "Never." Once upon a time, she would have welcomed the attention for solving a cold case that only her abilities could solve. It would have fast-tracked her career to becoming a detective, maybe even the youngest one on the force. And female to boot. She spins on her heel and juts out her chin towards Scarlett. "How do you know that this case from the past isn't already solved?" Wren's Caribbean dream could be only that, a dream.

"I just have a feeling." Scarlett shrugs. "In my bones, I know there is unrest for the victims, for whoever I was before this life." Her eyes are hopeful now that she's found a lifeline. "And I like to believe everything happens for a reason. Like finding you." Scarlett's lips form a flat line, not yet ready to crack a smile.

Wren turns back to pacing the dull, low pile carpet towards the back of the room. "Have you ever tried psychotherapy? Hypnotherapy, regression therapy?"

Scarlett stirs in her chair, turning to face Wren. "Once, but the intention wasn't to learn more about my nightmares, it was to try to get them to stop; you can assume how well that worked."

"Okay, so we're basically starting from scratch." Wren wipes a piece of mascara mixed with eye goo from the corner of her eye. A warmth spreads into her limbs, but she ignores the sensation. Years ago, she told herself she wouldn't let her temptation to see people's secrets drive her actions. She tells herself that this time she's doing it for the paycheque. It's a means to an end. A way to start over and focus on something new without having to work shit jobs to keep herself afloat. However, now is not the time for Wren to dwell on what she is going to do with the rest of her life.

"I'm willing to try again. I'm willing to try almost anything," Scarlett blurts.

"That's good. Here is what we'll do." Wren returns to the table and takes a seat. "Tomorrow morning, you'll come pick me up at my place and I'll come back with you. You can put me up in a hotel. One of those nice ones with a business centre. I'll need access to a printer and good Internet. And you follow everything I ask you to do." It dawns on her that she's never had such a willing participant to touch. She stuffs her hands into the pockets of her jeans.

"It's a seven-hour drive."

It takes Wren an extra second to process Scarlett's words. "What? You drove seven hours because some guy from therapy told you I might be able to help you?"

"Like I said, I'll do almost anything." Her dark eyes plead

with a fixation on Wren.

"Fine—wait, why didn't you fly?"

Scarlett picks at a tiny piece of balled wool on the hem of her sweater. "I don't know. It just seemed simpler to get in my car and drive."

Wren tilts her head, perplexed by the rich girl's availability for being able to hop in her car and drive for seven hours. If she had Scarlett's money, flying would be the way to go. Wren's only been on a plane twice, many years ago, and she thought it was the best. High above the world. Soaring above everyone else. Even when she was a kid, she knew she would love to ride in an airplane one day. The day she touched Kyle Farr, the new kid in her class, she knew he must have once been a pilot, because she felt his weightlessness. The feeling was intoxicating, addictive, and eventually branded her as 'cootie girl', but she didn't care. She knew what it felt like to fly. Wren shakes off her digression and returns her focus to Scarlett. "So, we drive back in your fancy BMW."

"Have you ever helped someone like me before?"

"No, can't say that I have."

"Have you solved any cases before?"

Wren answers with a hesitant nod, refusing to let the past escape her lips—pieces of her life she promised herself would stay in the past.

"I would love to hear about..."

"Here, give me your phone." Wren changes the subject. "I'll put my number and address in there. You can pick me up at eight. I'll be outside waiting."

"Yes, of course." Scarlett pulls her phone from her pocket, unlocks it, and passes it to Wren.

Wren punches in her information and hands the phone back. "I have a few more deliveries to make tonight, but I'll see you in the morning."

"Wren." Scarlett calls.

Wren pauses mid stride with the door open. "Yeah."

"Thank you."

"Don't thank me yet," Wren says, and closes the door behind her. She holds her breath on the brief walk to her car. A breeze kicks up and slaps her face. Small yellow leaves twirl around her worn, scuffed sneakers with each step.

Chapter 5

2006

Standing in front of the office door with his name, *Chief Instructor Payne*, printed in bold black letters on the opaque glass, Wren can't help but think that it is a fitting name for a chief. She thinks of her own name and wonders what a fitting title for Roussel would be. The only thing she can think of is Detective Roussel. She swallows her uncertainty and frowns.

Knock. Knock. Her fist raps on the wooden part of the door. Her breath traps in her lungs.

"Yes, come in," his booming voice beckons.

Wren's eyes don't know where to look as she enters. Chief Instructor Payne is exactly who you would envision running a police college. Male, Caucasian, tall, broad shoulders, a thick dark mustache that conceals his thoughts, creases of wisdom around his eyes, and an all-knowing air about him. She's never spoken to him one-on-one before, only seen him give the welcoming address to the class.

"Ah, recruit Roussel, thank you for coming to see me." He removes his glasses, folds them, and tucks them into his breast pocket. "I like to speak to all the parties involved when an incident takes place on my campus."

Wren finds her bottom lip between her teeth. She's not sure how to read the man who's made it his life's mission to read people. That's what police work boils down to, she's concluded: reading people. Who's good and who's bad.

"You don't need to be alarmed." He motions to a chair positioned in front of his large mahogany desk. "Recruits Lyle and Stevens have been asked to leave the campus. As we speak, they are removing their belongings from your shared dorm."

She keeps her face still and takes a seat. The idea that she no longer has to deal with those goons puts her tense muscles at ease a little, and she floats the idea to herself that maybe she should stay, but her stiff and tender glutes remind her she physically doesn't have what it takes. "Yes, Chief. Sorry, Chief." Wren's eyes meet his, and she immediately looks down.

"The way recruits Lyle and Stevens stripped you down and carried you outside, bound your wrists and ankles together, tying you to the flagpole, with only your cotton panties between you and that frigid metal pole..." The chief summarizes Wren's lived trauma. He leans back, resting his folded hands in his lap.

The word *panties* leaving the chief's lips sounds uncouth. Wren rubs her wrists. She keeps her eyes down and her feelings to herself. *I was there. I know what happened, he doesn't have to repeat the details.*

The chief continues, "Now, I should tell you, the actions

of recruits Lyle and Stevens were absolutely out of line, and they have been punished with a week's suspension and removal from living on campus. And they will issue you a formal apology." The chief shifts and rests his elbows on the leather top of his solid wood desk and leans in. "If it were up to me, or if they were men, they would be removed from the program..."

Wren is taken aback by his words, *if they were men*; what does gender have to do with it? She wonders. Wren knows in her bones these two women are bad news. Her brow twitches, and she thinks, *none of this matters because I've decided to withdraw from the program.*

"But there is a demand for female officers, and we can't spare losing two recruits." The sounds of his leather chair crinkling as he shifts fills the break in the one-sided conversation. "Recruit Roussel, so far you have top marks for all the in-class learning. Very impressive, and a good start to the year."

Her eyes make their way back to him. The apples of his checks are polished pink. *Is he smiling?* Wren keeps her attention on him. "Thank you, Chief, but my top marks aren't the problem." She fidgets, but catches herself and stops. The chief's presence is commanding.

He leans forward even more. "You know, when I enrolled in this very college, over thirty years ago, I was a string bean. A hundred and sixty-five pounds soaking wet."

The chief pauses, and Wren's not sure whether she

should speak. She gulps down the nerves that rise in her throat.

"You know it takes more than a couple of months to build endurance and stamina." He tilts his head and locks his eyes with hers. They are locked like a steel door, and she has no idea what's inside. "The ribbing from your fellow recruits will build character. Give you experience. Make your skin tough."

Wren didn't have to say a word. He reads her like a book.

"Can I show you something?" He raises a bushy salt-and-pepper eyebrow and leans back.

"Yes, Chief," is all she can say. The word 'no' probably isn't a word he hears often.

"Very good." He pushes out his chair and the leather creaks as he stands. "Please, stay where you are."

She's afraid to stare, so she lets her eyes focus on the painting hanging on the dark green wall behind his desk: a skillfully-painted piece of art depicting a hunter with a rifle strapped to his back, pointing to something outside the frame, with three regal hound dogs on the scent of whatever their master is hunting. And a flock of birds fly above in the distance. *Whack.* A heavy book slaps down on his desk in front of Wren, and she jumps in her seat. Her attention is startled back to the chief. The chief, who is now standing close enough that she catches a whiff of his woodsy aftershave.

He licks his index finger and begins to leaf through the pages of the book. "Yes, here it is." He flattens the crease of the pages with his palm. "Class of '67." His cheeks are still tinted pink. He leans in for a closer look. His leg grazes Wren's thigh. His pine scented aftershave now envelopes them both.

Wren holds her breath as the chief's closeness stuns her. She's looking at the page where his meaty finger points, but her eyes glaze over. A weight lands on her shoulder and every achy muscle in her petite frame hardens.

"Take a look. That was me. All limbs, no muscle. My fellow recruits nicknamed me 'Officer Gumby'. I wouldn't grow into my body for another few years, but I was still a handsome lad, eh?"

From the corner of her eye, she can see his hand on her shoulder. Heat builds under her skin. She wants to wiggle out from under his weight, but her mind refuses to send the appropriate signals to the appropriate muscles.

"Go on. Lean in and take a look," he coaches, using his hand on her shoulder to guide Wren forward. "Wasn't I handsome?"

She can't stop blinking. Her eyes won't focus. *Are authority figures handsome?* The question has never crossed Wren's mind before. She searches for the right words to leave her lips. "Yes, handsome." That's not what she wants to say.

His thick finger continues to tap on more of the graduates. The chief's words sound like static.

Wren refuses to look at the faces of the people on the page before her.

"See. I wasn't big either, and look at me now. Chief Instructor Payne." He finally removes his hand from her shoulder and surveys his office with a look of satisfaction. His uniformed chest puffs as he stands there like an oak rooted in the wooden planks beneath his large black shoes. He leans down casually on his desk in front of Wren. "So, you will stick it out with us a little while longer?"

His breath is hot, stale with a hint of smoke. His eyes linger in her hazel eyes, and all Wren wants to do is pop her head into her shirt like a small turtle hiding from a coyote.

"Recruit Roussel?"

"I don't think I want to be an officer anymore," she squeaks, and summons her legs to stand, mentally preparing herself to make a run for the door.

"I was hoping I could change your mind." His calloused, warm flesh reaches out and touches Wren's hand.

A marble statue of a man on a horse through the window. Men speak a foreign language behind us. (I can't understand but the tone is heated.) Someone is stuffing something into a wall. It looks like artwork. Stacks of paintings. The weight of someone's hand collides with our cheek. Nascondilo velocemente! *a man yells. And our hands move quicker to help slide the artwork into the slot behind the wall. Another voice whispers next to us, "I have a contact who will be able to sell these, we just need to wait for the inquest to die down. You have very stealthy skills, my friend."*

Wren stumbles back, taking the chair with her. Its legs scrape against the floor. Her hands jerk to her sides. *The chief was a thief.* A mystery forgotten by time. No murder, no blood, but a real mystery. Wren's mind hums. *I need to see more.*

"Recruit Roussel, don't be alarmed." The chief treads lightly towards Wren.

Her mouth gaps open. "Let me think about it," Wren says. She beelines for the door. Before she leaves, she tells the chief she'll be back with her decision. Walking as quickly as her legs will carry her Wren thinks she needs to be smart about this. She needs to think her plan through to touch the chief again and see more of what he did in his past life.

The next day Wren has a window of time after lunch and before her criminology class. She decides this is the best time to visit the chief. Last night she planned out how she would touch him. She would return to let him know that she thought about their talk and that she has decided to stay. She would extend her hand for a handshake to thank him. It's simple, and no one would suspect anything out of the ordinary.

At the chief's door, Wren knocks and waits for his voice. The door swings open.

"Recruit Roussel, how wonderful of you to stop by." The chief steps to the side and ushers her in.

Wren smiles back at the chief. This time she can clearly see the man grinning under his mustache. They exchange pleasantries. The wheels in Wren's mind feed her the next step of her plan. "Chief, I have decided...."

He cuts her off: "Roussel, come here I want to show you something." The chief saunters over to a bookcase and eyes a framed photograph.

This is the first time the chief hasn't prefaced her name with *Recruit*. It throws Wren off. "Chief, sir, umm..."

"I don't bite." The chief chuckles. "Just come here for a moment."

Wren steps closer to him. She can see the photograph of the chief on his graduation day.

He waves for Wren to come closer. "Come, I want you to get a good look." When Wren is next to him, he lays his hand on her shoulder. "One of the proudest days of my life."

Wren's body is frozen. *He doesn't need to keep trying to convince me. I'm going to stay.* "Chief, I came here today to tell you I'm going to stick it out," she blurts.

"That's terrific." He spins to face her and pulls her into his embrace.

Her arms don't move. His action is unexpected. Wren's body is squeezed in the chief's arms. She wants to ask why he is hugging her, but she hastily decides that it would be rude to ask her superior for his motivations. She feels his hold loosen.

"I'm happy to hear that you're going to stay with us," the chief says. He moves his hands to the top of Wren's arms. He stares down at her.

Wren does her best not to fidget under his grip. The only thing she can think of doing is the next step in her plan. "I want to thank you for the chat yesterday," Wren says and extends her hand. She has miscalculated the distance between them, and her fingers press into the chief's crotch. Wren gasps and whips her hand back. "I'm—I'm—so sorry..." Wren trips over her words.

The chief laughs and takes Wren's small hands in his solid paws.

We're sitting on the grass in a shady spot under a tree. Our teeth chomp down on the sandwich in our hands. I'm picking up flavours of cheese and tomato. "By god, Hugo, you did it!" The guy next to us playfully punches our bicep. "Stole those works right from under their big fat, greedy snouts." We smile and take a big bite from our sandwich. "They won't think to look anywhere in Italy."

A name. Hugo. Wren opens her eyes back to reality. The chief is standing within ten inches of her body.

"Not to worry, Roussel. It was an honest mistake." The chief looks Wren up and down and returns to his desk. "What would you think about weekly check-ins here in my office? Sort of like a mentor program." He leans back in his chair and rubs a pen between his fingers.

Wren's blunder pops back to the top of her mind and

overshadows the name Hugo. *The back of my hand accidentally grazed the chief's penis.* Her cheeks flush and she spins on her heels to leave. "Okay. Yeah. Sure." Wren blows out a shallow breath. What she agrees to is not quite registering. "I've got to go to class now," she says, and marches out of the chief's office.

Muscle memory takes Wren towards her classroom. Her knuckles turn white from gripping the straps of her backpack. *Hugo and Italy.* Two key pieces of evidence she saw today. Yesterday was the marble statue. Wren doesn't know how she'll be able to stay focused for the rest of the afternoon when all she can think about is researching stolen art in Italy paired with the name Hugo. The unknown is all so tantalizing. The hazing events of yesterday are already forgotten, although it takes strength to think about the visions the chief showed her rather than her grave misjudgement in timing on shaking the chief's hand. Her face will remain flush for a while.

Wren thought it would be best to grab dinner from the cafeteria and eat it in her room so she could at least do research on her computer while she ate. Eating alone in the dining hall isn't appealing anyway. Everyone in her class seemed to form groups, except her. Always the odd man out: story of her life ever since her nan passed away. Wren didn't mind; she got used to being on her own.

She turns on her screen and notices a new email. It's from the chief. Pink returns to her cheeks. *It was an unfortunate accident; he didn't seem bothered, so neither should I. He's the one that gave me a hug. That was weird, but maybe he's just a friendly man.* Wren's heart quickens as she reads the subject line; *My office tomorrow at 8AM.* Her heart rate returns to a normal beat once she reads the contents of the email. The chief wants to start their mentor meetings tomorrow. A vague memory of saying yes to something comes to mind. She was too frazzled with the touching and the vision. Wren types back with a simple formal response: *Confirmed receipt of email. See you tomorrow morning.*

Last nights internet search turned up nothing. Wren needs to touch the chief's hand again. The visions before were good, but she needs more concrete facts, like full names and glimpses of newspapers to see dates and locations, to dive deeper into this case. She decides this mentor program may not be the worst idea, but the trick would be making touching his skin seem natural or accidental.

"Recruit Roussel, good morning," the chief greets from behind.

Wren turns to see the chief strolling down the hall with a mug in hand. "Good morning, Chief," she responds. Wren readjusts her bag straps on her shoulders. The bright lights in the hall highlight the chief's grey hair. Nerves cause an instant parchedness. She coughs and scoots ahead to a nearby water fountain.

"You okay?" The chief's brows draw together.

"I'm fine," Wren squeaks after a quick sip of water. She waits for the chief to enter his office, then she follows. She crosses her fingers behind her back; in her vision with Hugo, he's reading a newspaper.

"Welcome, have a seat," the chief offers.

Wren spins to see him standing behind the door with his mug. She watches him take a sip and close the door.

"You have inspired me to start a mentoring program. Each year I will choose a deserving student and personally mentor them." The chief steps closer to Wren. He takes another sip.

He is standing close enough for Wren to smell the sweet coffee on his breath. She nods.

"Oh, here." His hand reaches in his pocket, and he pulls out a handkerchief. "Let me get that." The white fabric dabs Wren's cheek. "You had a few drops of water."

Wren stumbles back into the chair. The back of her fingers reach up to where he touched her. She has no real interest in this mentor program he mentioned, she just wants to see something else through Hugo's eyes. "May I borrow a pen?" She looks up at him, trying to keep her butt on the chair. Her backpack is still anchored to her back and taking up most of the sitting surface.

"Of course." He sits on the desk and reaches over to a pen next to a stack of folders. He twists back with a black ballpoint pen in his grip. "Here you go." The chief smiles down at her, the same smile as yesterday.

Wren reaches for the pen, wrapping her fingers around

his.

"Money, lots of money if you are up for it," a man's voice whispers. He's standing in front of us, but it's dark. It's difficult to make out his features. The scent. It's different. Like stone or damp concrete. In the distance water is dripping. We can hear it. We nod our head. Take me there tonight, so I can learn more, *our voice speaks in English with a thick accent.*

Pressure digs into the top of Wren's thigh. She pulls her hand back from the pen and sees the chief's other hand is no longer holding his mug, but rather onto her leg. Her eyes widen and her mouth goes dry again.

"Sorry about that." The chief pulls his hand back. "I was losing my balance." He immediately stands and walks behind his desk.

Wren doesn't know how to respond. The thought of Hugo planning another robbery is fresh in her mind.

"You know what?" The chief leans back and rubs under his nose with his finger. "Perhaps I was too eager in starting this program today. Let me put together a plan with a schedule and we can make this mentor program more official."

"Okay," Wren says, and stands. "I need to go work on my biological perspective on criminal behavior assignment." The next few seconds are a blur. She finds herself heading for the doors to the main entrance. A walk always helps her clear her head. *I can go pick up some cereal or snacks in town.*

The main street in this small town doesn't offer much other than an overpriced convenience store, a flower shop, a pizzeria, a post office, and a bakery. A few people speckle the street: seniors doing their daily walkabouts, a mother pushing a child in a stroller stopping ahead to take in a window display. The small child waves at Wren. The hand waving is wearing a blue mitten, while the other hand holding what looks like a stuffed cat is bare. Wren offers a weak smile and a wave back. She spots the solo blue mitten on the curb about three feet behind the woman. The mother doesn't know her kid lost a mitt. Wren quickens her step towards them to retrieve the mitt and return it to the child.

"I think this belongs to you." Wren smiles at the mother and crouches down to offer the mitten back to the child, babbling and laughing. Their mouth is spaced with tiny white teeth. Rosy chapped cheeks and drool down their chin.

The mother smiles back at Wren with an airy laugh. "Hilary, stop taking off your mitten."

Little Hilary reaches out for her mitt and grabs Wren's hand.

Chapter 6

2023

It's dark. Wren knows what to expect. She leaves no lights on to welcome her when she returns to her apartment. She flicks a switch and the dome light illuminates the front hall enough for Wren to enter, remove her shoes, and put them neatly on the shoe rack. The furniture is sparse, no knickknacks or photographs hanging or set lovingly on a shelf. There is one framed photo that hangs above her couch: a snowy owl taking flight, a Robert Bateman print that the previous tenant left behind. The image is peaceful and soothing, so Wren decided to keep it where it hangs as a little daily reminder of nature and how precious it can be. Sometimes she wonders who that owl once was or who it became, and if the artist captured the essence of that soul.

Wren flicks on another light, and the hall to her bedroom is lit. There is no life other than herself in her apartment. No pets, no plants. She knows the risk in keeping the smallest houseplant, which could attract bugs, that could hold a past that she does not wish to see. Not anymore. On paper karma is a nice thought. It even makes sense to most logical, spiritual people. A greasy pervert being reborn as a cockroach seems just, but Wren knows that's not always what happens, and life is never fair. Once she awoke to find a spider crawling across her arm. That early morning, she also had a dream of a child playing and running through a playground. It could have been a random dream, or it could have been a vision of the little arachnid's past life. The dissection of the vision consumed her day. *Did the child die too soon and wish to come back as a spider? Did the person who now inhabited this spider love his childhood and wanted to share a memory they cherished most? Was being a spider a punishment or a reward? A short life lived in fear of being squished or a welcomed escape to a life of simplicity?* From that night on, Wren slept in a long-sleeved shirt. She has her own life to figure out; she can't constantly be bothered with the weight of everyone else's. Not anymore.

In the hall closet she finds her duffle bag and carries it with her into her bedroom. It's a worn black nylon bag with some beer company's logo on the side. Wren doesn't even remember how she acquired the bag. She doesn't even drink beer. Enough clean clothes to keep her afloat for a week should suffice. And if she would have to stay longer, she's sure the hotel would have a laundry room she could use.

Staring into her closet, all her pants and nicer clothes hang motionless in front of her. She grabs a pair of jeans off a hanger and folds them neatly on her bed. Behind her something metal collides with the parquet floor. Wren spins to see a belt sprawled on the floor in the closet. She walks to go pick it up and return it to the special hanger designed to hold a variety of belts, ties, or scarves. The tail of the belt rests on top of a plastic storage tote she keeps in the back of her closet. Wren gulps and stares at the box. She knows exactly what it conceals: a family quilt, photographs of her grandparents and mother, and the seven journals she kept growing up where she documented everything she saw—in this life and past ones. She reaches out her hand to lift the lid off the tote and snaps her hand back. Nothing good can come from reading the past. And with that thought, she questions her decision to help Scarlett. Every time she digs too deep, nothing ends as she expects. The very first time she called the police to share tips on a double homicide, she didn't get the recognition she thought she would. She thought that by helping the police solve a decade-old cold case, her Nan would see that her ability was a good thing, a gift to celebrate, instead of being constantly reprimanded or made fun of for always touching people. *Ew, don't let cootie girl sit near you. She'll touch you and infect you with her cooties.* The chants of her classmates echo through her head. Wren wonders if, in her next life, if someone like herself touches who she is reborn as, would they see the vision of kids being cruel to her?

She forces herself to think about something not as depressing. *The money, think about the money.* Finally, someone recognizes her gift and is going to compensate her fairly.

She forces her hands to pop off the lid of the tote, despite her initial judgement. It feels like a lifetime since she breathed in Nan's scent of fresh linen fabric softener and saw the warm creases of her smile. Wren wants to believe once her Nan had passed that she would somehow find her again.

She knew she was gone, but not really *gone*. And for years Wren searched for her Nan, a mission of finding a needle in a haystack with eight billion pieces of hay, until the day she found another woman from her life. A woman she wasn't looking for. The woman that ruined her life. That's when the life she once knew stopped and the Earth stood still. She didn't want to think about the woman who was her mother. She couldn't. With a deep breath, she tilts the lid off the tote and peers at its contents. She slowly contorts her body to sit cross-legged on the small patch of floor in her closet.

It still smells like her, Nan preserved in time. There is still a chance their paths will cross again. On the other hand, she wants to believe being reborn into a new life could be a gift, a reward, if karmic intention aligned with whatever spiritual plane you went to when you died. *Nan could be living a grand life, so why would she waste time in coming back to visit me? Or maybe she* has *come back to visit me, in the form of a butterfly or hummingbird, and I wasn't wise enough to know it was her.* Wren's thoughts of her Nan fade quickly as she eyes her black and white journal that sits on top the contents of the tote. The last journal she ever kept, a journal that kept her secrets from what happened at police college. A lump rises in her throat and she crams the top back on the tote. She can still smell his dusty, mahogany office. She can see the slivers of sunlight cast through his closed blinds, hitting the floor in front of his desk. The way his dry cracked lips and coffee breath invaded her mouth. She hates herself for not stopping it. The risk was not worth the reward. There was no reward. Chief Instructor Payne may have been a thief in a past life, and karma must have been taking a nap the day he once died. He wasn't reborn as some slimy bug or snake; he was born into a life of power and bent the law to suit himself. Bubbles form in Wren's blood and her skin grows hot. He probably retired and lives a lush life on a lake in a cottage in Muskoka. After Wren was forced to drop out of school, she never let herself think about the Chief. Not until this moment.

Wren dabs her eyes with the sleeve of her sweater and shuts the closet door. *This time there is a reward. Fifty-five thousand.* Right then and there she decides that whatever she finds out about Scarlett's past life will bear no weight on her life. In her mind she draws a line in the sand. This is a job. Black and white. *I get Scarlett the information she seeks, collect my fee, and walk away.* Wren bets she can make that much last for two, maybe two and a half years in the Caribbean. Enough time for her to start fresh and figure out what she wants to do with the rest of her life. A shot at a normal life, where no one knows what she is able to do.

Chapter 7

With her back against the brick portico of her apartment building, Wren grips the handles of her duffle bag with a glove-free hand and combs the street with her eyes for Scarlett's black BMW. There is no need to wear her gloves at this moment, but there is always a pair in her purse just in case. She checks her watch and sees that Scarlett is five minutes late. Scarlett's tardiness could be an early indication of what it's going to be like to work with her, or Wren thinks she could give her the benefit of the doubt; she could have hit traffic or a patch of construction, depending on which way she took.

The BMW rolls down the street and stops at the stop sign. Wren can see Scarlett searching the buildings for numbers. Wren waves her down and walks down the cracked pavers that lead to the sidewalk.

"Good morning," Scarlett shouts out of the rolled-down passenger window as she pulls up to the curb. "Sorry I'm late. I stopped to get us some coffee and bagels for breakfast."

Stopping for food. Wren failed to consider that in her scenarios for why Scarlett was late. "It's fine." Wren opens the back door and sets her bag on the back seat before she climbs into the front. Black leather interior with indigo stitching. Wren knows little about cars, but she can tell this car is nicer than most.

"I didn't know what you liked, so I got a black coffee with cream and sugar on the side, and a cup of boiling water with every flavour of tea bag you can imagine." Scarlett keeps her car in park as she shares all of her Starbucks treasures with Wren. "And I got us bagels and muffins, you can choose first. I'll eat whatever."

Wren eyes Scarlett and the assortment of drinks and bags of baked goods before them. This version of Scarlett is much more jovial than the one begging for help at the motel yesterday. "You sleep well last night?" Wren asks.

Scarlett lets out a single laugh. "That's the first time anyone has ever asked me that question."

Wren buckles her seatbelt and stares forward at the bumper of the car parked in front of them. *This may have been a mistake. I barely know anything about this woman. This is how abduction stories begin. Women can abduct people just as easily as men. Women can tempt people to come with them because people find them the more trusting sex.* The rookie mistake of getting into a stranger's car weighs in the back of her mind.

"Since the drive is a long one, I figured it will give us time to get to know each other better." Scarlett's comment doesn't ease Wren's thoughts.

Of course, she wants us to talk, that's how victims grow to trust their abductor. Wren wriggles in her seat and calms herself by focusing on her breathing, forcing herself out of this rabbit hole of negative thoughts. *Of course, Scarlett's going to want to talk. She hired me to help her solve her past.* She wonders if Scarlett's going to want this bonding time to be a two-way street. "I guess." is all Wren can say. It isn't listening to Scarlett blather on about her life that worries her, it's what this woman is going to want to know about her own life. AJ already told her about Hilary Clarke, what else did he let slip?

Scarlett taps away on the large screen situated in the middle of the dash. The car boops and beeps in response. A map appears and the stats pop up for how many kilometers and hours it's going to take them to arrive at their destination. "What kind of music do you listen to?" Scarlett asks without breaking concentration with the screen.

This car is more advanced than anything Wren could have imagined. Compared to her old Civic, it's like sitting in a rocket ship. "Whatever you choose will be fine."

"Cannibal Corpse it is!" Scarlett stifles a snort. "I'm just kidding. I don't listen to death metal...unless you..." She flashes a toothy grin towards Wren.

"No, no. I don't listen to that either." Wren's brows knit together. *This is definitely a different woman than the desperate and sullen woman I met yesterday.* The gears in her mind twist, chronic nightmares, varied personalities in a short period. There could be a deeper mental health issue here. Or drugs. *But does it matter? She's paying me good money to complete a very specific job.* "Shoop" by Salt-N-Pepa blasts through the speakers from all corners to interrupt Wren's train of thought.

"Nothing beats the hits from the nineties as a soundtrack for a road trip." Scarlett bops to the beat, mouthing the lyrics, and pulls away from the curb.

Wren doesn't mind the popular dance tracks from the decade that defined her youth, but she prefers Tori Amos or Alanis Morissette. She's also come to be cautious of not rocking any boats, especially with people she doesn't know well. So, she keeps her musical preference to herself. "Yep, it's just fine." She stares ahead as the car directs them to the highway and thinks this is probably one of those self-driving cars, too.

Scarlett sips on her Starbucks and Wren grabs one of the extra beverages that was purchased for her. She never got into the habit of a morning tea or coffee but doesn't want to insult Scarlett's thoughtfulness. It's the most considerate thing anyone has done for her in quite some time. Wren chooses the black coffee and is scared to open the lid to add milk or sugar in the moving car, so she drinks it as is. The dark liquid touches her lips and its bitterness seeps into her tongue. In any other situation, she would spit the hot liquid out, but she has no choice but to swallow. She decides she'll only pretend to sip and then throw the drink out at their first stop.

"So, is there anything specific you'd like to ask me? Anything you think might help you with my past?" Scarlett keeps her eyes on the road, as it's busy on the highway today.

"You can ask me anything. I'm an open book." She glances at Wren for a split second. "I'm just so relieved to have finally found someone to help me. You know, it's been almost twenty years of living with debilitating nightmares."

Wren pretends to take a sip and nods along. Scarlett has a point. This could be a good opportunity to learn and record everything she knows. She secures her drink in the cup holder and retrieves the new notebook and a pen from her purse. On a crisp blank page, she writes the date and where they are. *September 30, 2023. Driving to Scarlett's.*

"What are you writing?"

"Just the date and where we are." Wren looks up from her notebook to the concrete barricades whipping by. "It always helps if there is written documentation. You never know what's going to be relevant and you never want to forget any detail."

"Old habits die hard, eh." Scarlett cracks a smile and keeps her eyes on the road.

Wren blinks and wants to give Scarlett the side eye but stops herself. *AJ told her I was going to be a police officer.* She clears her throat and flips the conversation off her. "Let's start from the beginning. Where were you born?" Wren never thought that where one was born has any bearing on who one was in a past life; it's more or less a question to start from the beginning. The very beginning.

"I was born in Japan. My parents work in business and finance and were living in Japan when I was born." Scarlett flashes looks to Wren when she can.

Wren scribbles this detail down. "Does that make you a Japanese citizen, then?"

"Oh, no, not at all. Japan is very strict on who can become a citizen. Nothing like the anchor baby stories you hear about happening in the US. I think some law official decreed the hospital room where I was born was Canadian territory for the day, or something like that." She takes a sip of her drink. "I'm sure it wasn't cheap, but my parents had money back then, too."

"How long did you live in Japan?"

"I didn't, really. Right after I was born, we flew back to Canada."

"Interesting." Wren closes her eyes and thinks back to the vision. None of the girls she saw looked Japanese.

"Growing up, my childhood was pretty normal. I went to private school; my parents loved me, spoiled me. Making friends came easily to me. I loved my horse, Sprinkles." She flashes another glance to Wren. "He was a birthday present when I was four, so don't laugh at the name, Sprinkles."

Wren doesn't laugh or even crack a smile. She was trying to imagine what life would be like with a mom and a dad that catered to your every whim. The edges of the triangular pen dig into the side of her finger as her grip tightens.

"Then around twelve years old, the nightmares began. Like I told you yesterday."

Without warning, Wren reaches out and wraps her bare fingers around Scarlett's bare wrist.

His voice is familiar. It's the same man as before. Yelling at the girl to stop crying. Her eyes are swollen shut. The lighting is dim today, but I can see a new girl standing in the hallway, scared and alone.

"Be thankful. I rescued ya. Ya want to go hungry or have your limbs hacked at with a machete while running, looking for sanctuary?" He shoves her forward and his deep laugh builds. "Soldiers, criminals would rape you. One after another. Giving ya no mercy. I'm nice. I give you a bed to lie in, clean clothes, food, shelter."

"That's enough." We shout and emerge from the darkness of a spot against the wall. "She's terrified."

The girl searches our face for comfort, and her sobs turn to heaving breaths.

"She's your problem tonight," the man scoffs. The curl of his upper lip makes me cringe. He turns and leaves us in the wake of the steel door locking shut behind him.

We inch closer to the girl. My best guess puts her at fifteen. Maybe younger, but I plead with a non-existent God that she's not younger. "I'm Fabienne." We extend our hand.

The girl stands there, her lips trembling. Too frightened to speak.

"What's your name?" we ask.

She shakes her head.

"Nom, non, nombre?" Our lips say.

"Imya." The girl I saw before says and lurks from the darkness to stand next to us. "Ya, she looks Russian, Serbian, Ukrainian, or you know, one of the countries he likes to collect us from. You know, like his dolls." Her accent is thick as she eyes me up and down. "Like the rest of us, but not you." Her smile is ungenuine, as if being different down here offers me some type of reward.

I can see the colour of the back of our hands and is not white like all the other girls; it's a rich brown. How could I have not noticed that before?

"Anya," the new girl says.

"I knew it, classic Russian name. I'm Sofia." Sofia studies Anya. When she's finished, she flashes me a glance to signal that she is smarter than me. She sulks back to the blanket on the chair.

Anya asks something in Russian, I think. I'm guessing that's the language she speaks.

All I can do is plead with my eyes to tell her I am sorry. So terribly sorry she is here.

Bojana moans from the bed while she clutches her protruding belly. All eyes are now on her.

Anya asks another question I don't understand, yet Sofia doesn't answer her. She looks to all of us for answers. When the silence fills with more of Bojana's cries, Anya cries with her.

"Dostatochno!" Sofia shouts. She continues speaking in her mother tongue.

I watch Sofia and listen to her explain, this time in English.

"You never fight back or try to attack the man. You will be removed and never come back. He won't think twice about killing you. You are disposable. You keep our space tidy, or you will be beaten. You lie in bed and open your legs when you are asked; if you don't, again he will kill you or threaten to hurt your family. The only way to escape is getting pregnant. Once you deliver your baby, you are returned to your home country and never allowed to return to this one." Sofia's face stays hidden in the darkness.

Once Sofia is finished speaking, Anya throws her body to the hard, cold floor and cries so hard her body convulses, almost like she is willing her body to shut down, as she cannot live like this.

None of us can, *I think.*

Bojana continues to moan in the distance.

We run to her side and attempt to soothe her with words. "You're almost out of here. You'll be free. Wherever you end up, you cannot stay silent, and we promise to do the same when our time comes. No matter what that asshole tells you. You tell our story until you find someone that will listen."

"I don't want to go back. I can't. I have no one left there. Canada is my sanctuary," Bojana tells me through heavy breaths. "This pain is too much. I'd rather die."

"It's going to be okay." We rub her back. Blood soaks

through the bottom half of her nightgown and spreads across the white sheet under her. "Oh, no!" We clutch her arm. "Bojana, are you in labour?"

She lets out another scream, this time louder in an effort to let the pain escape her body.

"Help. We need help!" we shout to the other girls. "Someone grab extra bedding, towels, anything." Blood rushes to my head. We have no training in this. No one here has training in this. Did that asshole think that because we are women, we would know how to deliver a baby? Fabienne's legs run us to the steel door and bang with our fists, pulling all our weight behind every pound. "Help, help! We need help, Bojana is in labour!"

"Bojana." Wren whispers her name under her breath. "Bojana, Sofia, Anya, Fabienne." She repeats the names until they are scribbled down in her notebook.

"What? Who are they? What did you see?" Scarlett's eyes bounce from the road to Wren. "Tell me," she demands.

Wren continues to scribble as she recites what she is documenting. "Bojana, the girl I saw before, she was in labour. The man brought in a new Russian girl, Anya—at least I think she's Russian. One of the other girl's names is Sofia; she is also Russian, I think." She looks at Scarlett. "Does the name Fabienne mean anything to you?"

"Fabienne." The name drips from Scarlett's lips. "Fabienne." The steering wheel squeaks under her wringing grip. "No, but there is something about that name. Hearing it knocks the wind from my chest."

"That kinda makes sense, because it's who you were." The car falls silent. Wren can't remember when Scarlett turned the music off.

She looks at Wren longer than she should. "What did I look like? Tell me you know what that woman looked like. I can hire a sketch artist, they can…"

"Woah, Scarlett! Eyes on the road." Wren drops her pen and points to the road as Scarlett yanks the wheel to put the car back into their lane. The pen clinks as it falls between the seat and the centre console.

"Sorry."

"I didn't see her face; like I told you yesterday, it doesn't work like that unless there is a mirror. And there wasn't." Wren wiggles her short fingers in the crevasse. She can almost pinch her pen with the tips of her fingers. "But she has dark skin."

"Like mine?"

"Darker." Wren manipulates the pen in her fingers until she can form a firm grip to pull it out. "Yesterday, he also called the woman you once were an African princess…"

"How come you never told me that yesterday?" Scarlett's voice is excited but she keeps her eyes on the road.

Wren puffs her breath to blow a piece of hair from her eye. She forgot about the ugly man's racist comment until now. "If I'm going to help you, I need to do it properly. And to do that, I first need to document everything I see, so I don't forget anything. Once I put structure to what I have seen, I will share with you." She nods at her own advice.

"Well, then can you please warn me or tell me when you're going to touch me? You caught me a little off-guard. And I wanted to grab a bite of a blueberry muffin, but I couldn't move for like ten minutes."

"Sorry, yes, I'll try to tell you ahead of time, but honestly, sometimes I see more interesting things when it's unexpected." Wren returns her pen to paper and continues to document everything she saw.

Scarlett waits for Wren's hand to stop moving to ask her question. "Can you look up the name Fabienne? It's interesting. You know, it's not a name you hear often. I've never known anyone with that name before."

"Sure." Wren grabs her purse and fishes out her phone. "Fabienne," she says as she types, pretty sure she has the spelling correct. "Fabienne Colas, Haitian-Canadian actress; Fabienne Shine, model born in North Africa."

"What else?"

"Videos on how to pronounce. The meaning of the name," Wren continues. "Fabienne means 'the noble'."

"Well, if she can't rest until she and these girls find justice, then I think that's pretty damn noble," Scarlett quips.

Wren clips her pen to the cover of her notebook. A part of her hopes this case isn't already solved. She wants to believe Scarlett's intuition, and that she can play a small part in finding justice for these young women. Something Scarlett said springs back to her mind. *A name you don't hear very often.* It's true, she thinks. Once she's settled in the hotel with her laptop, one of the first things she'll do is research the name Fabienne in missing persons in Canada. She clicks her tongue to the roof of her mouth. If they're lucky, they may have caught their first break.

"So, want to touch me again?" Scarlett dangles her wrist in front of Wren's face.

Wren wants to reach out and slap her hand away, but she knows better. *This could become annoying real fast.* She leans as far back into her seat as she can. "No, it's quite exhausting to experience what I do." Wren hopes this will be a subtle way of telling Scarlett she wants quiet time.

"Gotcha." Scarlett grabs her drink and downs the remaining liquid. "It's cold, but it's fine." Her fingers tap the wheel. "So, you said it can help when it's unexpected. What's something you have seen unexpectedly?"

Wren watches the corner of Scarlett's mouth turn up. "I once saw people having an orgy," she says with a tone of authority. Wren surprises herself by sharing that information.

"Oh, my god! Really?" Scarlett beams at the sound of this juicy gossip, even if it is about complete strangers. "When? Where? Tell me everything."

Wren folds her lips into her teeth. The memory surfaces as vividly as the day she saw it many years ago. She remembers the feeling of curiosity that filled her small, growing mind and clears her throat. "Dustin White. He was the boy in my class that, when I touched, I saw the naked people intertwined. I was in grade two, so I was six, seven, I don't remember, but I remember that seeing people naked is something we didn't talk about, so I told no one. I also remember not knowing exactly what I was looking at. I just knew they were naked men and women together in a room. I had never seen naked adults before. I wanted to see what they looked like."

"Well, naturally. I think any kid would take a peek if they came across that scene." Scarlett smiles. "I mean, that's way too young to witness an orgy, but what were you supposed to do? I was twelve when I experienced a man raping a woman, which we now know as Fabienne. Nightmare or not, that's way too young to see something like that. It'll scar you, ya know? And forces you to grow up too fast."

Scarlett's words ring true. This isn't the first time she's thought about not having a normal childhood like the other kids, and not just because she didn't have a mom or dad, but because she was privy to things that no child should ever have to know. "When I was twelve, I saw a man being stabbed to death." The words fall out of her mouth into the air for Scarlett to hear. She instantly bites her tongue. She's never been this open with what she's seen before.

"Please tell me you saw that by touching someone and not in real life." Scarlett lets her eyes linger on Wren until she answers.

"A vision," Wren blurts, and continues with the story. A story that's weighed on her shoulders ever since she saw it. Writing it in her journal helped, but releasing the words to another human felt freeing. "Jack Cunningham. A boy that my Nan and I used to babysit after school. He was a reincarnation of the man who was murdered in the house that he and his family lived in." She takes a sip of her drink to stop herself from reliving the rest of the story, but quickly remembers why she was only taking fake sips. The bitter coffee has grown cold and tastes even worse. She consciously forces herself to not make an expression of disdain.

"Jesus Christ! What did you do?"

Wren shrugs. "Nothing. I was twelve or thirteen." That's a lie, but she isn't ready to share everything with Scarlett, who is still somewhat of a stranger.

"I guess you never really know what people have lived through," Scarlett adds.

"That's for sure." Wren assumes Scarlett is referring to what the living have lived through, but the same applies to the former living, too.

Chapter 8

The rest of the drive passes quickly. Scarlett is one of those people who finds it easy to talk about themselves, whereas Wren listens and takes notes when something seems relevant, or just for something to do. And Scarlett didn't even leave probing questions hanging in the air to force Wren to shift in her skin, which she is grateful for. There isn't much of significance that's revealed by Scarlett blabbing on about her travels across the world, private schools, and more about her beloved horse, Sprinkles. The pieces of Scarlett's life that Wren finds interesting are the parade of doctors who tried to fix her nightmares with drugs, drugs, and more, newer, cutting-edge drugs, and shock therapy as a one-time trial out of desperation. Psychologists also tried their best with regression therapy and hypnosis, but nothing worked, hence why Scarlett had to track down Wren when AJ from her therapy group told her what she could do.

Scarlett never brought up AJ or how the conversation about Wren came about, and Wren isn't about to pull at that thread. Not yet, anyway. The fact that AJ told Scarlett personal things about her life still left a dry, ill taste in her mouth.

"That's where I live." Scarlett points to the extremely tall glass tower. "I can pull up to the entrance and the attendant can park the car or we can park it ourselves."

Wren imagines how wealthy Scarlett must be. *Valet at your house? I never would have thought that I would know someone who was this rich.* "You live here with your parents?" Wren asks while continuing to absorb the sight of the building.

Scarlett laughs. "No, silly. I'm thirty-four, I don't live with my parents."

Wren knows asking who pays for her condo is inappropriate, so she keeps her question to herself. She's also pretty sure she knows the answer to her own question. Wren was also right about Scarlett's age, only a couple years younger than she is. She wonders if, growing up in the same city as Scarlett, there would be a social setting where they would have crossed paths. Not likely with the giant gap in wealth, but from Scarlett's stories, high school was awkward for her, too. Wren knows that feeling, being who she is and living with a foster family after her Nan died. Part of her thinks that if she did cross paths with Scarlett when they were teenagers, she maybe could have helped minimize her years of suffering.

"It's nice, eh?" Scarlett jars Wren from her daydream.

"Oh. Yes. Very nice," Wren answers with a forced smile. Before she realizes, they pull into the entrance and park in the lane market with a gold sign that says 'valet'. "I thought I would stay in a hotel or motel, or whatever you have around here."

"I thought it might be easier if you stayed in my guest

room." Scarlett exits the car and stretches her legs. With little effort, she bends forward and touches her toes.

Wren is impressed and knows better than to attempt a novice stretch in public, as she hasn't exercised since police training. She retrieves her bag from the back seat and stands lost in front of the glass entrance. Like a red dot among black and white stripes, she looks down at her off-brand denim and pilled taupe sweater. She doesn't belong here.

Scarlett can read her apprehension and waves her forward. "Come, just let me show you my place. You can decide if you want to stay here. It's nice. And I never have company." She smiles and hands the man in the navy suit with gold buttons her key fob. "Thanks, Charles, you're the best. Can you also bring my bag up?"

The man obliges with a wink and a smile. "Certainly, Miss Scarlett."

Wren nods to the man and quickens her pace to catch up to Scarlett—a glimpse of a well-tailored woman in her natural habitat, the opposite person from the one in the motel ordering takeout less than twenty-four hours ago. Part of her is curious to see inside how Scarlett lives. How one lives and keeps one's home can say a lot about a person.

"Come, I'm on the eleventh floor. We can take the stairs if you like. I usually do, for exercise."

Flashes of grueling physical tests form behind her eyes. *Pull! Pull! Faster, Recruit Roussel! If you can't do this, you'll never become a cop.* Instructor Turner's voice rings in her ears, even after all these years. Her shoulders tense. "Maybe another day; the elevator is fine," Wren answers.

"You got it. It's probably smart after sitting for so long; we don't want to overdo it, ya know." Scarlett waves to another man in a navy suit with gold buttons standing in front of the elevator. When they arrive, the door is open and waiting for them to board.

"Good afternoon, Miss Scarlett. How lovely to see you have a guest today." The man smiles at Wren and Scarlett.

"Yes, I'm incredibly grateful to have Miss Wren Roussel in my life." Scarlett looks at Wren and reaches out to squeeze Wren's hand as a form of gratitude.

Out of instinct, Wren snaps her hand back.

Scarlett's eyes blaze like a wounded lion as she pulls her hand back.

"Sorry, I..."

Scarlett interjects, "No need to apologize. I know you don't like to be touched. I should have known better." Her eyes flutter from Wren to the elevator attendant. She leans closer to the man and whispers, "Her father used to hit her." Her nose and lips scrunch in pity.

Wren's jaw hangs open as she follows Scarlett into the elevator. Her ears can't believe what they just heard. She even questions her comprehension, as she may have misunderstood what Scarlett whispered. The heavy mirrored doors close before them and they stare at each other in their reflection. "What the heck was that?" Wren blurts.

"I was only saving face with Lewis. I see him every day, and you embarrassed me in front of him," Scarlett says while standing perfectly still, watching the numbers rise on the screen above the doors.

"So? You didn't need to lie. No one hit me as a child, and if they did, it most certainly wasn't my father. I don't have a father, I never have." Wren shifts her stare to her shoes, which are scuffed beyond repair. She's surprised someone like her would be permitted to enter a residence like this.

"It doesn't really matter, does it? What is Lewis going to care?" Scarlett waves it off.

Wren's ears burn. She doesn't want anyone to take pity on her, even if it is a strange man who presses buttons on an elevator for a living. *That's not even an actual job, a monkey could do it!* She wonders if Scarlett touching her was all a game. An unexpected vision. Based on everything she's gathered about Scarlett so far, a conniving move like touching Wren out of the blue doesn't seem out of the realm of her character.

Ding. The elevator notifies them that they have arrived at the eleventh floor and Wren wishes she didn't come. Miles away from the comforts of her own apartment, she scrambles to put on her black latex gloves. The action calms her nerves.

Scarlett marches on towards her door and flashes a glance back to make sure Wren is in tow. "For heaven's sake.

You don't need to put your gloves on when it's just us."

Wren keeps her lips screwed tight and follows.

"The staff here are going to find you even weirder if you wear those gloves about." Scarlett pops a key card from her purse and waves it over the handle of her door. It beeps, and the lock retracts, letting them enter the apartment.

Wren stares in amazement. "Just like in a hotel," she utters to herself.

"Pardon?" Scarlett enters and places her purse on the hook on the wall.

"Sorry, nothing, I've just never seen anyone use a card to enter their apartment," Wren says.

Scarlett lets out an airy laugh. "I guess that would be amusing." She turns and smiles at Wren. "Hotel-inspired living is all the rage."

Wren leaves her bag by the door and follows Scarlett's lead by removing her shoes and placing them in the closet. They walk further into the apartment and the lights magically turn on. "Energy efficient."

"Oh, yes. This entire building is powered by green energy."

Wren takes in the contemporary décor and art. It resembles a museum or gallery more than it does someone's home. Nothing out of place. No evidence of personal effects. She's convinced that Scarlett doesn't live here full-time, or that there is daily housekeeping services.

"So, this is my place." Scarlett waves her hand to the open-concept kitchen, eating area, and living room. Floor-to-ceiling windows line the south side of her condo. "The bathroom, my room, and guest room are down there, and don't worry, the bathroom is all yours. I have an ensuite." Scarlett swings over to the fridge, grabs a bottle of water, and offers one to Wren.

Wren extends her gloved hand to take the bottle. *All this state-of-the-art sustainable technology and she still uses bottled water.*

"Please, take your gloves off. It's just me here, and I know your secret." Scarlett smirks.

"I'd feel better if I left them on." She looks down at her dingy sock feet on the glossy ceramic tile floor.

"And I'd feel better if you took them off," Scarlett states.

Wren is caught between a rock and an alligator's open jaw. If she removes her gloves, she risks some surprise touching, and if she doesn't, she's not sure she wants to test the temperature of Scarlett's tantrums. She wishes she didn't touch Scarlett by surprise in the car.

"Go on. Take them off!"

"Umm, one of my conditions was to stay in a hotel. Alone." Wren twists the bottle of water in her hands and feels the friction against her gloves.

Scarlett stomps down the hall. "I think I'd rather be alone, anyway. Go talk to Lewis, he'll find you a place to stay." A door slams.

Wren stands alone in the kitchen, baffled by their interaction. She takes her water, puts on her shoes, grabs her bag, and exits the apartment. *When Scarlett calms down she can call me. I have enough to begin my research. Alone.*

Chapter 9

"Excuse me." Wren makes eye contact with the elevator attendant. "Lewis?" she calls from behind, wondering how she arrived at the main level and exited the elevator without his acknowledgement. *Maybe he only greets residents, and without Scarlett, the staff just knows I am out of place.*

He spins. "Oh, yes, Miss Hernandez's new friend." His voice is not as warm and welcoming as it was when the ladies rode the elevator up. Wren takes notice.

The name 'Hernandez' throws her off guard. She didn't know Scarlett's last name until this moment. But that's not what strikes Wren as curious; there is something telling in the way Lewis's expression rests, like he's already exhausted with what she has to say. His lips are flat and his brows angled. "Sorry, I don't mean to bother you, but Scarlett told me you could help me check into a local hotel?" Wren asks.

He chuckles silently. "You couldn't last ten minutes with her, could you? That's understandable."

All Wren can do is glare at his uncouth demeanor. "And what is that supposed to mean?" Her own defence of Scarlett surprises her.

"Nothing. I shouldn't have said anything. I apologize." Lewis straightens his jacket. "Please, visit our front desk and

Anita will be of assistance in booking you a room at one of the fine hotels our city has to offer." He eyes Wren from bottom to top with a judgy eye. "And I'm assuming Miss Hernandez is covering your stay?"

Wren doesn't dignify him with an answer. She grips the nylon handles of her Molson Canadian promotional duffel bag and marches in the direction of the front desk. *He has no idea what Scarlett has gone through. Thinks she's another spoiled rich girl.* And although part of Wren's thoughts may be true, his attitude leaves a sour taste in her mouth. As the space grows between Lewis and Wren, she wonders what he meant by her having only lasted ten minutes.

The ride in the building's car service is short, and the Plaza Hotel's exterior is just as grand as the building Scarlett lives in. "What do I owe you?" Wren asks the driver, as she doesn't see a meter like in traditional cabs or know how these town cars work.

"Nothing, ma'am." The smile on the driver's face has an air of delight. Wren knows he, too, doesn't belong in this world. He tips his hat, and his pillowy white hair shows itself.

"Thank you very much." Wren clutches her bag and climbs out of the car. She does her best to match the warmth of the smile the driver offered her.

"Enjoy your stay. The check-in desk will have all your information."

"Thank you." Wren closes the car door and watches the kind, old driver pull away.

Wren is invisible to the hotel staff once she obtains her room key card. There are tons of people coming and going through the lobby and halls, and all these people don't bat an eye at the cost of staying here. Looking up the rates at the Plaza was the first thing Wren did after she buckled up in the car that drove her here. *Scarlett must really want or need my help to pay me and put me up here. Or she has zero concept of money and value.*

Wren's room is every bit as nice as she expects to match its price tag. She runs her gloved finger over random surfaces and inspects her findings. Not one morsel of dust. Before she forgets, she grabs her notebook from her purse and tosses it down on the solid wood dinette table. She removes her gloves, grabs a hotel pen off the desk, and records her interaction with Lewis. This has nothing to do with the past she was hired to detangle, but rather the enigma of Scarlett herself.

Wren sets up her workstation at the desk with her laptop, notebook, and her new Plaza-branded pen. Even the pen from the Plaza writes smoother and feels nicer in her grip than the ten-cent Bic she has in her purse. She flips open to the page where earlier today she wrote the names Bojana, Sofia, Anya and, of course, Fabienne. The next step is at her fingertips, yet she can't force herself to sit and search these names in the missing person database. She knows it's not difficult; in fact, she tells herself this will be the easiest thing she's had to do all day, but the thought of Jack Cunningham and Doug Wannamaker won't leave her head—the victim from the case she solved when she was thirteen. Wren's first real mystery. The only mystery she's ever solved. A robbery turned homicide where the detectives had zero leads.

Doug lived and died in the same house Jack lived in. He didn't leave. He stuck around and was reincarnated as Jack. But Jack never had nightmares of his past. He never once revealed to me he saw or felt Doug was killed, he only knew the parts of the story his parents told him. Wait, Jack was only seven or eight when we used to babysit him, and Scarlett didn't have her nightmares until she hit puberty.

After Wren's Nan passed away, she lost touch with Jack and his family. She was placed in a foster home on the other side of town and had no reason to keep in touch with them. And once Doug and his wife's murderer were caught, it bookended that part of Wren's life.

She flips open her laptop and waits for the machine to boot up. Wren taps her fingers on the desk as she waits. *After I get paid, the first thing I'm buying is a new laptop.* Wren does some quick math in her head and guesses that Jack would be around twenty-seven, twenty-eight; a full-blown adult now. She wonders if she'll still be able to recognize his face. The browser window pops up, and she types 'Jack Cunningham' into the search bar and hits the enter key with more force than normal.

First, she searches the picture results. She figures that will be her best chance of recognizing who Jack became. Pictures of vastly distinct faces in an array of backgrounds fill her screen. She scans each face, looking for traces of the boy she once knew. Her finger grazes the trackpad, scrolling, waiting for his face to jump out. She tilts her head as she examines one image of a guy who looks to be in his late twenties. He has shaggy dark hair under a backwards baseball hat and he's blowing smoke out of the side of his mouth. There is something about the twist of his lips that's hauntingly familiar. "Jack?" Wren says to herself. She clicks on the picture, and it takes her to an Instagram page for a @Puff_Pass_Cunningham. It doesn't take long for her to notice this person is all about smoking marijuana. She scrolls through his photos and begins to wish she left the sweet, innocent memory of Jack undisturbed. One picture causes Wren to click for a closer inspection. She picks up the laptop and pulls the screen closer to her face. A faded Pizza Junction marque sign still stands in the backdrop on main street. *He still lives there. It's him.* She scrolls back to the top. *Over fifty thousand followers and he reviews different types of weed?* Out of all the things she could have guessed Jack would grow into, pothead influencer was not on her list.

Wren's next thought is that it's very possible that nightmares could have driven him to a life as a stoner, but she would need to talk to him to know for sure. She also knows Roger and Colleen Katz were tried and found guilty of second-degree murder, so there is a chance that Jack never had nightmares. There was no reason for Doug to cause Jack unrest.

She returns the laptop to the desk and stares at the painting of a vase of pink tulips that hangs above the desk. *Without my tip to the police, without subjecting myself to the horrors of Doug's attack, they never would have found Roger and Colleen. Doug and his wife never would have found justice.* Wren paces her room. The idea that Doug would stay close to his home strikes her. *Why would he do that?* She's tried hard to leave that part of her life in the past, yet here she is, sucked into another crime that's gone unsolved. But this time the reward is her driver, not the accolade of single-handedly solving a cold case at the age of thirteen.

Wren grabs her gloves and key card off the table, and swiftly makes her way to the door. She wants to make sure she has access to a printer in the business centre before she begins her search into who Fabienne is. Her stomach turns, and she exhales. It won't be long until hidden secrets are exposed, and then there's no turning back.

Chapter 10

"Wren, hey, where did you go?" Scarlett asks.

Wren pulls her cell from her ear in a moment of confusion. "Uh, you told me to go talk to Lewis, your elevator attendant, to help find me a room at the closest hotel." She traps her next breath behind tight lips.

"Oh? Did I? I must have been tired. Where did he send you? The Plaza?" She yawns into the phone.

"Yes, Anita, the woman at your front desk set me up and the building's car drove me over."

"You spoke with Anita? Was she nice to you?"

"Yeah, she was pleasant." This line of questioning seems misplaced in Wren's mind. Instead of probing more into why Scarlett cares about how Anita treated her, she changes the subject. "The Plaza is very nice, thanks again for the accommodations."

Before Scarlett even has a chance to fully listen to Wren's comment, she blabs on. "So for dinner, I'll come to you. We'll sit down at the restaurant and talk about everything so far and what the next steps are."

"Actually—" Wren scans the business centre, spots an empty workstation with cables popping out of the table, and takes a seat. No one else is in the room with her so she is not worried about disturbing anyone with her conversation. "I was hoping to focus on the case alone tonight."

"No, I think it's best if we work together. You need me. I'm the key. Don't you think?" Scarlett insists.

Wren adjusts her phone against her ear. "Yes, but a lot of research is needed, and I can do that alone. I think it'll be boring for you to sit around and watch me work on my computer." A thought pops into Wren's mind and she blurts it out before Scarlett has a chance to speak. "Plus, I don't want to interrupt your life. I'm sure you have hobbies and a job, and you don't want to miss work."

Scarlett laughs. "I work for my parents at their foundation for helping refugees get settled in Canada. It's only really a title I hold. I show up whenever I want. My parents think it's for the best, as trying to hold down a traditional job with my state of mind would be challenging and stressful. Don't you agree?"

Wren scratches at a mark in the table and struggles to find the right words. "I guess so." She never thought how chronic nightmares would affect all facets of someone's life.

"Let me shower and I'll be right over. I'll text when I'm on my way and we can meet in the lobby."

"Okay," Wren answers, positive that there is no other answer that Scarlett would accept.

They spot each other and Scarlett waves through the revolving door. Wren offers a slight smile, Jack still on her mind, and the common location of him and Doug Wannamaker. Something about Scarlett's birth in Japan fidgets in her mind. From what Wren has learned in her experience with reincarnation, she doesn't think that the location of a person before they passed has any weight on who one is reborn as. The exception is Jack and Doug. There was a trauma there, and now Wren is attempting to draw possible parallels with Scarlett and Fabienne, but she needs time to research.

"Wren, how are you?" Scarlett marches to Wren with open arms.

Wren's not sure what to do with her arms, and she intertwines with Scarlett in some sort of awkward embrace. It's been a while since Wren hugged another human, and this hug feels forced. Moisture builds between her skin and the latex protecting her hands as she pats Scarlett's back. She will not chance a random touch from Scarlett. The gloves stay on. "Hi, Scarlett. I'm fine."

Scarlett beams. "Great, I made a reservation for us. Come. The *pasta primavera* here is the best in the city." Her pointy heels click on the polished marble floor as they walk toward the restaurant. "Chef Asselin is fantastic! I hire him for all the dinners the foundation puts on."

Wren walks silently next to Scarlett. She's happy she changed into a pair of black dress pants and a button-up top, as her jeans and hoodie would most likely not be permitted in an eating establishment such as this.

Brass wall sconces cast arched light patterns on the damask rouge wallpaper. Soft, upbeat jazz from a trio of musicians is creating a classy, intimate eating environment. A tightness presses Wren's lungs when she wonders whether she will be asked to remove her gloves to eat in an establishment so fancy. She stuffs her hands into her pockets.

"Don't be nervous." Scarlett picks up on Wren's body language. "You'd feel better if you took off your gloves. I promise I will not touch your hands." She snaps a glance at Wren.

Wren eyes the well-presented patrons dining among them as they weave through the tables. "Fine." She plucks the loose rubber on her fingertips until her gloves are off and discreetly tucked into her purse, the air cool on her moist hands. She dries them on her pants. "Wait, Scarlett, don't we have to wait to be seated?" Wren whispers.

Scarlett smiles, exposing teeth only a high-paid dentist could have crafted. "No, I always get this cozy table, no need to wait."

"Cool," Wren says as she studies an older man dining with a younger woman enveloped in deep conversation. They are all people who make Wren feel like a fish out of water. If Scarlett never pressured her out for dinner, she would be enjoying pizza alone in her room right now, hunched over her laptop.

"See, isn't this cute?" Scarlett ushers Wren to the climb into the tan leather booth.

The table is cozy, like it was designed for a couple on a date, Wren thinks while she scoots in next to Scarlett. Within seconds of sitting down, a waitress comes and pours water into glass goblets.

"So, you seeing anyone?" Scarlett breaks the tension with a personal question.

Wren fiddles with a napkin and lays it over her lap. She chokes on trying to spit out an answer and takes a sip of water. "No," she manages to say. "But I hardly see how that's important."

"I know, I'm just trying to get you to loosen up a bit. You're so serious. For what it's worth, I think you would have made a good cop," Scarlett says.

Wren doesn't know what to say or where to look. No one has ever said those words to her before. "Are you seeing anyone?" is the only retort that comes to her.

"Nah." Scarlett takes a sip of water. "I mean I date men casually, but never anything serious."

"You ever date AJ?" Wren blurts from behind her glass of water, instantly regretting her words.

Scarlett purses her lips. "Who?"

"AJ, my friend who told you to track me down." Wren is thrown off by Scarlett's confusion. *How could she forget who AJ is? Maybe her memory can't be trusted, or she lives in her own fantasy world and she can't keep anything straight.*

"Right. No." Scarlett takes another sip and waves down a waitstaff in the distance. "We're ready to order, please." Scarlett inspects her silverware and lines up the bottoms with the edge of the table. "I would never socialize with or date anyone from therapy," she adds with an air of self-righteousness. "Wait," Scarlett leans in closer to Wren with a smirk. "Yesterday, when you came to the motel, didn't you say you were married to AJ?"

Wren clears her throat, clenching her jaw enough to cause her teeth to sting. Embarrassed with herself, she forgot she let that slip. "No, not exactly."

"What do you mean?"

Wren knows there is no point in lying if Scarlett can ask AJ herself. She swallows her discomfort. "I met AJ when I was in Italy. We were like two magnets who just had to touch, but not in a sexual way. When I touched him, it was like nothing I had ever experienced before. We were married in a past life, except I was the husband who went off to war and died, and he was the wife who was left a widow to raise our son." Wren's eyes linger on Scarlett waiting for a reply. She's a little surprised that AJ blabbed all about her and her abilities yet didn't tell Scarlett about their past connection. He used to get a real kick out of sharing that tidbit of information to people to get a reaction. As a joke AJ would sometimes call Wren husband as a corky nickname.

Scarlett raises her eyebrows. "How interesting."

"Good evening, ladies, have you decided on your meal

for this evening?" the waitress interrupts their conversation.

"Two *pasta primavera* and two house salads," Scarlett answers. "Please."

Wren frantically searches the table for a menu, but there isn't one.

"I ordered for the both of us. You'll thank me later," Scarlett whispers to Wren, and sends her a wink.

"Excellent. Thank you." The waitress nods and retreats toward the kitchen.

Taken aback by the archaic way of ordering, Wren is confused by her own wondering. *Can I be upset about another woman ordering for me? What if I had a severe food allergy or didn't like pasta? Maybe Scarlett had a sense I wouldn't know what to order or wanted to avoid a lingering waitress.*

"I hope you don't mind. My family eats here frequently, and we order whatever we want, even if it's not on the menu." Scarlett unfolds her napkin and lays it over her lap.

"Sure. I've just never had anyone order for me before." Wren stares off at the band in the distance. A warm pressure ripples through her cheek. *Flashes of a man taking off his pants appear before her eyes. I can't see his face, but she can hear his warm, heavy breath behind her. We're too frightened to move. We're in the basement, but in an unfamiliar room, she can tell by the stronger musty book smell and harsh lighting.* With great focus, she forces her head to the side to get away from Scarlett's touch. "What the hell was that?" Wren fumes through her teeth to avoid strangers gawking their way.

Scarlett sits there with her palm lingering in the air. "Sorry, did you not want me to touch your face?" Her eyes are wide like a naïve child asking for forgiveness instead of asking for permission first.

All Wren can do is stare back at this conniving woman and wonder what she has gotten herself into. Her chest thumps with anger.

"Well, what did you see?"

Wren slides as far as she can from Scarlett without falling out of the booth, refusing to tell her what she saw. "Never do that again! Do you understand?"

Chapter 11

After Wren and Scarlett finish their meal in silence, Wren is adamant about retiring to her room alone. She understands the best and quickest way out of this situation is to figure out what happened to Fabienne and the other girls, hand everything over to Scarlett, and get the hell out of here. Money or no money, she is beginning to wonder if it is worth it. Scarlett lives in a world with her own rules, and Wren isn't about to play her games because there is a carrot attached to fifty-five thousand dollars being dangled above her head.

The blue light from the screen of her laptop bounces off her face in the dark. No more stalling, she thinks as she calls up the database for missing persons in Ontario. The province is a shot in the dark, and so is Canada, but she knows she has to start somewhere, and America is too large. *If I had a last name, this would be so much easier, but so far everything Scarlett has shown happened in this basement where there was no need for full names to be spoken.* She scrolls through the list of people with names starting with the letter F, but no Fabienne. She repeats the name out loud, "Fabienne, Fabienne, where are you? Fabienne." She stops scrolling and pilots the curser back to the browser bar. "Of course!" She says the name again, this time in her best French accent. *"Fabienne."* She types in missing persons of Quebec into the browser and clicks on the top result. Her fingers can't keep up with her mind. The page loads with results. Pictures of women who share the same name, their images stacked one on top of the other. Wren blows out her trapped breath. This is a popular name in Quebec. Without knowing what Scarlett's Fabienne looks like, what her last name is, or some distinct fact about her, scrolling through this list is pointless, but Wren continues and reads every word written about each woman of colour.

Knock, knock. "Wren. It's Scarlett. Can I come in?"

Wren jumps in her seat at the sound of raps on her door. She's paralyzed by her choices. Sit in silence and hope Scarlett goes away, or answer her and not prolong the relentlessness she knows Scarlett is capable of. "I'm busy," she shouts after five seconds of contemplation.

"I just want to tell you I'm sorry. Can I come in, please? There is something I need to tell you."

Wren stands and shakes her head. "Fine. Give me a sec." On her way to the door, she flips on a light and blinks until her eyes adjust. She can't imagine what drama Scarlett must release tonight. *Couldn't this wait until tomorrow?* Wren unlocks the door, opens it, and turns to walk back to her computer.

The door clicks closed behind Scarlett. "First, let me just tell you I am so sorry for my behaviour in the restaurant. I shouldn't have touched your face, and ordering for other people isn't polite. My mother would be disappointed if she found out I wasn't minding my manners." She takes a breath.

"I'm a little bit of a control freak." Scarlett laces her fingers and twists her hands. "My therapist told me I look to control every aspect of my real world because I can't control my nightmares."

Wren sits back down at the desk and bends her neck so she can see Scarlett. That makes sense, she thinks. She keeps her expression blank.

Scarlett takes another deep breath. "And I used to be an alcoholic." She paces. "Well, I still am, but I'm recovering. Every day can be a challenge. In a few months is my third-year anniversary of being sober."

Wren's shoulders drop. "I get it. Self-medicating, trying to dull the nightmares."

Scarlett laughs. "Except liquor always made the nightmares more intense, I just remembered less of them." She stops pacing and plops down on the plush chair in the corner of the room. Under the light, the dark circles under her eyes become more apparent.

All Wren can do is stare and nod. *In her mid-thirties and already a recovering alcoholic. You never know what someone is dealing with.* "It's okay. Thank you for telling me."

"What are you up to? Find out anything juicy?" Scarlett asks. Her slight frame sinks deep into the chair, the plush leather hugging her tired body back.

Wren turns back to her screen. "I wish. The only thing I have is that we were pronouncing Fabienne wrong. Try it with a French accent. *Fabienne,*" she says.

"*Fabienne.*" Scarlett lets each letter roll off her tongue as if she's been speaking French her whole life.

Wren licks her lips and blushes at her attempt to say the name correctly. She twists to look back at Scarlett. "Do you speak French?"

"Heavens, no. I struggle with learning languages. I'm lucky to grasp the English language." Her arms pat the puffy arms of the chair. "I hated school. I guess I'm lucky my family has money. I'm smart enough to know that." She laughs.

Wren's not sure how to respond, so she spins back around to her screen and scrolls, scanning the faces of the missing and forgotten. "It's sad to think that these women and young girls will probably remain missing."

Scarlett hoists herself from the chair and saunters over to see the screen of faces. "Yep, life is a bitch, and the world is shit." She touches Wren's shoulders and instantly removes her hands. "Sorry, I didn't mean to do that."

The warmth of Scarlett's hand lingers through the fabric of Wren's shirt and spreads like lava across her skin. She wasn't caught off-guard with a gruesome vision, but rather by the friendly interaction. A fleeting smile crosses her lips. "It's fine. Nothing happens when you touch the fabric I'm wearing."

"Oh, good." Scarlett reaches out and gives Wren's

shoulder a squeeze. "Now, let me see these women; maybe if I see my Fabienne, it will trigger something in my mind, and I'll know it's her."

Wren knits her brows. "Are you sure you want to try that?"

"Why? Does it frighten you not knowing what might happen to me?" Scarlett laughs and pulls the chair from the table next to Wren at the desk.

"If you're cool with it, then I'm cool with it. But I should tell you I have zero first-aid training, so if you have a seizure all I can do is call for help." Wren digs her phone from her pocket and sets it on the desk.

"I'm just kidding. I'll be fine." Scarlett scooches her chair in to get a better look.

Wren clicks back to page one to start at the beginning, although she thinks looking at the people named Fabienne born after Scarlett seems like a waste of time. "Maybe we should start on the last page and work our way up to the eighties, when you were born."

"Brilliant. That's some good detective work."

Hearing Scarlett say those words with her nonchalant air of speaking makes Wren feel like a child. She nibbles on the inside of her cheek. On the last page, the oldest date of the missing Fabienne is 1959. She guesses at some point they remove people based on the fact they would most likely be too old to still be alive, or the family who would still be looking for them are too old. Wren's mind spirals with depressing possibilities.

"Slow down a bit," Scarlett asks.

"Oh, sure." Wren must have sped up her pace without knowing.

"Well, at least there are only five pages."

"Yep." Wren nods. The French faces are forever trapped in time. A wire twists around her heart as she wishes she could reach through the screen, touch their cheeks, and see something, anything to help. But she knows that would only help if their past life had something to do with their disappearance, which would be impossible. The tension in her chest loosens, and she's reminded why she used to be obsessed with touching people and animals; it's because they could hold the key to the mysteries of the past.

"Stop!" Scarlett shouts and jabs her finger into the screen. "Wren! Do you see this?"

Wren climbs out of her thought spiral and focuses on the face staring back at them. "Fabienne Delva."

"Not the name. The face. Look at her face!"

Wren squints at the woman staring back at her; she's seen this woman before.

"Wren, look at me." Scarlett stands almost sending her chair toppling backwards. She rips off her oversized fake reading glasses, pulls her dark curls off her face, and smiles, showing her teeth to match the woman in the photo. "Do you see it?" Scarlett mumbles through her perfect smile.

Wren's eyes flash back to the screen, then to Scarlett. "She looks like you. Or rather, you look like her." She blinks to make sure what she is seeing is correct. Wren reads the blurb next to Fabienne's picture. "Date of birth, 1969. Reported missing in October 1985 when she never returned home from school. Lived with her family in Montreal, Quebec, and immigrated here from Haiti. Last seen leaving St. Francis High School walking to her after-school job at a local restaurant."

"This is her. It must be her!" Scarlett lets go of her hair and examines the photo with a more critical eye. "How can this be?"

Wren blows out the air trapped in her cheeks. The resemblance is undeniable. "How?" She mutters under her breath. "How is it possible to look like the person who you are a reincarnation of?" Wren chews on the inside of her mouth again. The shock of pain startles her as she accidentally bites through her tender mouth flesh.

Chapter 12

"You need to relax." Wren stands and addresses Scarlett.

Scarlett rummages through her purse, chucking its contents all over the room, searching for something.

"For all we know, this could be a very weird coincidence." Wren worries Scarlett is searching for something dangerous, like a pill or a little bottle of alcohol she carries around like a security blanket.

"Fuck, finally." Scarlett holds up her phone and taps away at the screen. She rushes over to the laptop to check the website where they found Scarlett's twin from a previous decade.

Wren keeps out of Scarlett's way. "What are you doing?"

"I'm finding this page so I can take a screenshot of Fabienne on my phone." The phone screen is inches from her face, as if it's a precious stone she can't risk leaving her sight. "Wren, I expected you to be smarter than this."

Wren's lips twist as blood rushes to her face. "What the hell do you mean by that?" She crosses her arms and keeps her eyes glued to Scarlett.

Scarlett looks up from her screen for a second. "Facial features, the way people look, traits are inherited through genetics.”

“Fabienne was from Haiti, is your family from Haiti?”

“No, that’s the point. Someone is lying to me.” Scarlett huffs and jams her phone in front of Wren’s face. “Look! Look at those people.”

Wren adjusts the screen in Scarlett’s hands to focus on what she is trying to show her. “Are those your parents?”

“Yep! My dad is white, and my mother is Black. Both Canadian. Their families have been here for generations.” Scarlett moves beside Wren to inspect the photo with her. “Tell me which one of my parents I look the most like.”

“Well—” Wren is lost for words. She’s searching the photo for something to latch onto. “Your mom has brown eyes; you both have similar hair. Same height.” In all honesty, Wren thinks if she saw this family walking down the street, she would never question that they weren’t a family bound by genetics. “Family members don’t always look similar. I don’t think I look that much like my mom,” Wren adds.

Scarlett’s fingers spread across the screen to zoom in. “My mother is wearing a wig. But look at their smiles, the shapes of their jaws, their eyes.” Her dark eyes land on Wren. “Those are not features you find anywhere in my face.” Scarlett takes the phone, finds her newly-gained photo of Fabienne, and zooms in so the edges of the device frame her face. “This is my face.”

There is no denying the similarities between Scarlett and Fabienne. Wren crosses her arms. "Fabienne's skin tone is a little darker than yours," Wren answers. "And it's said that we all have a twin out there somewhere. I mean, there are almost eight billion people on the planet; some of us are bound to look like each other, even if we're not related."

"This picture was probably taken in summer. She's tan. I get darker in the summer, too." Scarlett pulls her phone to her chest and locks eyes with Wren. "What do we do now?"

"The first thing we need to do is not jump to conclusions. We're not one hundred percent sure this is even the right Fabienne." Other than this uncanny resemblance to Scarlett, the only other piece of the puzzle that fits is what Fabienne was wearing when Wren experienced her vision. It looks like clothing from the eighties. "Scarlett, what are you doing?"

Scarlett drops to her hands and knees, cleaning up the contents of her purse that she haphazardly discarded moments ago in a panic to find her phone. "I'm cleaning up. I'm not a slob."

"Then what are you doing?"

"I'm going to go pay my parents a visit tonight."

"No." Wren rushes to her and grabs her shoulder. "Please, don't do that. It would be a huge mistake," she pleads.

Scarlett lifts herself off the floor and returns all the items to her purse.

Wren can feel the heat radiating off Scarlett's body.

Scarlett turns to face Wren, her eyes wide and full of fire. "I am who I am because of them. They're ashamed of me. Embarrassed. They never really wanted me to get better. I always knew there was something off. And now I have proof."

"You have proof you look like Fabienne Delva." Wren's eyes soften. "That's not enough."

"It's enough to get them talking. Maybe they can explain why I look like this stranger who went missing all those years ago more than I look like either of them. Huh! Isn't that good detective work?"

"A good detective would do nothing to spoil the case before they have concrete evidence." She holds her eyes in Scarlett's. "If your parents are connected to this, and you accost them with this piece of information now, it could spook them, and maybe they'll try harder to hide evidence that could be useful."

Scarlett slumps down on the plush leather chair. Her rigid body folds into putty. "You're right. I'm so confused. Seeing her face that looks like mine got me all fired up. I can't see straight, ya know?"

"I know." Wren takes a seat on the bed across from Scarlett. *How could a spirit or soul be so strong to force their new body to look so much like their old one? Why would they even want that?*

"You're a good person." Scarlett sits up in the chair. "I know I'm paying you, but you're still a good person." She tilts her head and stares at Wren.

Wren keeps her arms crossed tight against her chest. Scarlett's scrutiny makes her uncomfortable. "What?"

"He was right about you." Scarlett offers a slight smile.

"Who?" Wren stares back at her.

Scarlett breaks her contact and fiddles with a tassel on the side of her purse. "Your friend. You know him."

"AJ?"

"Yeah, he said deep down you were a good kid who just always wanted to do what's right." Scarlett quickly looks at Wren, then back down to her purse.

The word *kid* stands out in her mind. *AJ would never call me* kid. *I'm older than he is.*

"Can I stay with you tonight?" Scarlett changes the subject.

"Why? You have a beautiful apartment. Or you can afford to rent your own room here." Wren remains seated on the bed.

Scarlett can't help but let out a laugh. "I don't sleep much. Plus, I'm feeling very motivated to have a drink right now." She eyes the mini fridge. "And I know I won't do anything if I'm here with you. And you don't want me to go see my parents." The whites of her eyes are bright, looking for sanctuary.

"It's fine, I guess. I can sleep on the loveseat and…"

Scarlett cuts Wren off before she can finish her sentence. "That's not necessary. You keep your bed, and I'll take the loveseat. If I do sleep, it's short little cat naps, anyway. I'll just curl up into a little ball and you won't even know I'm here."

"That's fine." Wren stands and returns to her computer at the desk. "I still have Sofia, Bojana, and Anya to look up. Hopefully Russians missing in Canada won't be too hard to find." She opens her notebook and documents everything she can on Fabienne Delva. She even types her name into a search engine but comes back with nothing fruitful. The word *kid* still lingers in the back of her mind. *Did AJ actually call me* kid *or was Scarlett paraphrasing and mixed up the word? Either way, AJ isn't the endearing type; he is more of the push-you-in-the-water-and-hope-you-can-swim type.*

A curled-up Scarlett watches Wren from her chair, her eyes fluttering between real life and the escape of a brief slumber, her phone displaying Fabienne Delva slipping from her grasp.

Wren peeks back at Scarlett, who has been quiet for the past ten minutes. *I wonder if a nightmare is going to jar her from her sleep?* She prepares her mind by imagining different scenarios. Maybe Scarlett will wake up screaming, or physically hurl herself to the floor in a struggle with her past captor. Wren's heart thuds; it's all she can hear. She opens her notebook and reads her recap of events surrounding Fabienne Delva. It's inevitable that she'll need to touch Scarlett again to gain more information. She cranks her neck to check on her again. Scarlett is curled up, the same as she was the last time she looked at her. The thought crosses her mind that she could walk over to her right now and gently place her hand over Scarlett's, but Sofia, Bojana, and Anya's names call her attention back to the search online, their faces etched into her memory. Unlike Fabienne, if she finds the missing person report for any of these three girls, she'll without a doubt know it's them.

Wren opens a new tab and searches the name Bojana on the Quebec missing person's site. She starts with her because Bojana is another rare name. The results yield one woman who is older, Italian-looking, and not an ounce of resemblance to the Bojana she is looking for. She switches back to the site for missing persons in Ontario.

Before typing 'Bojana' into the search, she opens another tab and types in the name, reminded of when Scarlett asked her to look up Fabienne in the car. Another beautiful actress dominates the top few results. Then the meaning of the name, a Slavic-given name, derived from the Slavic word 'Boj', meaning battle. *Whoever this Bojana was definitely fought the battle of her life.*

Wren clicks back to the missing person search and types in the six letters. This time there are only two pages of women. Two pages too many, she thinks, and she scrolls, inspecting their faces with a quick study. The picture of the

Bojana she is searching for hits her like a punch to the gut. "It's her," she whispers. Thin, dark blond hair falls over her narrow shoulders dressed in a purple t-shirt. Her clear olive complexion forces a toothy grin in what appears to be a school photo. Wren reads on. *Bojana Milosevic, missing since May 1984. Last seen walking home from Massey High School in Oakville, Ontario. She and her family arrived in Canada as Serbian refugees. DOB: May 17, 1970. Any information on the whereabouts of Bojana Milosevic should contact the Oakville police.* Wren does some quick math in her head. If she's still alive, she'd be fifty-three.

"Well, I've seen her. I just can't tell you where, or when exactly," she says to herself, and scribbles down Bojana's last known location into her notebook.

"Why are you doing this?" Scarlett says.

Wren whips around to find her still in a deep sleep. "Scarlett, are you okay?"

There is no answer. Scarlett's eyelids flutter and her forehead creases with deep lines.

"Fabienne." Wren tries a different approach. Her lips moving independently from her mind, as if her heart knows not to overthink this. "I'm here." She rushes to her side and kneels on the carpet, mindful not to touch her.

"Where did he take her?" Scarlett asks through a whisper.

"Where did he take who?" Wren leans in closer to Scarlett's lips. Her heart races. She's only ever had the privilege of seeing what a past life wants to reveal to her through their own point of view. She's never had the opportunity to talk to them, and never fathomed that she could talk to them.

"Bojana."

"I want to help you. You need to tell me the man's name."

"He calls himself Roman. He is so mean and cruel. None of us deserve this." Scarlett speaks softly, as if it's another voice inside her. In the little time Wren has known Scarlett, she has accomplished nothing softly.

"You need to find out where he took Bojana," Wren says.

"Something isn't right. He's back. Go away. You'll get us all in more trouble. Wait," Scarlett says. "No, don't go. He's going to take me to the room. I don't want to go to the room." Tears well in the corners of her eyes.

"Fabienne. It's okay. I'm here." Wren hovers her hands over Scarlett's arm, bracing herself to experience Fabienne's lived trauma.

"Wren!" Scarlett's eyes shoot open.

A tingle of ice slithers up Wren's spine. "You're awake. You were having a nightmare, but I was talking to you, to her, Fabienne."

Scarlett picks a crusty bit from the corner of her eye and sits up. "What do you mean talking to her? Was I talking in my sleep?"

Wren attempts to sort through the explanations firing off in her mind. "Her, yes, she was talking through you, you were sleeping. The nightmare, your nightmare, Fabienne's life, you were telling me what was happening." She slumps to the floor and leans against the chair. "Regardless of who was communicating with me, they told me his name."

"What? You found out his name?" Scarlett is fully awake now, staring through her blinks at Wren. "Tell me."

"Roman." Wren twists her neck to stare back at Scarlett.

Scarlett puckers her lips, digging deep in her memories for a connection to a man named Roman. "Roman?" She squints.

"Yeah, Roman. That's what you, or Fabienne, told me." Wren picks herself off the floor and goes to her notebook to document the new discovery. "Don't get too excited, criminals often have many aliases. But this is a start."

"Like Birdie." Scarlett winks at a frowning Wren. "Don't give me that look. I was only joking." She stands and stretches, reaching her long arms towards the ceiling. "What else did I say?"

Wren continues to scribble. "Something about not letting him take you to the other room, and you wanted to find out where he took Bojana." Her pen stops writing and falls to the paper. "I found Bojana." Her eyes wide at the sound of her own discovery that was overshadowed by the sleep talking.

"You know where he took her? How?"

"No." Wren twists in her chair. "I found her missing person entry." She turns back and taps the screen. "Here on the computer. She went missing in 1984 from Oakville."

Scarlett joins her and looks blankly at the screen. "She was there with Fabienne? She's so young." Scarlett chokes back the lump in her throat and wipes her eyes. "She was pregnant. Are you sure?"

"Yes, I'm sure. I saw through Fabienne's eyes. And apparently Roman took her somewhere. That's what Fabienne wanted to know."

Both women stare at Bojana's school photo, forever paired with the report that she went missing at the age of fourteen. "Maybe she's still alive."

"Or maybe she's haunting some other girl's or boy's nightmares, looking for justice," Wren responds. She turns to face a pale Scarlett, the solo light from the lamp making her look older and more tired than usual. "Because that's what Fabienne is doing to you."

"Stop." Scarlett wipes her eyes with the sleeve of her shirt. "Don't talk like that. She was abused and raped, and we have to find Bojana to let her know Roman, or whoever the fuck did this, will not get away with it. Even after all these years." Scarlett's hardened confidence softens.

Wren isn't acclimatized to Scarlett's rollercoaster of emotions. "Look, we already found more information in twenty-four hours than the cops probably found in twenty-four years," she says to comfort Scarlett. "And once we connect all the pieces of the puzzle, you can take the information to the police, or we can submit what we found anonymously." A pinch in her stomach tells her it doesn't matter how they deliver the information to the police, someone else is going to take credit for their work, her work. History always repeats itself, and even if she single-handedly solved the Wannamaker case when she was thirteen, she learned people of authority would steal credit if the opportunity presented itself. She massages her own shoulder to calm herself and tells herself this isn't about her; it's about bringing Scarlett peace.

"Is your shoulder sore?" Scarlett asks.

"Oh." Wren stops and pulls her hand back to her lap. "No, I was just thinking…"

Scarlett's tears instantly stop, like someone turned a tap to stop it from dripping. Her eyes grow. "I have an idea. Tomorrow, let's go to the spa to relax. Go in the sauna, have a soak, a massage."

The little hairs on the back of Wren's neck stand at attention at the thought of a massage. A stranger's hands rubbing her naked flesh. She quivers at the thought of not escaping visions of their past life. *What if it was disturbing? Or it could be a pleasant vision. Or there could be no vision at all.* "I'll take a hard pass on the massage, plus we need…"

Scarlett cuts her off again and laughs. "Right, I forgot."

She raises her hands and wiggles her fingers. "The whole no touching thing."

"Not only that, I have more research." Fabienne and Bojana's faces flash before her eyes. "Montreal and Oakville, they aren't geographically close, yet these two girls ended up together. I need to find out where they ended up and how they got there."

"Well, we now know an ugly man named Roman had something to do with their disappearance." Scarlett slides her sleeve up to her elbow and holds out her arm. "Go on. Touch me. Let's get this over with."

Wren eyes Scarlett's bare arm. Her body remains motionless. She knows she's going to have to touch her again, but she doesn't want to keep seeing the same scene. Her eyes meet Scarlett. "Not yet. I need you to try something."

"Can we go to the spa tomorrow?"

"No."

"Then I don't want to try it." Scarlett says with closed eyes and tight lips. "Wait, what do you want me to try?" She opens one eye.

"I need you to tell yourself to go back, back to the time when you got abducted." Wren's never had someone she could experiment her ability with. Well, other than AJ, but that doesn't count because he didn't live through some horrendous trauma, and she doesn't want to think about him right now.

"Oh, yeah, that's good." Scarlett is fully alert and paying attention. "I can, and will, do that, with all my might, but you need to come to the spa with me tomorrow."

The corners of Wren's mouth turn down.

"I'll buy you a new bathing suit if you didn't pack one."

"Why would I pack a swimsuit?" Wren interjects.

Scarlett shrugs and runs back to the chair to find her phone. "I'll order one online right now and it'll be here by noon tomorrow." She eyes Wren between tapping away on her phone. "One piece, size small, black. Simple. Classy. You'll love it. Done. Easy-peasy."

Wren stares at Scarlett, folding her lower lip between her teeth.

"I try something new. You try something new." Scarlett points her manicured finger at Wren. "I'll call the front desk and have them send up a razor."

The struggle to make a connection between Montreal and Oakville slips from her mind as she tries to remember the last time she had to wear a bathing suit. Childhood memories spring to mind. *Is this really happening?*

Scarlett collects her purse and makes her way to the door after she grabs a bottle of water from the mini-fridge. "It's getting late. You better get some sleep. I'll pick you up tomorrow once your suit is delivered. Night-night, Wrenny

Wren." She turns back. "Good detective work today. Don't worry, you don't need to get a massage tomorrow." Scarlett leaves with a wink.

"Night," Wren says to Scarlett. She bites her lip to prevent a laugh from escaping her mouth. No one has called her Wrenny Wren before. *What a stupid nickname.* She tries to come up with a logical explanation for why Scarlett wants to go to the spa with her, and why she suddenly left when an hour ago, she didn't want to leave. *Maybe all rich people are this bizarre.*

Chapter 13

Wren holds up the black swimsuit Scarlett tossed at her when she entered the room. Her nose scrunches at the smell of plastic packaging that still lingers on the garment. How someone can order anything online and have it delivered in less than twenty-four hours still boggles her mind. She knows how the delivery systems work; she delivers food for a living, anyone with a car can deliver anything for anyone, but Amazon is on another level in terms of having inventory ready at a moment's notice.

"Come on now, throw it in your bag and let's go. It looks like it's going to fit fine."

"Do I need to pack a towel?" Wren asks as she stuffs her new swimsuit into her bag.

"Don't be silly." Scarlett waves her to follow.

Wren grabs her notebook from the desk as she passes and tells herself she'll tell Scarlett about her latest discovery once they are in the car. It isn't much, but it is something. Just another piece that doesn't fit with anything else she knows so far.

Wren waits for Scarlett to get the navigation sorted. The screen tells her that they will arrive at their destination in approximately thirty-three minutes.

"You ever been to a spa before?" Scarlett asks.

"No, can't say that I have." Wren shakes her head. The thought of her exposed skin being so close to other people with exposed skin makes her itch. She tells herself she will stay alert and mind everyone's personal space.

Scarlett merges with traffic and tails the car ahead of them closely, a driving maneuver Wren would never do out of fear of rear-ending someone.

"It is going to change your life. You'll love it," Scarlett adds.

It baffles Wren how Scarlett can start the day with zero recognition of yesterday's events. No mention of Fabienne, no questions about if Wren found out any other information after she left. No wandering conversations about how she can look uncannily identical to the woman she might have been in a past life. "I found Sofia and Anya," Wren blurts to steer the conversation in a meaningful direction.

"What?" Scarlett looks to Wren. "They are alive?"

Wren's face turns red at how she phrased her fact. "No, sorry, I meant I found their missing person profiles." She sinks into her cooled leather seat. "I don't know if they are still alive."

"And..." Scarlett slams on the gas, and the women get pushed back into their seats.

"Sofia Petrov was from Russia and Anya Adamovich was from Ukraine, but both of their families immigrated to

Canada and lived in Toronto.”

Scarlett remains quiet.

“So, we have Fabienne from Montreal, Bojana from Oakville, and Sofia and Anya from Toronto.” Wren focuses on a graffiti tag on the side of a cement bridge as they whip by, just as confused by what it says as the link to these three cities.

Scarlett readjusts her sunglasses. “Sounds pretty random to me. And Roman? Anything on him?”

Wren didn’t even search for Roman; there is nothing to look up without a last name. “Nothing yet.” She pulls the sleeves of her sweater over her hands. “What about what I asked you to do?”

“All night I’ve been talking to myself like a damn fool. If my walls weren’t soundproof my neighbours would think I’m crazier than normal.” Scarlett chuckles and stifles a snort. “Show me when you were abducted, show me something different. Show Wren something that we can use to help. Show me clues of where you are.” “Any answers in your nightmares?” Wren smirks.

“No, nothing yet. But I didn’t sleep after I left the hotel. I just went to my building’s gym and walked around.”

Wren eyes Scarlett’s exposed wrist, wearing what she guesses is an expensive watch. *Now is not the time. Not yet.*

The bathing suit fits surprisingly well. Wren wraps the complimentary white towel around her torso and exits the change room to find Scarlett, women gabbing and changing freely in the rows between the lockers.

"Wren, over here. Put your stuff in the locker."

She rolls her shoulders inward and looks for a path to Scarlett with the least amount of people. Hugging her arms, she thinks about how she's never bared so much of her flesh in a space with other people baring so much flesh. Her skin stings with the jolt of electricity at the thought of accidentally coming in contact with someone. She pretends she's the tweezers in a game of Operation, and all these women are metal edges, ready to shock her with visions of their past at any moment.

"I'll keep the key safe." Scarlett slides the curly jelly bracelet over her wrist as Wren sets her bag in the metal cube. "I figure I'll show you around first, then I'll go get my massage. And you can pick how you want to relax."

Wren settles on a sauna that looks like a giant's cedar barrel laying on its side with a smokestack protruding out of the top. It's quiet, with only one other person inside. She takes a seat on the bench the furthest away she can sit from the furry man glistening in sweat. The heat makes it hard to breathe. She can't recall ever being in a situation so hot. Even the hottest summer days as a kid, where she thought she could fry an egg on the sidewalk, weren't as hot as this sauna. But she is going to give it a shot. Apparently, it is good for you. Helps release toxins—that's what Scarlett told her on the grand tour. She settles in and releases her towel. She wants to smile but holds it back. Wearing nothing but a bathing suit in a public setting as an adult is new, and for the first time she doesn't feel different, she feels like everyone else. *I bet the man doesn't even notice me through all this steam.* Wren invites the hot cedar aromas into her senses. Her skin sucks moisture from inside her body and releases it through every pore. *The wealthy sure know how to enjoy life sometimes.* She never would have come to a place like this if it wasn't for Scarlett. At peace with being in the moment, she closes her eyes and lets the reality of her life dissolve into tiny vapours and get carried off by the steam.

It's loud, so loud. Cheering, screaming, crying, reaching out. I'm trapped in a sea of young women. The energy of the mob pushes and pulls my body. Before us is a stage. Four men in formfitting suits stand behind their instruments, a cord of music ripples through the air, and the energy around me erupts. The base thumps my chest. Someone squeezes my hand. "Paul! It's Paul. It's really him. I'm going to die!" the girl latched on to me with her death grip screams into my ear. This song. I know this song.

Wren's eyes shoot open, and she springs from her seat as if the cedar plank bench burns her bum.

"Sorry, I didn't mean to sit so close," the young girl sitting next to her says. "It's getting full, I had to scooch down."

Wren sees blurred faces through the steam. Her heart quickens. *I need to get out of here.* She beelines for the door to escape. Her flimsy complimentary flip flops slip under her feet with each squeaky step. The fall air blasts her face, and she's never felt more relief in letting the cold air smack her skin. Her sinuses sting from the instant switch from hot to cold. She stands on the path, unsure where to go. Unsure what to do. She chooses a direction and hopes it will lead her back to the change rooms. Her plan is to get fully clothed and wait for Scarlett in the car. A faint ring still echoes in her ears from the crowd of screaming fans she experienced.

"Woah, Wren. It looks like you just saw a ghost." Scarlett casually walks towards her.

"You could say that." Wren makes her way past Scarlett. "I've had enough for today." Her skin is still vibrating.

"Did someone touch you?" Scarlett frowns.

"Yes, but it's fine. It's over. It just zapped all my energy. I wasn't expecting it. I was so relaxed..." Wren pauses to find her breath.

Scarlett walks next to her, mindful not to touch her. "So, what did you see that's got you all hot and bothered?" Her tone insinuates something naughty.

She gives Scarlett the side-eye. "Nothing like that. It was a Beatles concert with a million screaming girls. I thought I was going deaf."

"Wow, you know how many people would have loved to experience that? To see them perform on stage, alive, together."

Wren stops and stares back at Scarlett, the cold now seeping into her skin. She uses her breaths to calm her nerves and tightens her towel around her shoulders.

"Look, you're shaking now, let's find a hot pool. I'll stay with you, and I'll make sure no rando comes near us." Scarlett stands there in her white designer swimsuit with a cutout on the side, seeming more calm than she has in the last two days.

Wren watches the couples and single people sauntering along the pathways, and she recalls a time in her life, when she was much younger, where a place like this would have been her playground. Body after body of exposed flesh she could accidentally touch and peer through a window that only she can see. The secrets of past lives on full display. A concert never would have drained her before, it would have excited her, left her hungry for more. Like Jenny from third grade, who when she touched, she would always hear funky music, and everyone would be dancing and twirling in rhythm with the beat. Years later she pieced together that Jenny loved to go to disco clubs in her previous life, and she thought that would have been a great time to be alive.

"Do you remember your past life?" Scarlett asks as she lowers herself into the hot water.

The water burns the bottoms of Wren's feet with a white-hot sensation before the one hundred-and-four-degree water warms her skin. "Um, no, but I know I was a man, a soldier in the war who died in battle." She submerges the rest of her body up to her neck into the biggest hot tub she has ever seen.

Scarlett's eyes light up. "You can touch yourself and see this?"

"Not at all. I've only seen fragments of who I once was when I met AJ. We were like two souls drawn together like magnets." Wren stares at her hands under the water and wiggles her fingers. "The randomness of how we found each other a half a world away I will never understand." She looks at Scarlett, who's staring back at her intently.

"Where did you two meet? Does he have the ability to see past lives, too?"

Wren tightens her lips. Scarlett's simple question raises the hairs on the back of her neck. *Why would AJ tell her all about me and nothing about himself? Normally he's an A-class narcissist.* "Did AJ not talk about himself to you?" *He loves to blab on about his adventures to anyone who will listen. Tell them he's a citizen of the world. His opening line to people is the fact that he's been to over fifty countries,* Wren recalls.

Scarlett turns her attention from Wren and stares at the couple across the pool. "Meh, doesn't matter. Forget I asked." She sits lower under the water, so her shoulders are submerged. "The heat feels so good, doesn't it?"

Wren can't deny the soothing effects the hot water has over her body. The ringing in her ears caused by the concert has disappeared and she forgets that moments ago her body was more rigid than a wooden ruler. She decides not to dwell on AJ. She'll worry about how to handle him later. The silence lingers between the two women, and they take solace in the quiet. There are no words to be said in this moment, but Wren knows what she needs to do. She looks down to see the location of Scarlett's hand under the water. It's floating freely next to her. She reaches out and grabs it. Wren and Scarlett are now linked hand-in-hand in the relaxing confines of the water. To an onlooker it would only appear as two people showing innocent affection, their secret of trying to solve a long-forgotten case of abduction, abuse, sexual assault, and nightmares remaining invisible.

Cots line what looks to be an abandoned classroom. They're speaking fast to each other. The other men, women, and children talk. It's French. And with the current of the water another memory takes its place. Bobbing and weaving with the motion of the water it's difficult to pin it down and watch. Kids laughing at her, taunting her with mean words. Now in English. 'You're dumb. Why is your hair so frizzy?' A pain deep inside I don't understand. She doesn't want to be here. Warm tears streak her face. The next memory ushers itself in with the current. Eating ice cream with two smaller children. They have her smile and the same hair. A boy and a girl, twin siblings. We take their little hands in each of ours and tell them we need to help Ma with dinner and clean up tonight and be on our best behaviour. Their two innocent smiles fade into the next clip. We're walking down the sidewalk. A man in a car with big sunglasses and a hat asks us for directions, but in French. I piece together the words and context based on the map he holds up. We ignore him and keep on my way, but his tires roll slowly behind us. He's following us now. We look around for someone, for anyone and our legs move quicker. We glance over our shoulder. Roman. His hat and sunglasses are now removed. Closing the distance between us. He's on foot and he's fast. Faster than us. The next memory bobs in and the motion turns my stomach. It's black. We're moving. Our mouth is so dry, and our wrists and ankles are bound. We attempt to wiggle. Something cold and jagged jabs into our back. Panic has set in and our breaths are quick and shallow. Our stomach lurches and I'm blinded by lights. After a minute our eyes adjust. A swell of pain pulses my entire body. It hurts. There is pressure down there. We look down and all we see is blood. Someone says it's stuck, and something is wrong. A girl yells in the background, but I don't know what she is saying. The pain is too much. We scream out to release the agony. There is no relief. The pain continues to hammer and squeeze at our insides. My limbs turn cold and I'm above. The scene is a picture taken from the ceiling. Fabienne's body lays lifeless on the bed. Deep crimson soaks everything around her. No, I think, but cannot speak. A vacuum of oxygen pulls me down. I can't breathe. I claw my throat gasping for air, but I have no hands. A force is pulling me down. NO. I cry.

"Wren, holy fuck, calm down." Scarlett slaps my hand away from hers. "Everyone is staring."

Wren lets her eyelids relax. She's afraid to look. Her hands pat down her body and her head dips below the water. She pops up gasping for air.

Scarlett doesn't know what to do. Her own hands are like

a trigger to another painful, public scene. She spots a towel close by and wraps it around Wren's shoulders. Half the towel is now soaking wet, but she doesn't care. "Wren, it's okay. It's me, Scarlett. We're at the spa. Remember?"

Wren's eyes snap open. "She died. I watched her die."

"Shhh, keep your voice down," Scarlett scolds, and pulls her finger to her parted lips. "People are starting, and someone is probably on their way to come tell us to leave."

"You were there." Wren stares deep into Scarlett's eyes.

"Get out of the pool." Scarlett climbs out over the lip of the poll and yanks on Wren's towel wrapped arm. "Now, Wren. Let's go," she hushes to her.

Wren does as Scarlett instructs. Still in a daze, the cool air is a welcomed refresh to remind her she is alive. Together, they scurry down the path, mindful of their bare feet on the cobblestone. "I've never experienced that before."

"Experienced what?" Scarlett returns to her normal volume of voice now that no one is in earshot. "Touching someone in water?"

"Yes, that. And feeling someone die and be reborn."

Scarlett pauses and can only stare into Wren's pale face. "I don't follow."

"She was reborn into you, seconds after she gave birth to you."

"What?" Scarlett crosses her arms. The cold is settling

into her skin. "You're not making sense."

With each thump of her feet against the cold stones, pieces of Wren's thoughts click together. She pauses and takes a step back. She reaches out to Scarlett but pulls her hand back. "You were right about being related to Fabienne. I think she was your birth mother."

Chapter 14

All Scarlett can do is laugh. She stands there and laughs. Wren stares back at her with no clue about what to do next.

"I did tell you!" Scarlett's voice is low and deep. "The second I saw Fabienne's face I knew my entire life was a lie. A dead birth mother making my life hell from beyond the grave and a living mother who tried to pawn me off to different facilities once she discovered I was so damaged." She turns and marches down a path. "I need a fuckin' drink."

"Scarlett, wait!" Wren charges after her. "Don't. We can talk this through."

"Ha! What's there to talk about? I blackmail my parents into telling me the truth, mystery fuckin' solved."

"What about Bojana, Anya, and Sofia? Maybe this isn't just about finding justice and peace for Fabienne." Wren comes up on Scarlett's heels, her purpose slipping away like the cold, wet towel falling off her shoulders. *Could getting the answers from Scarlett's parents be that simple? Would we get the truth?* She can't imagine what Scarlett is feeling. Everything she once knew was all an act. Scarlett's life was all for show. Wren's stomach gurgles.

"Those girls are probably dead, too, so what does it

matter?”

“Fabienne wanted to protect them, to help them, even when she, too, was facing danger.” Wren grabs on the glass door as Scarlett flings it open.

“Well, I’m not really her, am I?”

“Yes, you kind of are.”

Scarlett practically pushes people out of the way to get to the bar. “A bottle of your most expensive red.”

“No. Please, Scarlett, don’t let this throw your sobriety out the window.”

Scarlett flings her head back. “Ha! Sobriety is for losers.” She looks at Wren and a devilish grin creeps across her face. She lets her tongue wash over her lips. “I know you wouldn’t understand, but your daddy does. He’s a loser just like you.”

Wren lets the towel finally drop to the ground. The noise around her comes to a halt. “You know what, you’re right. He ran out on his family, so he must have been a big ol’ fat loser, but don’t you dare compare me to him. I didn’t want to help you, but here I am dealing with all your shit.”

Scarlett slaps the bar, waiting for her wine. “Don’t kid yourself, Bird-ie, you only agreed to this adventure for the money.” She eyes Wren up and down. “You’re more like him than you know. And perhaps if you didn’t get kicked out of police school you would have been better at solving real life mysteries and not ones set in the past.”

Wren reaches over the bar and snatches the bottle of wine from the bartender's grip. "What the hell is that supposed to mean?"

Scarlett tilts her head. "It means I don't know who the fuck this AJ guy is that you always talk about. It wasn't him who sent me to you. It was your daddy, Dave, we met in therapy." She adds air quotes over the word 'therapy'. "AKA Alcoholics Anonymous."

The bottle of wine slips from her moist fingers and smashes against the white marble tile, sending green shards of glass in every direction. Wren freezes like a statue fused to the floor, very aware that she is barefoot. If patrons dining on their watercress salads and cucumber bubbly water weren't staring at the two women before, they are now.

"You idiot." Scarlett keeps her feet perfectly still.

"Dave? You think I'm going to believe that garbage?" Years of letting people walk all over her erupt. "I don't need this." Wren knows she can take a cab and ask maintenance to open the locker so she can retrieve her belongings.

"It's okay, don't move. We'll get this cleaned up right away." The manager rushes over to reassure the women.

"Believe what you want, but I know where to find him. Another mystery you could never solve." Scarlett inflates her chest and takes a gulp from a glass, making half of the liquid disappear.

A glass of wine Wren didn't even notice the bartender

pour.

Wren's mind whirls around her father, a man she believed never existed. *How could she know my father? I never even knew his name. The crumbs of information my grandparents would leave lead me to believe my mother didn't even know his name. Is it possible he knew who I was, where I was, this entire time? Why wouldn't he have come forward after Nan died? Dave. Is that really his name? Sounds made up. Why now? Why Scarlett?* Her body shrivels as if a laser beam has shrunk her, like in that movie she saw when she was a kid. Except this isn't fun, this is a nightmare; instead of being chased by a giant bug, she's chased by an invisible man she never believed actually existed. At this moment she would prefer if a giant bug was chasing her. It would feel more real than having someone tell her that her father knows where she is. *How can a man I never knew have this kind of control over me?*

"Excuse me, miss?" An unfamiliar voice jabs at Wren's ears and a finger taps on her shoulder blade. "You need to take your friend and leave now."

Friend? Wren's eyes open to see the marble floor perfectly clean and free of green glass, just a glossy finish left behind from a wet mop. All eyes in the restaurant penetrate her exposed skin. She knew she never should have come here. Scarlett's body sloughs over the bar, the glass in front of her hand empty. Wren searches the ground for the towel she remembers acted as a flimsy shield, but it's gone.

"Your friend is clearly inebriated. Can you please help her stand up?"

Scarlett's designer bathing suit doesn't offer much coverage, and Wren hesitates with how to touch her with no fabric to act as a barrier. "Doesn't it feel good to finally have a drink?" Scarlett's carefree smile widens as her head rests on her arm, resting on the bar.

"Christ, how much did you serve her?" Wren asks anyone who is listening.

No one answers.

"She's recovering. I don't know the last time she's had alcohol." Wren's lip curls. She steps closer to Scarlett as if she is trying not to step on glass. There is no way of walking out of here alone now. If she can get her arm around her side, there may be a way to hold her up and keep the white layer of Lycra and spandex between them, she strategizes. Wren reaches her hands out and doesn't know what to do with her fingers. They now resemble lobster claws. With precision and gritted teeth, she slides her hand around the top half of Scarlett's torso.

"Hey, Wrenny Wren. Did you have a drink, too? You should. The wine here is divine. Excellent vintage." Scarlett twists her body, not fully supported by Wren yet.

Scarlett's arm collides with Wren's arm and Wren's instincts signal her body to pull away, letting Scarlett crumple to the floor.

"Wren, Birdie," Scarlett pouts. "Why did you let me go?" she asks. "It's cold down here."

"Can someone get me a towel, please?" Wren's chest deflates as she can't see any other way of getting herself and Scarlett out of this situation and away from all these rubber neckers. The true reason for her towel is unbeknown to everyone in this room, except for Scarlett.

The manager nods and ushers to one of the waitstaff to honour Wren's request. Within a minute, a new white towel is tossed in her direction.

Wren drapes it over Scarlett and helps her rise. "Scarlett, we need to leave now. Come on." The truth is Wren wants to leave by herself, but Scarlett drove and deep down she knows this woman needs her help. Questions about Dave will have to wait.

Scarlett walks with the footing of a newborn fawn. "Charge the wine to my account. Scarlett Hernandez. But maybe that's not even my real last name," she giggles.

Wren apologizes as they make their way past the manager, her ears burning with embarrassment. Once outside, Wren tries to get Scarlett to not rely on her for support. "How the hell did you get so drunk, so quickly? Christ, Scarlett."

"Shh, don't tell, okay? I popped an Addy after my massage." Scarlett playfully taps a finger to her lips as Wren pulls her towel-wrapped arm. "Don't worry. I'll be fine, okay?"

"Adderall? Do you even have ADHD?" Wren whisper shouts, then looks around to make sure no one overheard.

Scarlett shrugs and stammers forward.

Wren guides Scarlett down to sit on the bench in the change room. She carefully removes the bracelet with the key to their locker. The giant breath of trapped air blows out of her lips. She wasn't aware she was holding her breath.

"I wasn't lying, you know."

Wren looks back to Scarlett. "About what?" An air of contention in her voice. The key clicks and the door to the locker pops open.

"Your dad. I do know him from AA." Scarlett laughs and shakes her head. "I guess I'm not sober anymore. Dave's going to be so disappointed."

In dealing with Scarlett, Wren temporarily forgot about this new piece of information. The sound of Scarlett uttering the name 'Dave' pinches her gut. She doesn't want to talk about him right now. Wren pulls out Scarlett's bag and finds her neatly-folded clothes. "Here, put these on. I'm going to get changed."

Scarlett ignores the ask and just sits there, cold and alone on the wooden bench. Her eyes and mind are drifting off to a place somewhere else.

"Scarlett, come on. Get dressed and I'll drive you home. Okay?" Annoyance firmly settles into Wren's demand.

"I need help, Wren."

"Yes, I am going to help you," Wren says, and whispers under her breath, *that's an understatement.* Really, Wren thinks it's quite the loaded ask. *What doesn't Scarlett need help with?*

Scarlett manages to shed the straps of her bathing suit, and her breasts are exposed.

From the corner of Wren's eye, she sees what has happened as she tries to pull out her own clothes from her bag. "Scarlett, here." She abandons her search, grabs Scarlett's bra, and passes it to her.

"Help me."

"I'm not helping you put on your bra, you're a grown woman." In her mind Wren shakes her head. She pulls out her bag and rummages in search of her gloves. She is in no state to touch Scarlett. Not now. Her mind is spinning as it is, how could she focus on Fabienne's troubles when she has her own mess to mop up at this moment? Guilt pains her as she has the thought that her own problems are worse than Fabienne's. They aren't. Even what she dealt with in the past could never compare to what Fabienne was forced to live through.

"Wren." Scarlett swings her arm out and latches on to Wren's boney wrist.

It's summer. I can tell by the scent of barbequing hot dogs and freshly-cut grass. Our barefoot toes absorb the heat from the sand. Children run, slide, bounce, swing, laugh as they play on the wooden structure. "Be careful, Ricardo." We shout, and watch a boy swing across the monkey bars. I've seen this little boy before. Fabienne's little brother. "Is that your brother?" a man beside me asks. I want to scream. I want to force Fabienne's legs to get up and run, however they feel like cement bricks, and I'm reminded that there is no way for me to alter her future; I am merely a helpless observer. Fabienne is smart and doesn't answer Roman. She probably doesn't know who he is yet. This could be their first encounter. "My daughter is over there." He points aimlessly to a pack of kids by the swings. "You come here often?" Fabienne continues to ignore his interaction. Good girl, I comment to myself. "I'm Roman, Roman Moore." We stand, slide into her flip-flops, and move swiftly towards the play structure.

"I don't need to wear a bra today," Scarlett announces, and brushes her bra off her lap.

Wren returns to the present. *Roman Moore,* she repeats to herself.

Scarlett slithers out of her bathing suit on her own. "Today, I'll pretend I'm from France and I won't wear a bra. My boobs are small enough. I can get away with it." She looks up to Wren. "You, too. You don't need to wear a bra today, either. It'll be fun. You know what else would be fun? Going to Europe. Wren, ever been to Paris?"

Ignoring Scarlett's ramblings, Wren grabs her notebook and pen from her bag and opens to a fresh page. Laying it flat against the locker door, removing the pen lid with her teeth, she writes 'Roman Moore and little brother Ricardo'.

"It stinks like chlorine in here." Scarlett remains on the bench, struggling to pull her white tank top over her head. "You know where it doesn't smell like chlorine?"

"I don't know," Wren mumbles with the pen lid still between her lips.

"France."

Wren finishes writing and clicks the lid back on the pen. She looks over to Scarlett, who is sitting there naked trying to pull her tank top down. "For Christsakes." She returns her pen and notebook to her bag and turns her attention to Scarlett. Carefully placing her fingers on the fabric of Scarlett's tank top, she pulls it down.

Scarlett instinctively raises her arms like a child who knows the routine of getting dressed. "You're a good friend, Wren." Her lips bend into a goofy grin. "My only friend."

It's been a long time since Wren had a close friend. The thought of AJ comes to mind. He was the closest friend she ever had, but they fell out of touch a long time ago. She feels bad for thinking he was the one who blabbed all her secrets. Deep down she knew it couldn't have been him. Even though they drifted apart over the years, he would never share her secrets. AJ may be an aloof nomad, or citizen of the world as he called himself, but Wren knew she could trust him. Their marriage, love, and devotion from another life carried into this one, and although it took on a different form, the two of them mutually understood their connection. Wren theorised that being born as AJ and given the chance to explore and experience the world was a reward for being a war bride and raising a son on her own in a past life.

"Would you be my friend, even if I wasn't paying you?" Scarlett asks.

Wren finds Scarlett's underwear folded neatly on her pants and stretches the lacy band so Scarlett can easily step in. "Sorry, what?" Wren shakes from thoughts of AJ. All she heard was something about a friend.

Scarlett's grin turns upside down. "My friend! Would you be my friend if I wasn't paying you to help me?" Her eyes lock on Wren and she keeps her feet firmly planted on the black-and-white honeycomb tile floor.

The words Wren choose to answer Scarlett could decide how the rest of her day unfolds. She licks her lips and studies Scarlett's face: the face of a woman searching for help, searching for answers. The face that she inherited from her birth mother—a face shrouded in so much deceit and pain. "Of course, I would be your friend. You're a good person, Scarlett. And you deserve so much more."

Scarlett's smile returns and she slides her feet into the holes of her panties one leg at a time. "I'd be your friend, too. And that's not the wine or Adderall talking." She waves her hand in the air, signalling some imaginary victory. Scarlett reaches for her underwear to pull them up and her fingers intertwine with Wren's bare fingers.

It's black. We can't see anything. And something hard presses against our spine. Fabienne's words are in French, and at this moment, I wish I had studied French more. Our breaths align with the quickness of Fabienne's racing heart. I let her senses engulf me. It's bumpy, and I can hear rubber tires speed over asphalt. We're moving, too, and rough carpet scratches our cheek. It's the trunk of a car.

Scarlett finds her footing and stands to secure her underwear.

Wren steps backwards. "You were kidnapped and put in the back of a car."

"I was never kidnapped," Scarlett slurs.

"Not you, you. Fabienne. Remember?"

Scarlett plops back down on the bench. "I don't want to talk about her anymore."

Now that Scarlett is somewhat covered up, Wren grabs her own clothes. She debates changing in a change room but worries about leaving Scarlett unattended for two minutes. Who knows what other trouble she would get into? There is no one else in their row of lockers and she's already experienced so much from Scarlett today. Wren lets down her guard, peels off her damp bathing suit, and lets it fall to the floor, quickly pulling on her own plain black undergarments. Today is not the day to adopt a Parisian way of life.

"Wren, pass me my purse."

"Give me a second. I'm trying to get dressed." Wren waves her folded jeans and climbs in, pulling the worn denim over her butt.

"What's the code for abduction?"

"What?" Wren crinkles her brow at Scarlett.

"The police code. You know, like ten-four, we have a twelve-eighty-five. Like when you radio for backup."

Wren lets a laugh escape from her lips. She's forgotten most of what she learned in police college, but she knows it is buried deep in her memory somewhere. For the most part she doesn't let herself think about that time in her life. Like redacted memories in her brain, she doesn't want to remember it. But she remembers attempting to commit the one hundred codes to memory before attending college in preparation. "There is no twelve-eighty-five. They all start with ten," Wren retorts without thinking.

"Oh!" Scarlett exclaims. "You know who would know?"

Wren pokes her head through her sweatshirt, ready to move on from this topic.

"Dave. He's a cop."

Wren halts her movements while putting on her sweater, her arm bent like a chicken wing trying to find the arm hole. *Dave is a cop?*

"Or I can just look it up." Scarlett laughs off her comment and stands, wobbly, making her way to the locker, reaching for her bag.

"Ten-fifty-six, missing person. Or ten-eighty-one, if a child is abducted by a parent," Wren blurts, proving to herself she still has it and there is no use for the Internet or Dave, the man who allegedly impregnated her mother. Her arms find their way through the sleeves, and she pulls down her sweatshirt. She secures her ponytail behind her head and a lightness fills her chest.

Both women are dressed, and they double-check to make sure they have all their belongings. Exiting the change room, they pass an unattended maintenance cart. Bottles of disinfectant and an array of cleaners crowd the top. A box of blue gloves catches Wren's eyes. She's familiar with that box. They pass the cart, and she keeps her fingers to herself.

Chapter 15

Wren secures Scarlett in the car, hustles around to the driver's side, and climbs in. She searches for the ignition, but only finds a button that says 'start'. *Well, isn't this fancy?* Her finger presses the button and nothing happens. The digital screen tells her to press the brake plus push the ignition start. She follows the car's instructions, and the engine comes to life. Never in her wildest dreams did she ever see herself behind the wheel of a car so new or futuristic.

"It's a step up from your shitbox, eh?" Scarlett adds.

"You could say that." Wren can't help but smile to herself in the rear-view mirror as she reverses out of the parking space. The events of the day are packed away in luggage in her mind; she knows she'll have to unpack later, but right now she focuses on the task at hand, getting Scarlett home and not fucking up her expensive car. "Which way do I go to get you home?" Wren asks as she rolls up to the stop sign.

Scarlett leans forward and taps the screen in the center of the dash, the weight of her upper body supported by the seat belt, without it she may have just folded over. "Easy, listen, the car will tell you." She leans back. "It's a good thing, 'cause I don't have a clue. I just drive where my GPS tells me."

"Gotcha." Wren flicks on her signal when the British

female voice of the car tells her to make a right. "How did we all get around before we had GPS?" she asks rhetorically. People had better memories, and paid attention more, she thinks.

"Wren." Scarlett turns to face her stand-in chauffeur. "Can we make grilled cheese sandwiches today? I would really love a grilled cheese sandwich. With a big fat juicy pickle on the side."

Wren scrunches her nose. *This chick just dropped a bomb in my life, telling me my estranged father sent her to me, we think she is adopted and she is a reincarnation of her dead birth mother, and all she can think about is eating a stupid grilled cheese sandwich and pickle?* "Sure, okay." is the only response Wren can muster. It wouldn't surprise Wren if Scarlett got into the habit of popping Rohypnol every now and again to forget what she's seen.

"Dave told me you would make an excellent detective one day," Scarlett blabs. "He's sad he wasn't there for you. And that's probably why he's in AA now." Her lips turn out like a duck's.

Wren's heart tightens and drops into her stomach. Nausea hits her like a wave. She doesn't want to talk about him. *He doesn't deserve my thoughts.* She changes the subject. "Do you need to go to a meeting? Call your sponsor or something? You know, after your setback today?"

Scarlett shrugs. "Probably. But who cares anymore? Life is such bullshit. Everyone is a goddamn liar." She thrusts a fist in the air. "That's why I told you about your dad. No more lies."

"Yep. That's for sure." Another wave of nausea crashes against the side of Wren's stomach. She focuses on the directions for her next turn. Everything in her life now feels foreign—the car, location, family. The past twenty-something years she thought she was an orphan, but the whole time a man that claims to be her father was watching her.

"At first, I thought Dave was just another weirdo alky, but he's the one who told me about my nightmares being from a past life. It was the first time an adult didn't think I was crazy or faking it for attention. I didn't know if I should believe him when he sent me to you for help, but you know you have his nose and chin, and he's short, too." Scarlett looks at Wren. "I can see the resemblance."

Bringing up AA backfired on Wren. A light snaps on in her mind and she glances at Scarlett. "Did he ever touch you?"

"Gross. No. He's not a pervert."

"No. I mean, like how I touch you."

Scarlett reflects before she speaks. "Not that I can remember. If he grazed my hand or arm, it was nothing more than a harmless accident." Her voice grows with a heaviness to signal she is tired.

Wren never thought of the possibility that her ability

came from her dad. She always assumed it was inherited from her mother, with the way her Nan always wanted her to ignore her gift and how upset her grandpa got when she would ask about her mom. It made sense, but now, what if she is who she is because of him? The question takes shape in her mind.

"Hey, can you swing by the liquor store on our way home? I would love some Southern Comfort." Scarlett's eyes close.

Wren ignores the request. She is not going to enable an alcoholic, and she doesn't even know where the liquor store is. Instead, she focuses on her own thoughts, now a runaway train. *Did Dave boost my chances of getting into police college? Did he know the chief? Did he know what the chief did to me? He knew about Hilary. And if he knew about Hilary and he has the same ability, he most likely figured out Hilary was a reincarnation of the woman he once loved. Well, maybe not loved, but definitely had some sort of relationship with.* The scars of her past break open like fingernails scratching at scabbed skin. She refuses to let the memory of the chief's stale coffee breath on her lips surface. Or the way his giant hand slid down her sweater to cup her breast. The stillness and darkness of his office. *No! If Dave knew what the chief was doing, why didn't he protect me? Why did I have to be a victim? It's most likely he didn't know what the chief was doing to a female recruit. How could he? I've never told a soul. If I did, I never knew what else the chief was capable of. And finding Hilary was a terrible coincidence.* The thought of Dave not being privy to the chief's perverted ways brings Wren a slice of peace. It's the only conclusion she lets herself believe at this moment.

"Make a U-turn," the smooth British voice says. "Recalculating route."

Wren glances at the screen and realizes she missed her turn. Scarlett is lulled to rest from the motion of the car and effects of the wine she hammered back an hour ago.

The rest of the way back to Scarlett's building, Wren can't shake the sweat collecting down her back or in her armpits. The thought of being face-to-face with Dave may be inevitable. Or maybe she's already seen his face in a sea of everyday strangers and never knew it, she wonders. Heat radiating from the leather seat and steering wheel isn't helping, but she can't figure out how to turn it off.

"Scarlett. Wake up, we're here." Wren gingerly shakes Scarlett's shoulder and removes her seatbelt.

"Please, take me to a doctor." Scarlett's voice barely above a whisper. The same voice from the other night. "Something isn't right."

Wren knows this is an opportunity to learn more, so she asks Scarlett, or rather Fabienne, where she is.

"I don't know."

"Is there anything, anything at all that sticks out about where you are?"

"It smells weird."

Wren is already aware of the musty paper and chemical smell of the building. She searches Scarlett's face. "Is that it?"

"It really hurts."

"I can imagine." Wren strokes Scarlett's clothed arm. "We know his name, Roman Moore, we'll find him."

"There is another one."

"Another one?" Wren's brows come together.

Without warning, Scarlett reaches for the door handle and swings the upper half of her body out of the car. Burgundy-stained vomit paints the cement curb.

Wren clicks her own seatbelt , so she can react to the situation with no restriction. She presses buttons on the centre console to find a napkin or tissue. Thankfully, she finds a few napkins leftover from Starbucks in the glove compartment.

Scarlett rolls herself upright back into her seat and takes the napkin Wren is offering her. "If Fabienne was my bio mom, who the fuck is my bio dad?" She wipes the creases of her mouth with the napkin. A look of disgust can't be wiped away as easily as the spittle that was dangling from her lips. "Some nasty, random criminal? A rapist?" Scarlett covers her mouth with the napkin as if the final contents of her stomach are ready to vacate her body.

Wren falls back into her seat. It never dawned on her who Scarlett's biological father might be. Roman? This other character Fabienne just revealed? Her limbs turn numb.

"What if I inherited some criminal DNA from some rapist?" Scarlett lets her body slump into the seat. If she wasn't sitting in such a well-crafted car seat, she would have easily let herself flop over out of the car, or land on Wren.

"Have you ever committed a crime? Or been charged and gone to jail?" Wren asks, thinking her question would offer some comfort.

Scarlett remains motionless and silent.

"Let me take you up to your apartment." Wren reaches in the back for her purse.

"No. I can't go back to my place. It's full of my parents' deceit." Scarlett stares forward. "Take me to the hotel."

"Sure. Whatever you want." Wren presses the ignition, buckles them both back in, and pulls away from Scarlett's building. She pulls back next to the curb. "Don't exactly know how to get to the hotel." She pokes at the screen and taps 'Plaza' into the search.

Scarlett's able to walk on her own, and walks next to Wren into the lobby. She grabs the sunglasses from her purse and places them on her face. Her eyes are sensitive to the well-lit entrance. "What a shit day," she mumbles.

"You don't have to remind me," Wren retorts. Her patience for Scarlett is waning. She's wondering if the payoff is worth this drama, or maybe Fabienne's past and Scarlett's present are over her pay grade. A tiny voice deep down tells her that no one else can do what she does. *Except for maybe Dave.* Dwelling on the negative helps no one, a lesson her Nan taught her from a young age. To herself, she sifts through the shit and remembers, *Roman Moore.* That could be a huge lead if that is in fact his name. Her heavy steps lighten through the corridor towards the elevators.

"I don't think you actually get it." Through tinted lenses, Scarlett's eyes spit fire at Wren. "I am a product of rape, my parents have lied about it my entire life. Hell! It's been so long they probably believe I am their bio baby." She stabs the up arrow. "Jesus Christ!" None of the four elevator doors open at her command.

"Least you had parents that love you and raised you," Wren adds. She's tired of Scarlett's complaining. Maybe if she understood how the world actually worked and how many people struggle day-to-day, she wouldn't be so high and mighty. "My mother is dead, my grandparents who raised me until I was fourteen, dead. My father was a question mark, until today, that is." She gives Scarlett the side-eye as they step into a vacant elevator.

"You don't get it." Scarlett adjusts her bag sliding off her shoulder. "I feel violated. Abused. I would rather have been molested by a junkie on the street."

An embellished laugh is all Wren can gather to contain her disdain at what just came out of Scarlett's mouth. "You didn't just say that."

"Yes. Yes, I did."

Wren's secret rolls from her brain along her sinus track and halts on the tip of her tongue. The words she's never shared with another soul are ready to leave her body. "You're right, I don't know how you feel, but I know how it feels to be sexually assaulted." Her voice is unwavering.

Scarlett's breath falls heavy. She gulps. "You never told me that."

"I've never told anybody that."

"I don't even think your dad..."

"Don't. I don't need your pity." Wren keeps her gaze on the numbers counting above her head. "You hired me to help you. I'm not going to burden you with my problems. Sounds like you have enough of your own shit to shovel out of."

"Ha!" Scarlett throws her head back and laughs. "Is every woman fuckin' damaged?"

The number of their floor flashes and the elevator dings. Wren steps out first and Scarlett follows. "His name was Chief Instructor Payne. He was head of the college. He could smell my vulnerability like a bloodhound." Like a faucet, Wren's past flows, and this time she doesn't want to turn it off. She pulls out her room card from the front pocket of her purse. "The bigger, stronger girls bullied me, and part of me wanted to quit. First his words were kind and encouraging, and I liked how they made me feel. Our hands touched. At the time, I thought it was innocent enough. To be honest, touching strangers used to be my guilty pleasure." Wren taps the card and opens the door. The piped-in fresh air refreshes her senses. "I saw stuff. I liked it and wanted more. For years and years, I convinced myself that I lead him on."

Scarlett keeps her eyes on Wren. All she can do is follow along in silence.

"Then one day he's undoing my bra, grabbing my breast, and unzipping my pants. I was paralyzed with fear." She turns and faces Scarlett, who is now sitting on the edge of the bed.

"What did he do? What did you do?" Scarlett's dark eyes inflate.

Wren's unsure if Scarlett is asking what the chief did to her or what he did in a past life. She can almost taste his wine dipped cigar on her lips. Either way, Wren is done talking about this. Wren sets her bag down on a chair at the table. Her shoulders slump in a deflated stance. Whatever energy she had is now drained. Her body is weak, and she remembers she has eaten nothing all day. "You hungry?"

Scarlett lets her body fall back onto the bed. "I could go for a drink." She smirks, trying to lighten the heavy mood that occupies the room.

"No one needs a drink." Wren finds the room service menu in the desk's drawer. She gives it a once-over and makes her choice. The beige room phone blends into its surroundings. In any room other than a hotel, this phone would look out of place. Wren sits down on the bed and picks up the receiver. When a voice comes on, she asks for two Greek salads and their four most popular appetizers.

"Oh, I love a woman with authority," Scarlett jokes when Wren hangs up the phone.

"You order for me. I order for you. I thought that's how this worked?" Wren's sarcasm surfaces. "You need to eat something." Wren makes a beeline to the fridge, searching for something that she can't find. She forgot there might be those little bottles of alcohol hiding in the mini fridge.

"Looking for the booze?" Scarlett sits back up.

Wren doesn't turn to look at Scarlett, but continues to scan every cubby and shelf in the mini fridge.

"You won't find any. The people in my building are on strict orders to not bring me alcohol, or subject me to a situation where I might be tempted." Scarlett crosses her legs. "That includes hotels. Lewis, or whoever made the booking, requested no alcohol be stocked in this fridge on the chance that I came to visit you."

"Smart." Wren abandons her search and closes the fridge door. "Well, then, let's get to work." She takes a seat at the desk and opens her laptop, the name 'Roman Moore' itching at her fingertips. The screen flashes and beeps, and she types in her password. It's best if she focuses all her attention into Scarlett and Fabienne's past; Wren knows this is the best option if she doesn't want to talk about her own tainted history. The question Scarlett asked ten minutes ago, *What did I do?* lingers in her mouth like sour milk. She hopes the food will wash it away. Wren's search engulfs her, and Scarlett fades into the background.

"Hey, where's your corkboard with pushpins, yarn, and photos of suspects and victims?" Scarlett asks to monopolize Wren's attention.

"Don't be daft," Wren answers while keeping her eyes glued to her screen. "That shit's only in the TV shows."

"I'm going to order all the supplies, and we'll hang it right there on the wall." Scarlett points. "It'll be fun."

"No, I don't want that." Wren's voice is stern. "Stupid Roman Moore. I don't think that's his real name."

"Come on. I need something to do, too. A distraction," Scarlett whines.

Wren grinds her teeth. "Fine. You want to pin your picture on a board next to Fabienne's— be my guest." Opening a page for the *Toronto Star,* she tries to search his name there. Nothing. The *Montreal Gazette.* Nothing. Her fingers glide over the keys, clicking and hitting 'enter' with more force than needed.

Scarlett clicks her tongue to the roof of her mouth. "I know who might know something." She moves herself into the plush chair and lets her body sink in. A few taps on her phone, and it rings. She taps the speaker.

"Hello, darling."

"Hi, Mama." Scarlett coyly beams.

In seconds, Wren swivels in her chair to face Scarlett. *What the hell is she doing?*

Scarlett's narrow gaze is devious. "I don't want to alarm you, but I know what you and Daddy did. I'm not mad. I mean, I was absolutely fuming when I found her. You know, my birth mother..."

"Scarlett! Hang up the phone." Wren rushes closer.

"...But I'm okay now. I took a pill to help with that."

The other end of the phone is silent, except for a faint, shallow exhale.

"It's smart not to speak and just listen, because we need your help with this next piece..."

"Hang up now." Wren reaches to grab Scarlett's phone, but Scarlett slaps her hand away. "You're going to ruin everything." Fury sets her eyes ablaze. She attempts to snatch Scarlett's phone again, but fails and stumbles, catching herself against the wall.

"Roman Moore. Who is he? Please don't tell me he's my biological father. He's ugly." Scarlett pouts. "He haunts my nightmares and I hate his face."

"Scarlett, dear, I can tell you're not well. Where are you?"

Knock, knock. "Room service."

"Fuck!" Wren shouts and marches to the door. She's pissed, not just at Scarlett foolishly trying to get information from her mother, but also at herself for not anticipating Scarlett's hasty action. *How could I be so stupid?* She swings the door open and takes the tray from the man without saying a word, and lets the door close behind her.

"I'm safe, Mama, don't worry. I did have a teeny tiny setback, but I'm better now. My friend is helping me."

"Who is there with you?"

"Just someone. Her name is not of importance to you. But she's smarter than you." Scarlett repositions the phone against her knee. "Stop trying to distract me with all your questions and answer the questions I am asking you." She stares at the screen of the phone.

"Hang up, Scarlett!" Wren tosses the tray on the table and the dishes clang together.

"Well, Mama, my friend seems to believe it's best I end the call, so I will, but…" Scarlett licks her lips. "I came home last night and collected samples of DNA from you and Daddy, so you don't need to utter a word. The truth will soon be revealed." And on that last note, Scarlett taps the red circle on the screen to end the call and tosses her phone to the side.

Wren stands limp in front of Scarlett and looks down at her through a squinted glower. "Is that true?"

Scarlett climbs out of the comforts of the plush chair and saunters towards the tray of food. "Maybe."

Wren's eyes follow Scarlett's movements. She may have underestimated Scarlett's level of giving no more fucks. "Think about this." She steps closer. "If there is something really bad that your parents were once part of, if they knew of Fabienne's death, they might get scared and run. All this—" Wren flails her hands. "Can be gone in a blink of an eye." The sudden snap of her fingers startles Scarlett. "Your money. Poof!"

Scarlett removes the lid off one salad and nibbles on a piece of lettuce she pulls to her lips. Her grin resurfaces. "So, what am I supposed to do? Sit back and do nothing? Just like you did after that chief or whatever molested you?"

There are no words for Wren to say. Scarlett can read her like a book, and knew she did nothing to make the chief pay for what he did. "You're right." Wren pulls out a chair and takes a seat at the table. "I did nothing. Absolutely nothing." Her head tilts, and she blankly stares at the salad. "I was so afraid I didn't even say 'no' or fight to get away." She looks at Scarlett. "But I didn't consent, either."

Scarlett uncovers the rest of the dishes and sets the table for the two of them so they can eat. "Now we *are* doing something. And it may have been a lifetime ago, but that chief has what's coming to him."

Wren jabs at an olive with her fork. The chief would be long retired by now, most likely in a retirement home if he's even still alive, she thinks.

"I don't care what happens. I'm tired of always being in

the dark. Being the odd one. Mentally drained from living this nightmare and reliving Fabienne's nightmare when I close my eyes." Scarlett inspects the mushroom caps like she's some sort of food critic and places one on her side plate. "Please tell me karma is real. 'Cause if it is, I want to come back as some majestic animal at the top of the food chain."

The savoury feta, a sharp piece of onion, and a sliver of green pepper coated in vinegar crunch together under Wren's slow chew. She pulls the napkin to her lips to cover her mouth. "I like to hope karma is still real," she says, but in her mind the jury is still out. The fact that the chief was a thief in a past life and reborn into a position where he abused his power never sat well with her. Her mind spirals with the nature versus nurture debate. Perhaps nature did its best in death to reward the good and punish the bad, but somewhere along the way fate had other plans to weasel a soul out of punishment, like an ill-behaved orphan being adopted by an eccentric millionaire who encouraged bad behaviour, or a rat destined to live a life in the gutter picked up by a boy and given much love and attention. Wren eats in silence as the age-old deliberation takes up more real estate in her mind.

Chapter 16

The room is full of absolute darkness thanks to quality blackout curtains installed in every room of the Plaza. Wren feels around in bed for her phone to check the time. When she rolls over, a pale blue light illuminates Scarlett's face. "What are you doing?" She wipes the sleep from her eyes.

"Can't sleep." Scarlett looks up from her phone and the light from her phone highlights her lips and white teeth as she talks.

"What time is it?"

"Almost five," Scarlett answers. "You fell asleep after we ate."

Wren sits up and swings her legs over the side of the bed, relieved to find herself still fully clothed. "And you?"

Scarlett clicks her phone off and her eyes blink in the complete darkness, adjusting to the absence of light. "I've drifted in and out. Like usual." She gets up from the chair and navigates to the window to open the curtains. Filtered light from the city enters their room. A crescent moon hangs in the sky and holds Scarlett's attention. "Isn't it weird to think back to a hundred or five hundred years and know our distant relatives stared at the same moon?" Scarlett strains her eyes to study the moon's surface. "Do you think they ever looked up at the sky and wondered if the future generations would remember them?"

Wren joins her at the window and pulls back the layer of sheer curtain to see what Scarlett is looking at. "Do you look at the sky and wonder if future generations will remember you?" she asks.

"I am right now." One corner of Scarlett's mouth twists up. "My name is going to be sealed in time as part of some scandal. I know it. Readers feeling sorry for me, wondering how I was forced to live a lie for so long." The other corner of her mouth moves and Scarlett is now smiling at the moon. "Or someone like you is going to touch whoever I become in my next life and see the shit I lived through."

"I just hope whoever this someone like me is doesn't use their ability as some type of perversion to go around touching people."

Scarlett's smile dissolves. "That's a pessimistic thing to say. What if they want to use their gift to help people, like you?"

"Ha!" Wren keeps her eyes on the moon. "It's still very self-indulgent, isn't it? I was lured here to help you because you dangled a wad of cash in front of my face."

Scarlett turns to Wren. "I sense something good about you. Like you do really care, money aside." She pats the top of Wren's arm, where her shirt covers her skin. "Maybe me finding you and paying for your services is the universe rewarding you. Like you can finally get a leg up and stop delivering fast food to sad people in your sad car."

Wren can't help but laugh again. "I've never thought that anything in my life has been a reward." Scarlett's words sat with her and made her wonder if this life was originally good karma for being sent off and killed during the war, but a strange twist of fate made her mother run away and turned her father into an absent alcoholic. The thought of her own actions weighs on her conscience. Her compulsion to touch people was always in her control. How the chief took advantage of her in a moment of vulnerability was wrong; even if she touched his hand first, he was the adult, he should have never forced himself on her. She looks out at the sea of city light twinkling before her. "What would you do to your abuser?"

Scarlett scrunches her nose. "Where did that thought come from?"

Wren remains silent gazing out of the window.

"I think I would track him down and punch him in the face," she says. "But I'm a little crazy and have nothing to lose. If I were you, I would track down other girls who went to the college when he was chief and see who else's life he fuckin' ruined."

Wren nods in agreement with Scarlett. "Right, but first I need to finish what I started. You've been living with Fabienne's nightmares for long enough." She marches over to her duffel bag to find clean clothes for the day, a warmth spreading through her body. "We need to visit your parents.

I want to see how they physically react when we talk to them."

Scarlett seems to disregard Wren's latest suggestion. "For the sake of honesty and our new friendship, I didn't collect my parent's DNA samples. I just want them to quake in their boots." She rubs her wrist like she's fiddling with an invisible bracelet. "But I did sign up for an online DNA test. My saliva-testing kit should arrive tomorrow." Her eyes move down to stare at the floor.

"What?" Wren says.

"The DNA ancestry thingy. You know, they tell you your ancestry, and apparently, they can connect you with potential family members," Scarlett answers.

Wren takes a set next to her bag and stops rummaging through her clothes. Her bottom lip folds under her front teeth. "Interesting."

"Once I send in my saliva, I'll have the results in three to four weeks."

Well, I sure hope to get to the bottom of what happened to Fabienne, Bojana, Sofia, and Anya in less than three weeks. Wren selects a button-down mustard cardigan and a pair of plaid pants.

Chapter 17

The Hernandez house, or estate, as Scarlett refers to it, is as grandiose as Wren imagines. Even though it's fall, she can picture how colourful and impressive the gardens must be in the summer months.

Scarlett catches Wren staring. "You must think this is all pretty bougie, eh?" She pulls into the crescent laneway and stops her car in front of the main entrance.

"It's very nice." Wren musters a smile. Unsure how the next hour is going to play out, she keeps her comments neutral. On the tip of her tongue is the question asking Scarlett if she grew up here, but she swallows her words. The answer could have potential to send Scarlett spiraling down some awful memory of being shipped off to private school or being sent to stay at some sleep institution to be studied.

"Come on." Scarlett jolts Wren from her thoughts. "They're home. I called ahead and asked Magdalene."

"Who's Magdalene?" Wren asks, climbing out of the car.

"My parents' live-in maid. She's great. Not old, stuffy, or British." Scarlett laughs at her own joke. "Magdalene always got me, you know?" Scarlett walks towards the front door. "She even said she'd leave the door open for me, so we can really surprise my parents."

Wren reaches out and grabs Scarlett's clothed arm, causing her to swirl around to face her. "Before we go in there, we need to discuss the plan." Wren's voice is a shade higher than a whisper.

Scarlett's eyes rest on Wren's face. "Yes, good idea. I confront them about how I'm really adopted and show them Fabienne's photo."

The temperature of Wren's blood rises. *How could I have not gone over why we're here before this moment? Shit.* "No. Mention nothing about being adopted. This is not the time to berate your parents. This is a fact-finding mission." Wren demands, "We need to see what we can find out about Roman Moore. Then we need to ask..." Wren waves off her ramblings of a plan. "You know what? Just let me ask all the questions."

"My parents are steel traps. And they are smart. Smarter than whatever you had the chance to learn in Detective 101 or from *Law and Order*." Scarlett laughs at her own joke again. "I know how to play them like a fiddle. Trust me."

Wren's feet are firmly rooted in the wavy interlock pavers that form the driveway. Her idea to come here may have been a massive mistake. She looks down at her plaid pants and sneakers. *I look like some bum. No one is going to take me seriously.* In the confines of her hotel room her confidence somehow made its way to the surface, but now that she's in the real world she feels like a child whose age is lower-than-recommended to play this game of life.

"Scarlett," she softly beckons. She looks up to see Scarlett standing in an open-arched door. "Scarlett," she calls again. "Come back. We made a mistake."

Either Scarlett doesn't hear Wren's demands, or she chooses to ignore them. She steps further into the house. "Hurry up, Wren, get in here," Scarlett shouts over her shoulder, no longer trying to make their arrival stealthy.

Wren forces her jelly-like legs to the door. "Scarlett. There is another way. Come, let's go back." At this moment there is no plan B, and she realises there is barely a plan A. Her words are a futile attempt to coax Scarlett back to the car.

"Mommy! Daddy!" Scarlett's voice carries in the foyer with extra-high ceilings. "I'm here. I'm okay now. Sorry about my manic phone call yesterday." She waves for Wren to join her.

Wren enters and closes the door behind her. She notices it is taller and wider than a standard front door, and it doesn't make a sound when it closes. The thought of Scarlett sneaking in and out with no squeaking door is a luxury most criminals don't have. She still isn't positive about whether Scarlett did in fact steal samples of her parents' DNA, even though she told Wren she didn't.

"Scarlett, sweetheart!" A woman bounds out from around a corner and holds her arms out to pull Scarlett close to her body, like a good mother would.

Adopted or not, Scarlett has a mother who loves her,

Wren observes. It strikes her that Scarlett's mother does have the same rich, dark skin tone as Fabienne.

"It's fine. I'm just relieved to know you're okay. I know what happens sometimes when you haven't slept. And some characters you meet can be an awful influence." And on that note, the woman looks up to catch a glimpse of Wren, appearing smaller than normal in the oversized entranceway. "Oh, hello."

Wren's heel pivots on the tile floor. She's not sure what to say or do. Her hands latch together behind her back. She's out of her element and she knows it.

"Mama, this is my friend Wren." Scarlett pulls out of her mother's embrace and marches toward Wren. Caught up in the moment, Scarlett grabs Wren's hand. No safety of fabric or latex between them.

Nothing is clear, like Vaseline smeared over the lens of my eyes. What is happening? I'm not underwater because I can breathe. Voices chatter in the distance. I stop focusing on my sight and listen. 'She's in there waiting for you, Duane.'

"Wren, I'm so sorry. I didn't mean…"

"It's fine." Wren pulls her hands back and curls them into the sleeves of her sweater, the name 'Duane' on repeat in her mind. *A new name.* She's careful not to let her facial expression reveal her new discovery.

"She doesn't like to be touched," Scarlett turns and tells her mother. "We all have our quirks don't we?" she says with a wink, making her way back to her mom.

"Is that our little pumpkin's voice I hear?" a deep voice calls out, but it's indecipherable where it's coming from with the acoustics of the high ceilings. Scarlett's father appears from a doorway and jogs to hug his daughter.

"You look great, Daddy." Scarlett beams as she wraps her arms around the tall Caucasian man. She tousles his full head of white hair.

All Wren can think is that Scarlett is a convincing actress. She stays where she stands and observes the Hernandez family interacting. Although Wren never experienced a family dynamic so conventional, it seems normal.

"What have you been up to, kiddo?" The man stands next to his wife and puts one hand in his pocket and the other around the lower back of his wife. "Keeping out of trouble, I hope."

If he only knew! Or maybe he will soon enough, Wren thinks. She continues to watch like a fly on the wall.

Scarlett offers her parents a smile with half of her mouth. "Of course. And I made a new friend." She steps aside, signalling to Wren that it's her cue to step forward.

Wren feels the eyes of perpetually concerned parents crawl over her exposed skin, and she tucks her hands further into her sleeves. She clears her throat, "Hello."

"This is Wren." Scarlett bounces back and loops her arm around Wren's elbow, careful not to touch her hand this time. "I met her dad in AA, and she's great."

Wren's heart deflates as she hears Scarlett reference a man being her father as if it's no big deal. *What if they ask about him? He's clearly an alcoholic, and I know nothing about the man.*

The Hernandez couple read the fear in Wren's face, and smile. "Hello, Wren. Welcome to our home," Scarlett's mom offers. "I'm Gabby, and this is Hank."

Wren steps in rhythm with Scarlett. Her eyes study Gabby and Hank's faces for a sign of resemblance to their daughter. A ball in her stomach hardens, losing hoping that what they found about Fabienne to be false. She thinks Scarlett has similar cheekbones to her father, but she is only forcing connections that aren't there. She can't confront these people with what she knows about their daughter. It doesn't seem right.

Gabby and Hank jut their hands forward.

Wren's too occupied with taking in the visuals of the Hernandez couple to notice.

Trees, foliage, and the smell of rain surround me. A snarl tells me he isn't human. Close by, I see a small, furry moose.

"Yes, lovely to meet you." Hank releases Wren's hand.

Gabby hesitates and holds her hand back. With knowing eyes, she looks to Scarlett then to Wren, asking for permission without saying a word.

"It's fine," Wren says, and lets Gabby shake her hand. There is no vision. Her gaze falls to her hands and back to Gabby's caring, motherly face. *She's a new soul.* Like a breath of fresh air, Wren can breathe again.

"Yes, welcome," Gabby says.

"Well, we'd love to stay and chat, but we just came to look for something in my old room," Scarlett announces, and pulls Wren with her towards the stairs.

"Nice to meet you," Wren squeaks.

In the safe confines of Scarlett's sugary-sweet childhood bedroom, Scarlett asks, "Oh my god, what did you see when my parents touched you?" Scarlett plops down the bed with a pink frilly canopy.

Wren takes in the mural on the wall of a princess standing in front of a castle with forest animals surrounding her. Oddly, a moose in the forest catches her eye. Most likely a coincidence, but Wren's sure it's possible Hank has dormant memories of once roaming the forest as an iconic, stoic Canadian woodland creature.

All the toys she remembers commercials for (and desperately wanted as a child) line shelves on a wall in Scarlett's childhood room. Cherry Merry Muffins, Polly Pockets, and Littlest Pet Shops sit untouched in pristine condition, like they are on display in a toy museum. Not a speck of dust on these toys, and Wren wonders if part of Magdalene's job is to dust them once a week.

"Wanna play?" Scarlett asks teasingly.

Wren looks at Scarlett over her shoulder. "What?"

Scarlett rises from her bed. "Just kidding." She bounces to her closet. "I have a copy of my birth certificate in here somewhere. I used it in a school project on my family tree, way back before I knew better." She snorts. "How stupid do I feel now, but if we find it, maybe we can prove it was faked."

Wren follows Scarlett into the closet, which is the same size as her apartment. Wren doesn't hate the new idea to Scarlett's plan. The whites of her eyes expand as she takes in all the clothes, shoes, accessories, all that must be way too small for Scarlett now. *Why would they keep all her clothes from when she was a kid?* She catches sight of Scarlett standing in front of built-in floor-to-ceiling shelves, swaying in place. "Are you alright?" Wren asks.

"Never better." Scarlett stares blankly at the content on the shelf that is at eye-level. "I have a better idea. You distract my parents and I'll see if I can get into their safe in Hank's office."

Wren notices Scarlett now refers to her dad as Hank and not Dad. "Wait. What?" Wren bumbles through her words. All ideas for their plan on coming here have gone out the window.

"Yeah!" Scarlett twists her neck towards Wren with knit brows and pupils the size of marbles.

"Christ, Scarlett! What did you take?" Wren grabs her shoulder, the temperature of her blood rising. *How could I not see this happening again? Fuck.* It's very clear now, Scarlett's absence of friends. No one would want to deal with her rollercoaster of actions. She curses Dave's name under her breath. *Why would he saddle me with this whackjob?*

"Just a little something to take the edge off, you know?"

"No, I don't know." All Wren can do is stare back at Scarlett and think about how her brain is enveloped in a drug-induced fog. The hazy vision with the name Duane now makes sense. And the one back at the spa in the water. She's on something again and it's messing with her deep-rooted memory. Fabienne's memory. "Where's a bathroom in this mansion? I'm going to get you a glass of water." It's the only idea that comes to Wren.

Scarlett points a wavering finger. "Right next to my room. It's my personal bathroom."

"Stay put, okay?"

"Good thinking, you go distract my parents with a bathroom emergency. Like, clog the toilet with a stupid pink towel and then run to get them. I'll run to the office, find my birth certificate, and then come out and confront them with the photo of Fabienne, and we'll hit them with the truth." She punches her flattened palm.

"No! Stay right here." Wren backs out of the closet.

"It's go time." Scarlett follows with light, high steps, like a cat-burglar in a cartoon.

Wren pauses and rolls her eyes. "Okay, wait by the door and leave on my signal." A childish lie just might work, she thinks.

Scarlett gives a thumbs-up and runs to the door, placing her back against the wall, waiting for a signal that will never come.

Wren shakes her head and moves past Scarlett into the hall, wondering if she popped another Adderall or some other pill she keeps stashed away and takes when the mood strikes. It isn't hard to find Scarlett's bathroom. The towels and curtains are dripping in the same pink and lacy accents as her bedroom. *There must be a cup around here somewhere.* Wren opens all the drawers and cupboards. Only extra toilet paper, towels, hair accessories, and whatever else you'd find standard in a girl's bathroom.

"If you're looking for drugs, we don't have any." Scarlett's mother, Gabby, appears in the doorway. Arms crossed with an eyebrow raised.

Surprised, Wren freezes and slowly turns to look at the woman who is accusing her of searching for prescription drugs, she assumes. "No, it's not like that at all." She raises her hands and shakes her head like she is under arrest.

"How much is she paying you to be her friend? It's not right to take advantage of the mentally unwell."

The thought of the money turns Wren's cheeks pink.

Scarlett is paying her, but only to help her find peace from her nightmares. Her mouth hangs open.

"Don't think you're the first one she's dug up, playing the innocent card? Probably made you believe she was average, poor even, made you feel a little sorry for her. I won't let another selfish hoodlum take advantage of my daughter." Gabby's heels click on the slate tile floor. Her eyes locked onto Wren.

"No. I would never do that." Wren closes the drawer full of hairbrushes next to her hip. "I'm trying to help her. In fact, I came in here to look for a glass to bring her some water."

Gabby lowers her eyebrow.

"Look, I don't know what Scarlett took. She doesn't tell me. I'm usually blindsided by her unpredictable emotions," Wren says.

"What are you helping Scarlett with?" Gabby taps her shiny taupe nails on her forearm.

Wren exhales and her shoulders slump. She doesn't know if Gabby means what she is helping Scarlett with at this moment, or the bigger picture. The truth congeals in her throat. *What the heck do I tell her that won't make me seem crazy?* Talking about her ability is never something she does. Her grandparents forbade any discussion or mention of what she saw when she touched people. Her grandpa's stern words still echo in her ears: *Wren, don't you ever let anyone know what you've seen. Forget about it. Just stop touching people!* "Umm." She clears her throat. "It's true. Scarlett did meet my father, Dave, in AA. I'm not close with him. Actually, I don't really know him." She smooths her tongue over her back teeth. So far, that is the truth.

"That's not surprising, he's an alcoholic."

A statement Wren could not honestly confirm or deny, the fact that he is an alcoholic is secondhand information she heard from Scarlett, but who knows when she is telling the truth? "Right." She leans her hip against the porcelain vanity top. "Well, he thought I could help her overcome her nightmares." Her mouth is growing dry. "Without the use of drugs," she adds hastily.

Gabby's face is emotionless. Her eyes remain on Wren. "Scarlett's done so well to stay clean, and now she's using again. I'll double what she paid you to walk away and leave her alone."

How does she know Scarlett offered to pay me for my services? I know I never let that slip. Wren stands there stunned. The thought of a hundred and ten thousand dollars doesn't take over her thoughts. Instead, it's the thought of Fabienne. The woman who was abducted, held against her will, raped, and forced to give birth. *Gabby doesn't care how I'm helping Scarlett, she doesn't want the twisted truth getting out.* Scarlett asked Gabby about Roman and dropped the bomb of her parents of not being her biological parents on the phone yesterday night. *We're on the right trail.* Wren sways away from the vanity and stands as tall as her petite five-foot-two frame will allow. Her lips part to speak words her brain hasn't formed yet.

"Mummy!" Scarlett saunters around the corner and bends slightly to throw her arms around her mother's waist. "Is Wren telling you what she saw?" Her lips pout. "You're brand new. And Daddy was a moose. A big strong moose. With massive antlers. Before this life. You know, like, reincarnation."

Wren knows Scarlett is embellishing what she saw and relayed to her, and it doesn't surprise her. The truth that was just blasted into the air causes her spine to stiffen and her knees to weaken.

"Scarlett, what did you take?" Gabby grabs Scarlett by the shoulders and searches her eyes for answers.

"Nothing your quack of a doctor hasn't prescribed me before." Scarlett's smile is coy.

"Hank! Get over here now," Gabby shouts. "Scarlett, who gave you those pills?"

"A guy I know." Scarlett's smile is so wide it must hurt her cheeks. "Don't blame Wren, she's helped me more in two days than you have in thirty-four years."

Gabby looks down the hall. "Hank! Where are you?"

Wren stares at the two women, waiting for her secret to be called into question. She thinks back to a time when she told AJ her secret. He believed her. He embraced it. But when she was a child, before she understood reincarnation and what she was seeing when she touched people, a teacher she tried to explain it to only called her Nan and suggested therapy. *Maybe Mrs. Chadwick was right?*

"You need to drive your daughter to the clinic right now," Gabby spits.

Chapter 18

"Daddy, I'm fine," Scarlett babbles as she pries out of her father's embrace. "Jeez, I can stand and walk on my own." She tugs down her sweater. "Mom's crazy, you know that."

Wren notices Scarlett has returned to calling her father Daddy instead of Hank. She chalks it up to the drugs. Or maybe she is witnessing how Scarlett apparently plays her dad like a fiddle. She follows Scarlett, as she doesn't know what else to do, taking in more of the interior of the Hernandez estate as they walk down the halls. There are grand paintings in golden frames and fresh flowers in vases spaced about every thirty feet. The sounds of their steps rippling down the vacant corridor, Wren blows her breath out of the side of her mouth. This may take longer than she thought. If she needs to touch Scarlett a hundred more times to find the right information, then that's what she's going to do. She's into too deep now, and after Gabby's accusation of being with Scarlett for the money, the paycheque is no longer a motivator. There is satisfaction in proving someone wrong, she concludes to herself.

"Scarlett, your mother knows what's best, darling." Hank places his hand on Scarlett's back.

There is a tingle in Wren's bones that wants her to reach out and touch Hank's hand. To see what life as a moose is like. She's never spent more than a few seconds touching someone who was once an animal. It would be fascinating to focus on their feelings, their communication. *I could learn so much.* She looks down at her hands in front of her and holds them back. There was a time when the act of touching trumped her better judgement.

"I can't leave my guest high and dry, that would make me a terrible host." Scarlett looks at Wren over her shoulder and gives her a wink.

"Your friend can go home, I'm sure she needs a break from you," Hank adds.

"But I drove her here."

"Then pay for an Uber to take her home, or buy her a bus or train ticket." Patience wanes in Scarlett's father's tone.

The fact that they are discussing Wren's comings and goings in front of her without including her in the conversation makes her pick up her pace to walk beside Scarlett. "I'm perfectly capable of finding my own way home." Her expression is flat. They ignore her comment and turn down a hall, and Wren realizes she has no clue where she is. The sunlight filtered through the tall, stained-glass windows offers no assistance. They enter through a door, and they are now in a massive garage. Wren quickly counts the vehicles; there is a different one for each day of the week.

"Come, honey, it's for your own good. Your mother will bring a bag with your stuff later today." Hanks attempts to guide his daughter to a black shiny truck.

"Ha!" Scarlett lets an exaggerated laugh escape her lips. "How can my mother do that when she's really dead?" She pulls herself further away from him. "She's the one haunting me in my nightmares because of you, Hank!"

Okay, Scarlett's back to using Hank. Wren backs into a car, startled by its touch.

"See, you're not well." Hank approaches Scarlett with hands out. "Your mother is inside worried sick about you. We both worry about you, sweetheart."

"Wren, let's go." Scarlett points to Wren and signals to the door that will lead them outside. "I don't need to stay here and listen to you. I thought you could help! I thought you would understand!" She marches towards the door. A switch is flipped and Scarlett's calmish demeanour snaps to offended.

Wren jogs to catch up, and plans in her head that she'll drive, for both of their safety.

"Scarlett, wait, come back. Let's talk about this," her dad begs.

"Too little too late, Hank!" Scarlett accentuates the single syllable name. "You used to say you would do anything to take my nightmares away!" She stops and turns to face her dad before she and Wren exit the garage. "Why don't you go back to being a big dumb moose?"

Hank's eyes wrinkle. "What?"

"Wren told me you used to be a moose. A big, smelly one,

too!" On that last note, she spins on her heel and pulls Wren out of the garage into the fresh autumn air.

"I'll drive," Wren adds as she chases Scarlett around the grounds in the direction of her car, she hopes.

The estate shrinks in the rearview mirror. Wren's eyes bounce between the road in front of her, Scarlett next to her and the view behind her. It's possible Hank might attempt to tail them or call the cops.

"Well, that was a waste of time." Scarlett slaps her hands on her thighs. "Gabby and Hank are so dumb."

The events of the day unfold in Wren's mind. She looks at Scarlett, who is resting her head against the passenger side window. Wren's knuckles are white as her fingers wrap around the steering wheel. It dawns on her that she has no destination. She's only driving to put more distance between them and the Hernandez Estate.

"Wren, pull over and touch me. We need more information." Scarlett flips down the visor and stares at herself in the mirror. "Fabienne, Mom, you need to show us more. We need something good. Something we can use." Scarlett's face glistens on account of the sweat.

"Duane." The name appears on Wren's lips. She glances at Scarlett. "Does the name Duane mean anything to you?"

"Fabienne! Who's Duane?" Scarlett shouts at herself in the mirror. "Tell me who the fuck Duane is."

Wren never did get Scarlett that glass of water. And

come to think of it, she's barely eaten anything today. It doesn't take long for her to spot a Starbucks. "Scarlett, we're going to stop at Starbucks." She decides it's probably best if they go through the drive-thru instead of dining inside. "What do you wanna eat?" Wren pulls into the parking lot and eyes Scarlett, who is still staring at herself in the small mirror on the back of the visor.

"Fabienne, I need you, Mama," Scarlett mumbles to herself.

Wren remembers Scarlett picking at a muffin the day she picked her up. *Muffin and water it is.* She maneuvers the car into the row of vehicles in line for the drive-thru. There are seven cars in front of her. In the silence and time to spare, she goes over all the details she has so far. *Fabienne, originally from Haiti, living in Montreal; Sofia and Anya, living in Toronto; and Bojana, from Oakville, but she had given birth and never returned to the basement where they were being held. So far the evidence points to human trafficking or abduction with intent to impregnate these young women.* A cold shiver rattles up her spine. *The scent of the building is unforgettable. Possibly an old library or place with old books or paper. That could be a lead.* Wren shifts the car into park and roots around in her bag sitting next to Scarlett's legs. Once she retrieves her phone, she punches in 'abandoned libraries Canada', but the search comes back with nothing usable. A couple places in the States, but she thinks it would be way too risky to smuggle abducted girls across the border. Even in the eighties. Not impossible, but unlikely, she thinks.

Roman Moore, most likely a fake name, and now Duane.

Honk. Honk. An impatient SUV sounds off behind her.

Wren startles back to reality, drops her phone in her lap, and shifts the vehicle in drive to move forward a few spots. Her cheeks are pink from the embarrassment of not paying attention. Scarlett is now passed out in the seat next to her. Wren folds up the passenger seat visor.

At the speaker she orders two blueberry muffins, a water, and a tall latte. She's not really sure what size a tall is but guesses it's a medium. Wren chokes on her own saliva when she sees the screen displaying her order and the total is almost twenty dollars. Her phone vibrates between her legs. It's odd for Wren to receive a text. No one texts her. Her first thought would be Scarlett, but Scarlett is passed out next to her. It could be AJ, and somehow the recent discussion of his name and being accused of involvement in blabbing secrets has somehow sent invisible alarms his way. She taps her screen. *Private number.* Her lips twist as she reads the simple text that displays the name *Duane Strickland* and nothing else.

Honk. Honk.

This time, unphased by the sound of impatience, all Wren can do is stare at her screen, at the two words that spell the name Duane Strickland. Her stomach flips in her body, and she wishes she was back in her hotel room. If she's going to research her first lead not given to her through Scarlett, she needs to do it right, and not some hasty search in a Starbucks drive-thru. The fact that the clue came from a private number doesn't bother her; she now has a name. Plus, deep in her heart, she has a theory on who the private number is coming from. *Dave.*

Chapter 19

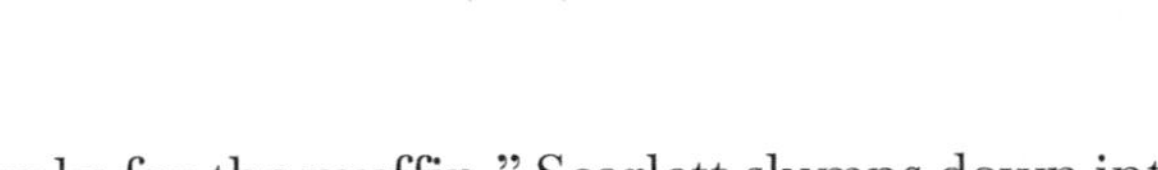

66"Thanks for the muffin." Scarlett slumps down into the plush chair in the corner of Wren's hotel room and plows the baked good into her mouth like a toddler learning to feed itself. "What a great day," she muffles between chews.

Turning her attention to Scarlett, Wren drops her bag and coffee on the table. Her forehead crinkles. "This is a good day to you?" she asks Scarlett with a hint of annoyance. Moments ago in the car, Scarlett was not happy about her parents' reaction. *Getting to the bottom of what happened to Fabienne and the rest of the girls is going to be impossible having to work with a manic like Scarlett.*

"The sun is shining. I feel good. Mommy and Daddy are shaking in their boots on account of the house of lies they have built my life on." Scarlett's grin exposes a hunk of blueberry caught between her teeth. "You have that new lead." She leans forward. "What's his name again? Dragon?"

"Scarlett, what did you take? You're spacing out." Wren pushes past Scarlett's clear cry for attention, grabs her drink, and sits down at the desk. The screen of her laptop beeps and flashes as it awakens. A newer machine wouldn't take so long to come out of sleep mode. She grabs her notebook and scribbles down the name 'Duane Strickland'. The blank white wall before her leaves an empty feeling in her chest. *Maybe Scarlett was right to want to get a cork board and pin all the evidence up to display.* Wren envisions a baby Scarlett pinned to the centre with red yarn weaving from her to Fabienne, to Roman, to the question mark labeled Duane. The idea of stumbling upon an underground adoption centre where young women are raped and forced to carry a baby hardens her insides. She rubs her jaw from the pain of grinding her teeth. This is the first time Wren's let her thoughts wander with the underground adoption ring theory. The theory first crossed her mind when she laid eyes on Fabienne's photo, but the reality of a crime this nasty was something she didn't want to let herself think about.

"Are you going to eat your muffin?" Scarlett asks, and yanks Wren from her spiraling dark theory. "I'm so hungry."

Wren twists in her chair and she studies the childlike behaviour of the grown woman waddling towards the Starbucks bag protruding from her purse. She can see her messy hands smearing muffin residue on her purse as Scarlett attempts to free the muffin. All she can think is, *It's not her fault.* Scarlett is a product of her environment. And if Wren's theory of the underground adoption ring is correct, Scarlett is the one paying the price for the crimes of others. *How many other babies were born there? Where are they now?* More questions than answers, but that's how it goes for any crime waiting to be solved. *The other babies!* Wren's eyes light up. "Scarlett! Isn't the DNA kit being delivered to your place today?"

"Oh, is that what I said?" Scarlett frees the muffin and nibbles at the top. A drastic change to how she consumed the first one. "I guess it was good that I accidentally touched you at my parents' place, eh?" She wavers on her feet, not registering that she hasn't answered Wren's question.

"Huh?" Wren responds, confused by the twists and turns of talking to an incoherent person.

"That name you asked me about before in the car, I'm guessing you got it from when we touched," Scarlett continues to nibble the side of the muffin.

Wren turns back to face her laptop. "You could say that." The text with Duane's full name from the private number, she keeps to herself. She turns back to the screen of her laptop, deciding to circle back to the DNA kit when Scarlett is sober.

"What do you mean by that?" Scarlett meanders closer to Wren. She may be high, but she can still read Wren's tone.

The search engine pops up, and Wren's fingers hover over the keyboard. "It means I only barely heard a first name. The vision was blurry because you're stoned on whatever you took." She keeps her focus on the screen and types in the name 'Duane Strickland'.

Scarlett's lips and muffin pull close to Wren's ear. "Maybe me being relaxed was the reason you got the name," she whispers, and reaches for Wren's latte.

I don't have time for this. The search page populates with article after article with the name Duane Strickland. *Dead. Hanged himself in prison.* are the top hits.

"Gross." Scarlett sticks out her tongue and wrinkles her nose. "This drink needs some sweetener." She traipses off with the muffin in one hand and the latte in the other.

Wren engulfs herself in the results and lets Scarlett fade into the background. *He's dead. And he was in prison.* His face tan, bold and brazen, hands cuffed in front of his navy prison issue jumpsuit. She knows right away this man is not Roman. The thought crossed her mind that Duane could have been an alias for Roman, but no, Duane was handsome in the conventional sense. Strong, square jaw with dark stubble and piercing blue eyes. Few people can pull off looking good in cuffs for a news cover story. A quick glance for the date tells Wren the news story covering his death is from July 1998. She would have been a teenager. She thinks back to that time to try to remember if Duane made national headlines, but she's made an effort to forget the majority of her teenage years ever happened. If his name topped the headlines, it meant nothing to her all those years ago. She had her own life in the foster home to worry about.

"Much better!" Scarlett plunks the cup down next to the laptop. "Who's that guy?" Her finger presses to the screen.

"Don't touch that." Wren swats Scarlett's hand away. "It's Duane. We can talk about him when you're sober." She doesn't watch Scarlett, but can feel her sway away towards the chair.

"Sounds good, champ. Good work today. I'm going to rest for a bit."

"Good idea, *champ*," Wren mocks. The ambient sounds dissolve, and Wren's focus glues to Duane. She sips her coffee, and the sickly sweet taste opposed to its original bitter one doesn't even distract her. She needs to know who this man is, and why the man who is allegedly her father would send her this clue.

Embezzlement, racketeering, tax evasion, Duane Strickland possesses a colourful rap sheet. Charged with all counts on January twenty-sixth, the judge ruled he be sentenced to twenty-five years in prison. However, Strickland's stay at North Shore Penitentiary ended after only six months, when the guard found Strickland unconscious in his cell early morning on July seventh and was declared dead an hour later.

The investigation surrounding his death is still ongoing, as a cause of death has not been made official.

Wren takes another sip of her latte and continues to read another article.

The RCMP arrested Duane Strickland today in his Toronto home. Reports say he surrendered peacefully as the officer cuffed him and led him to his ride down to the station to be charged and processed. Strickland simply smiled for cameras while officers carried boxes of presumed evidence from his primary residence.

The articles blur together as they all mention the same content. Wren scans for a connection to Fabienne, kidnapping, abuse, anything that might link Duane Strickland to Scarlett, except there is nothing she can see to make the link. No mention of a man named Roman, either.

Her thoughts grow foggy, and her limbs tingle, they feel like clouds attached to her body that are going to lift her and carry her away. "I don't feel right." She turns to Scarlett.

Scarlett is attempting to hide a gaping grin behind a half-eaten muffin. "You're so serious. I decided you needed to relax a bit." She pretends to chew. "Welcome to my world. Don't fight it. Enjoy it. Let the weight of the world be lifted and breathe with me," Scarlett instructs Wren, and exhales.

"Scarlett, what did you do?" Wren slurs.

"Come." Scarlett waves Wren over. "Sit with me. Hold my hand." Scarlett extends her hand that's not holding the muffin. She figures if Wren is relaxed, and she is relaxed, imagine what Wren will be able to see from Fabienne's life.

"Fuck you." Wren stands and keeps her feet planted in the carpet. "You can't drug me."

"It was only a teeny tiny bit. So just come sit." Scarlett pinches her fingers together.

Wren wipes her forehead with the back of her hand. Sweat builds along her hairline. "I need water."

"No, you're fine. Just come sit."

"No, I'm calling the police. You're absolutely insane." Wren pats her body in a search for her phone, but her own form feels foreign.

Scarlett pouts and sets her muffin down on the closest surface. "You're not going to want to do that, either. I'll tell them you got me high cause you wanted to rob me."

"What?" Wren stammers.

"I have five thousand dollars cash in my purse right now that I can plant in your bag, and my mommy already thinks you're using me for my money." Scarlett sits on the chair and pats the cushion that's big enough to hold the two women.

Wren's breath is now exaggerated. "Tell me what you gave me." Her lungs are tight and inflated at the same time.

"Come, hold my hand first," Scarlett demands. "Then I'll tell you. Just trust me, okay? Nothing bad is going to happen." She looks around the safe confines of the hotel room.

"But I just found something." Wren's brows arch like a clown. She glides closer to Scarlett and the comfy chair. "Duane. I found him online. He's in prison." She pauses and taps her finger to her lips. "Well, not anymore. He died." Her lips deflate and her frown ages her even more than time. "So close and yet so far away."

"Yes! You are so close." Scarlett bounces up, grabs Wren's wrist, and pulls her down into the chair. The two women, practically sitting on each other, huddle together like childhood best friends sharing secrets.

The haze is thick. I can't see a thing. My mind stops and starts. If I was a car, my limbs would be the tires, and they are sinking quickly in mud, spinning, losing traction the more I try to see. I'm nowhere and everywhere all at once. The girls. Their youthful faces stare at me from the cement wall. I blink, and the faces are different. Anger jolts me forward. My tires find dry land and I charge towards the girls. The girls that pushed me towards the chief. The girls that hazed me. That dragged me outside naked and tied me to the flagpole. I scream, but no sound comes out. A motion takes over my body. I look for something to hang on to. The haze is still thick. I'm going to fall. A man grunts. It stops. It starts again. It's coming from all around me. I let myself fall. His scent. A fragrance that makes me nauseous. Cracks splinter my brain. Weightless, the pain is too much; I don't care when I hit the ground. Death would be better than this. A palm and thick fingers grip into my shoulders. Why is he here? No, I shout. Nothing stops his hands. They move over my skin. Every bone in my body turns to ice. I will them to shatter into pieces to stop his touch, but my body does not listen to my demands. In the fog he still found me. No, he couldn't have found me. Hot breath falls against my face. I try to shove it away, but there is nothing there to shove. His lips are on my neck. Stop. I wiggle. Crying sounds off in the distance. It's not a baby. It's one of the girls. Anya. Don't touch her. A voice whispers in my ear, "You're the special one." I don't know that voice. My body held in place. He's too strong. I focus on my breaths and turn to the right. I can't make out his face, but he's tall.

"Jesus Christ." Wren awakens on the carpeted floor, her hands brushing invisible hands off her body.

Scarlett remains on the chair and leans forward to watch Wren. "You were spazzing out. I could barely hold on to your arm."

Wren licks her lips, and her eyes search the room.

"What are you looking for?" Scarlett joins the search. "No one else is here."

A heavy, invisible force keeps Wren pinned on her back. "Why? Why are you doing this to me?"

Scarlett shrugs. "I need your help. You know that." She climbs off the chair and joins Wren on the floor, laying on her back as if the carpet is grass and clouds float above them.

"I can't. My life is spinning." Wren closes her eyes tight to make this reality stop.

"Really?" Scarlett scrunches her nose. "Normally molly gives a more euphoric high. Like, it opens your heart, and all you can do is accept."

Wren can't speak. She needs to connect her body back to her present mind. All she can do is breathe. She knows she never wants to experience a vision like that again, Fabienne's experiences somehow tangled up with her own. Reliving her own nightmare was not something she ever wanted to do. "Go home." are her last words to Scarlett before she drifts off to sleep.

Chapter 20

Wren awakens on the floor. It takes her a few seconds to figure out where she is. Scarlett is nowhere to be seen. "Shit." She rolls onto her stomach to pull herself onto all fours. A desert dryness coats her mouth, and she extends and flexes her foot to alleviate the Charlie horse in her calf. She wants to heave the contents of her stomach, but can't. Something inside her knows it's not appropriate to vomit on the floor of a fancy hotel. Scarlett's actions crash into her foggy state. "That bitch slipped me something." Her limbs give way under her and she lays motionless on the carpet. In any other hotel room, she would have done whatever it took to hurl herself off that floor, but this place is different. The carpet feels soft and new against her cheek, and there is zero smell.

After a minute or an hour, Wren can't tell, as time doesn't seem to exist to her conscious thought, she peels herself off the floor and finds a sealed bottle of water in the fridge. Any shred of trust she had left for Scarlett is now gone. It's Fabienne's face she sees behind her eyelids and the cry of Anya. Wren isn't ready to face her own demons, but she could fight Fabienne's and get to the bottom of what happened to her and the rest of the girls thirty-something years ago.

After taking a shower and eating a banana she finds in

her room, Wren still doesn't feel right, but better than she did. *How did I let her slip me something?* She sits down in front of her laptop and taps on the trackpad, her heavy head resting in her palm supported by her elbow propped on the desk. Duane's mugshot is the first image that registers before her. It's his sharp blue eyes that the police photographer captured that jog her memory. *How are you connected to this?* All she is capable of is staring at the screen. No scrolling. No jotting down clips of vision she remembers. *He's dead. They caught him. There is nothing left for me to do.* Scarlett's promise of payment doesn't matter anymore. *Nothing is worth being drugged against your will.* Wren laughs to herself and uncurls her back. *Scarlett may look just like her biological mother, but maybe she behaves like her biological father, whoever that man behind me was. Too tall to be Roman, but a straight up sociopath. Or psychopath.* Wren knows she doesn't have enough information on the man to make an educated assumption on his condition, but based on Scarlett's behaviour, she is leaning towards psychopath. Wren's inclination for psychopath is because Scarlett demonstrated acts of caring (whether genuine or fake), where a sociopath would make it clear that they do not care how other people feel.

She decides the only course of action now is to pack up her belongings and find her way home. The thought of an anonymous call to the police from a landline from some random place (so the call can't be traced back to her) could be an option to let the police know Duane Strickland and his assumed buddy Roman Moore had something to do with impregnating women in some sort of underground adoption agency for the rich. Her hypothesis pairs nicely with Duane's list of charges, she thinks, and DNA tests could prove it. Wren isn't sure if Scarlett would ever comply with a request for her DNA from the police, but she no longer cares what Scarlett thinks.

Wren slumps in her chair as she scrolls aimlessly through the article open on her screen. *This would be another case I cracked that would launch some random detective into a promotion.* She can't help but think of Jack Cunningham and Doug Wannamaker again: the first and only case she solved— a case only *she* could solve. The reminiscing lump grows in her throat, and she sucks back the last of the water in the bottle. Every word through her shaky voice she told Officer Pritchett from the payphone that day when she was thirteen is now fresh.

I'm calling about a crime that happened years ago at 129 Foundation Street. There was a man named Roger, a real nasty looking man with a big scar through one of his black eyebrows, Caucasian, who killed Mr. and Mrs. Wannamaker with a shard of glass in their home. Roger stabbed them. He was about average height and had brown eyes. And a woman named Colleen was there, too, also Caucasian. She had short brown hair; light coloured eyes and her eyebrows were drawn on. Roger and Colleen wanted the Wannamaker's cash and jewelry.

Wren knew their names from hearing what Doug Wannamaker wanted her to hear using little Jack as a conduit. The screams and blood were real. She saw what Doug Wannamaker wanted her to see. Roger and Colleen never revealed their last names, but she bet with her description of Roger and Colleen, the police would find him. Wren knew she had to be careful on what details she shared with the officer. She couldn't invite any questions on how she knew what she knew. The payphone was her safest option back then as she could hang up when she was done and run. No one could trace the call back to her. No cameras on every street corner.

Wren shakes her head. The vision of the chief from his past life comes reeling back to her. He was an art thief. Chief Payne's face is hauntingly fresh. It comes to her; she saw him in her drug-clouded vision. She doesn't let the confusion of the replaying of his actions overtake her thoughts. *It was because of the drugs.* To change her stream of consciousness, Wren types Officer Deborah Pritchett into the search bar.

"Good, you're up," Scarlett announces as she enters as if the happenings in this hotel room have been nothing but copacetic.

Wren keeps her eyes on the screen. "Get the fuck out." She slams her laptop closed. Learning of officer Pritchett's career path isn't important. Her eye twitches at the thought of Scarlett stealing her room card or getting a spare from the front desk. *Little rich girl can do whatever she wants.*

The unsuspecting slam forces Scarlett to jump. "Calm down. You're fine."

"No, I'm not fine." She twists her neck in Scarlett's direction. "I've been drugged and blackmailed. And my body feels like it's been hit by an eighteen-wheeler."

Scarlett furrows her brow as she straightens the papers she's holding. "Well, then, I don't recommend you try molly again. You had a weird reaction to it."

"Molly? You slipped me ecstasy?" Flames ignite behind Wren's cheeks. Her eyes narrow. "What the fuck..."

"I did it in the name of science," Scarlett cuts her off. "Aren't you curious how different stimulations might enhance what you see?" She flattens her papers against her chest and stares at Wren.

Wren swings her sitting body in the chair to face Scarlett, who is keeping her distance. "Not when the stimulation is an illegal substance."

Scarlett stifles a grin. "Think what you want about drugs. I think you had a therapeutic experience." She walks and takes a seat at the table. "You were standing up to the chief. You confronted him. I heard you clear as a bell."

Hearing someone else speak his name in reference to what happened to her many years ago makes it real. Wren folds her arms across her chest and rubs her shoulders. What happened to her is in the past, and she tells herself it doesn't matter now. That man is most likely dead, just like Duane. Her actions against him now would only force her to relive her own trauma. Another man who got away with his past crimes. "Doesn't matter. None of this matters, does it?"

Wren's eyes are unfocused and stare past Scarlett to the empty beige wall.

"Maybe not. But I have something." Scarlett stands and walks back to Wren, extending the paper she came in with towards her. "Here. Maybe this will matter to someone, somewhere." The sharpness in her face softens as if she is extending an olive branch. "Look, I'm sorry, okay? Just take the paper."

All Wren can do is study Scarlett. For a minute she removes herself from her own body and examines their situation. *This is so messed up. I'm not a victim if I choose to keep staying here. Scarlett's an adult and made her own choices, too. She can't blame all her issues on her parents, adoptive or birth parents. It's Fabienne that needs help. Fabienne is the reason I stayed. If the truth is revealed, does it matter who brought it to light? Maybe it's better off I remain in the margins of justice.*

"Wren? What are you thinking about? You have a real pensive look on your face." Scarlett asks.

"The case is over. I think I know who was orchestrating the whole black market adoption agency."

Scarlett's hand holding the paper falls by her side. "Adoption agency?"

"Yeah, it's obvious. These men were getting girls pregnant and then selling babies to the rich who wanted to pass them off as their own." Wren's eyes stay fixed on Scarlett's face to read her reaction. "And your bio daddy isn't

Roman."

For once, no retort hastily leaves Scarlett's lips. The truth of her life hangs in the air. Her face is still, and she looks younger. "So that's it? My nightmares are over?"

Right, Scarlett's nightmares. The true test for whether Fabienne has found closure. "Go take a nap and find out," Wren adds.

"It can't be that simple. You can't just come here and magically figure it all out in three days." Scarlett lets the paper in her grip fall to the floor.

Wren shrugs. "You hired me for my unique talent, right?" She turns back to her computer and calls up the past search for Duane Strickland. Her findings fill her lungs with air, and the corner of her lip curls upward. "This guy, right here." She points to the screen. "He's the one behind it all. He has to be." She clears her throat. "I know it." Her voice is hoarse.

Scarlett looks down at the screen. "Uncle Dewy."

"You know him?"

"Yeah. Well, not really." Scarlett forces a breathy laugh. "He was a business associate of my parents'. Went to jail. Ruined a lot of lives. Thankfully, not..." She stops and doesn't finish her sentence.

"I asked you if the name Duane meant anything to you." Wren parts her lips. She eyes the paper on the floor and picks it up.

"I was a kid. And I only met him like a dozen times. And I always knew him as Dewy, not Duane." Scarlett leans in closer for a better look.

Wren glances down at the paper in her grasp. *Your DNA results have been loaded. Login to learn more about your heritage and connect with long-lost relatives.* Her eyes zero in on the date. *June fifth.* Wren grits her molars as she learns that Scarlett had submitted her DNA sample months before even meeting her. The lie fails to surprise her. Her eyes make their way back to Scarlett, who is still staring at the picture of Duane. "Scarlett, have you logged into this yet?" She raises the paper.

Chapter 21

Scarlett confesses to not logging in to see her DNA results yet, and that she submitted her DNA only because she always felt deep in her heart there was a connection absent between her and her parents. She also told Wren it was odd that she was told she never had aunts, uncles, or cousins and the test is a way to know for sure. "Before, when I first got notified when the results were in, I wish I never did it. I couldn't face the truth alone. My whole life, I have lived alone." She takes a seat at the table, and her eyes land on Wren. "You think I'm a mess, don't you?"

The room falls silent. Not even the faint hum of the minifridge can be heard. Wren takes Scarlett's story with a grain of salt. In the three days she's known Scarlett, she's faced more chaos than in her whole life, and she sees people's past lives when she touches them, so yes, Wren thinks Scarlett is a mess. A sane person doesn't drug someone, especially the only person trying to help them. She needs air. And something to eat. The dull ache pressing against her temple is a signal that she's gone too long without food. "I need to find something to eat." Wren rises and snatches her purse off the table. Before she slings it over her shoulder, she searches its contents to make sure Scarlett didn't plant something incriminating to have her arrested. Her mind runs with the thought of Scarlett's amusement of having

Dave the cop arrest his own daughter for possession of narcotics, and she wouldn't have the faintest clue, because she's never met the man.

"You really think Uncle Dewy was the mastermind behind all this?" Scarlett remains seated. Her eyes soften with uncertainty.

Wren knows better than to let that look of Scarlett's suck her in anymore. She heads for the door. "We'll know more when I get back, because I'm going to log in to see your results." The weight of the hotel room door clicks behind her.

Wren forgot how much the temperature could drop between a few days in the fall. The constant fluctuation of the Ontario seasons is something she is not fond of. She imagines herself living in a beach town south somewhere and wonders if fifty-five thousand is enough to pack up, move, and start a new life where not a soul knows what she's capable of.

About four blocks away she finds a European-style deli. She reaches for the door and realizes she doesn't have her gloves on. *It's fine. I'll be careful.* The salami and pastrami scent fill the inside of the shop, and it takes Wren back to the time she went to Italy. When she met AJ. It seems like another life ago. She stares blankly at a shelf of condiments, and it takes her a few seconds to realize the labels are in a different language.

"Good day, miss, what can I get for you?"

"Huh?" Wren pivots to the counter displaying a variety

of meats.

The man in a white apron with black hair smiles at her. "Would you like to order a sandwich?"

Wren nods and weaves her way through the vignettes of sweets and other delicatessens to the counter. The closer she gets to the man, the more she notices about him. His hair is dyed. The top button on his plaid shirt is missing. Hopefully, it didn't fall into someone's sandwich.

"First, let's start with the bread. Rye, pumpernickel, focaccia, baguette..."

"Baguette is good." Wren finds the sign, which outlines six different sandwiches identified with a number. "Number three," she blurts. "Please."

On the walk back to the hotel she eats her sandwich and lets her mind wander to where AJ could be. A real citizen of the world. He could be anywhere. She apologises to herself for letting herself believe it was AJ who blabbed her secrets to a stranger. She knew he would never do that. *Maybe I could travel with him for a bit after this?* She swallows her last, well-chewed bite and wipes her hands together. After witnessing and concluding isolation added to Scarlett's problems, the thought of returning to an empty apartment doesn't sit well.

"It didn't work," Scarlett announces the moment Wren steps back into the room.

Scarlett didn't steal her room card after all, it was in the front pocket of her purse. Wren removes her shoes and stays silent. She's not feeding Scarlett's demand for attention. The atmosphere has shifted to a mood more somber, like the last day of summer before you had to go back to school, unsure of what the next grade has in store for you. Pepperoni smell lingers in Wren's nostrils.

"I still have nightmares. I laid down and dozed off and there was his stupid, ugly face looming in the shadows." Scarlett remains on her back on the bed, dramatically staring at the ceiling with her arms stretched out like a starfish.

Wren nods and walks to her laptop. The paper from the DNA test is still on the desk where she left it. "Hey, they mailed this to you?" she waves the paper and asks. *Everything is digital now. It seems archaic to receive mail these days.*

"They email me all the time, too. I guess 'cause it's been so long and I paid for the top-tier package. It's nice to receive mail sometimes. You know?" Scarlett stays motionless on the bed.

Wren knew if she wants to sort this out, she can't keep giving Scarlett all the home court advantages. "I'm going down to the business centre to work." She stuffs the letter and her notebook in her bag, her laptop cradled in her arms.

"Okay." Scarlett pops up and swings her legs over the side of the bed, her eyes sunken and her hair matted from laying down. "Let me find my shoes." She shuffles around, scanning the floor for her misplaced shoes.

She must be coming down. Wren keeps her eyes on Scarlett. If she swallows, licks, snorts, or heaven forbid, injects something, she wants to know.

"What's your email?" Wren lightly taps her keys in anticipation. Her eyes rest on the space waiting for the email to be typed in.

"And you call yourself a detective?" Scarlett squirms in the chair next to Wren. "I would have thought you'd know all that basic information by now."

"I never claimed to be a detective." Wren chews on her lower lip, eyes forward.

"Well, you wanted to be one. And the way Dave carried on about you, you'd think..."

Wren snaps her neck toward Scarlett. "He talked about me like he knows me?" Her knee bounces under the table. "Nope, never mind. I don't care. Just tell me your email and password." *That man doesn't deserve to take up a single ounce of my time.*

Scarlett articulates each letter between her lips, smacking around a wad of gum. "S-L-E-E-P, underscore...."

When did she put gum in her mouth? "Password."

"Don't know."

"What do you normally use for a password?"

"I don't remember."

"Look, just type it in and try it. I won't watch."

"I honestly don't remember." Scarlett chews and stares at the screen.

Wren clicks 'forgot password'. *Enough of this garbage.* "Get your phone ready to confirm the password change." She puffs her cheeks but exhales her hot breath through her nose.

After a few minutes of senseless back-and-forth with Scarlett and her email, the new password is set, and Wren is in. *Welcome, Prudence.* "Scarlett, why does it say 'welcome Prudence'?" she asks before clicking anything.

"I'm not going to use my real name," Scarlett giggles. "The last thing I want is some stranger claiming to be my relative, constantly harassing me because they know my family has money."

Smart. Wren wrestles with the idea that maybe Scarlett isn't as dumb as she acts.

"The letter is addressed to Prudence, too. Didn't you notice?"

Wren can't help but give the letter a side-eye as it's sitting on the table to her left. *She's right. How did I not notice?* Wren gnaws on the inside of her cheek. The salty taste of deli meats still coats her mouth. *Right, I was drugged.* She carefully reads the options on the screen before clicking. *Ancestry, Connections, Health Insights...* Wren starts with *Ancestry*. A colourful pie chart pops up and dozens of countries form a list down the left panel of her screen. She clicks on *Connections*. Wren can't help herself. Evidence is at her fingertips. She twists back to check on Scarlett. The seat beside her is empty. "Scarlett?" She stands and sees her crumpled body squeezed on the windowsill, forehead pressed into the glass window.

"Nothing matters. What am I doing?"

Wren stays where she is and scans the business centre to see if anyone has joined them. They are alone for now. "You're doing what's right."

"I inherited Fabienne's trauma. We all inherit something we don't like. It's just a burden we're all to bear." Scarlett itches the window with her fingernail. Her gaze falls upon the grey horizon.

Wren's eyes bounce from the results on the screen to Scarlett. It crosses her mind that she's in way over her head. She has no experience dealing with trauma victims or addicts. Wren's Nan instilled her with compassion, and if you can inherit bad stuff, that means you can also inherit good stuff. She pushes her judgement of Scarlett aside. It doesn't matter if this is a manipulation technique; Scarlett is a human. In this moment there is a scared, sad woman in front of her, and Wren's heart can feel her pain. "Scarlett." She slowly walks toward her. "You don't have to do this alone."

Scarlett maintains her fixation on what's on the other side of the window. "I've always been alone."

"No, you haven't." Wren moves around the empty conference table. "You just didn't know where to find your people."

"No one wants me around." Scarlett looks at Wren. "Look at me. I'm a fuckin' mess. You try to help me, and what do I do?" Her voice is rising. "I drug you. For fun. To see what will happen."

"You found me for a reason. You need help. I'm alone, too. But for some strange purpose, here we are together. The universe is all kinds of fucked up, but here we are, alone together." Wren stops three feet from Scarlett. She wants to reach out and touch her trembling skin, but holds her hands back.

"Better put your gloves on. I might *accidentally* touch you." Scarlett puts air quotes around 'accidentally.'

Wren inspects the front and back of her hands and smiles. "If you think you have inherited trauma, then what the hell did I inherit?"

Scarlett blinks as she turns her attention to Wren's hands. "I guess Dave knew, eh? What a shit dad."

"Maybe most dads are shit?"

Scarlett offers a fleeting smile. "Hank with all his secrets is pretty bad, too, I suppose." She wipes snot that's dripping to her lip with the back of her hand and sniffs. "But especially the man that raped Fabienne and made me."

"We can always confirm that with his other daughter." Wren raises an eyebrow. She wasn't sure when to mention to Scarlett she probably has a half-sister, but now seems *à propos.*

Scarlett uncurls her body and sits in the window, with her feet now touching the floor. Her eyes flutter and dart around the room. "What do you mean?"

"I mean, I think you have a half-sister." Wren leans her backside against the conference table. "I think you have an uncle, too."

Chapter 22

"How could you?" Scarlett lunges forward and shoves Wren.

Wren's spine cracks as she bends back onto the table. *What is happening?*

Scarlett jolts Wren again with more might than she expected. "I can't unknow something like that. They are going to come looking for me now!" she screeches.

"Scarlett, stop!" Wren shouts back. "No one knows you exist." Scarlett's hands keep Wren's shoulders pinned to the table. "I didn't contact them. I just saw them in your profile."

"Ahhh!" Scarlett lets years of undirected anger exit her body.

Wren wants to shield her ears from the piercing sounds escaping Scarlett, but she is forced to listen. Scarlett's weight on her biceps forces her hands to remain locked at her sides.

"What on Earth is going on here?" a man barks.

Scarlett's attention pulls to the stranger, and she loosens her grip on Wren.

Wren instantly reaches for Scarlett's hands and propels her weight forward to pin her back. She wasn't in police college long enough to learn tactical take downs, but some maneuvers and the instinct to physically protect herself rush back, even though she was the weakest one in her class.

Fabienne's heart beats in a hollow chest. Fear and urine fill the cramped space we're currently in. It's the trunk. The snippet of vision that I've seen before reminds me where I am. Our mouth is taped, and it's getting hard to breathe through the sobs and mucus clogging our nasal passage. Fabienne focuses on keeping herself alive. Our breaths become shallow and less frequent. If we're not released soon, she is going to pass out. Even if she does, it doesn't matter, I know how this tragedy ends, I remind myself. We've stopped moving and I focus on the noise. I think I hear sirens in the distance, but know they are not for us. The sound of someone exiting the car and slamming the door is obvious. Roman. The trunk pops open and it's still dark. We're blindfolded. Fabienne's bound body is hoisted out of the back of the vehicle. His grubby hand finds itself on our butt. Fabienne has let herself go limp in an attempt to escape the only way she can, but I see a light. A sliver of light from the streetlamp lets itself under the bottom of our blindfold. Roman curses something about piss. I burn the sound of his voice to memory. Our legs are bound, too, but there is brown brick. I can see that much. I focus on the wall as he carries us away. My guess is to the basement. The surface changes for a second. It's bronze, I think. The streetlamp illuminates the words 'Historical' and 'Box'. They mean nothing to me.

"Are you okay?" a foreign man's voice asks.

Wren's body pushed up against the wall. Her breathing is still shallow, matching Fabienne's. She opens her eyes and sees Scarlett staring at the back of the man's head, seething through grit teeth. A stranger stands between them. "I'm fine." The words *historical* and *box* embossed in bronze flash behind her eyelids.

"Do you know this woman?" he asks.

"Yes," Wren says.

"Is she okay?" his lips ask, but his eyes don't care about the answer.

"She's just going through a tough time." Wren debates sharing Scarlett's story with the man. It's filled her for long enough, she needs to tell someone, but she agrees with herself, this man is not who should hear Scarlett's secret.

"I called security." The man straightens the collar of his sweater and walks away from the women.

"Scarlett," Wren beckons. "We need to go."

"Are you sure you are okay?"

"Yes. I assure you I am not hurt." Wren rushes to collect her things, including Scarlett. She doesn't have time to touch her hand, although the idea of touching Scarlett again is enticing. *Would my vision continue from where it left off?*

"She's strong, I really had to pry her off you." The man watches with authoritative eyes.

"Scarlett, come on. We need to leave." Wren holds the glass door open, waiting for Scarlett to return from wherever her mind took her to.

"What happened?" Scarlett breaks her trance and looks

around the room. "Who is this guy?" She points.

Wren waves her forward. "I'll tell you upstairs."

Scarlett gives the man a judging stare as she walks past him to leave. "Seriously, where did that man come from? Do you know him?"

"No." Wren wraps her fingers around Scarlett's clothed arm and ushers her away from the business centre, hoping to herself they don't cross paths with security on their way to the elevators. Chaos claws at her mind. She cannot afford to forget what she just learned from her vision and she needs to confront Scarlett on what the fuck just happened.

"The words 'historical' or 'box', do they mean anything to you?" Wren asks.

Scarlett gives her the side-eye without saying a word.

"I mean, do you recognize them? Fabienne showed me something new. She was blindfolded, but I saw where Roman took her."

Scarlett remains silent.

"It was a brown brick building; there was a bronze sign I saw for a second, and I could only make out the words historical and box." Wren jabs the up arrow on the elevator and shoulder-checks over both shoulders. They are still alone.

"We touched?" Scarlett rubs her eyes with her fists.

"What happened? Did you touch me or did I touch you?"

"It doesn't matter." Wren bites her tongue to not spill the part about finding a half-sister and uncle again. Whatever mental state Scarlett was in ten minutes ago cannot happen again. Especially if they are concealed in an elevator. The doors ding and glide open.

An older woman with a little yorkie in a stroller greets them. "Good day, ladies. Lovely autumn day to take Jonathan for a stroll." Deep wrinkles frame her thin, bright pink lips. Her lavender perfume fills the small space.

Wren forces a smile and nods, pulling Scarlett's shirt behind her.

Once back in the hotel room, Wren guides Scarlett to the plush chair and she rushes back to the peephole to check if security tracked them down, but the corridor is empty. Her muscles loosen now that they are back in the privacy of the room, although she's not sure how safe she feels with Scarlett. The only predictable trait about Scarlett is that she is unpredictable. "You good?" she asks.

Scarlett's body is rigid, her focus on the view of outside the window. She breaks her silence. "Why was I so angry back there? I felt angry, like I wanted to hurt someone, but I also felt like I blacked out."

Wren takes a seat at the desk. *She did hurt someone! How could Scarlett forget about a half-sister and uncle?* She chalks it up to drugs or coming down, and deliberates with herself that being alone in this room with Scarlett may not be the smartest move, but in this moment, this seems like the most logical option to find answers. *Now is not the time to dwell on her violent blackout.* The mission is still to gather all the information she can to relay to the police. "Maybe I'm the one angry with you?" Wren retorts.

"Why?" Scarlett scrunches her nose.

Wren wants to laugh out loud to keep her own sanity. Instead, she retrieves her laptop from her bag and places it in front of her. The back of her mind is still trying to piece together the connection between *historical* and *box*. "Maybe because you touched me without permission, took me to your parents and lied to me about your motive, are drinking and taking drugs behind my back…" Wren turns toward Scarlett. "Drugged me for your own amusement and forcefully pinned me down against a table."

Scarlett snaps to Wren. "Is all that stuff not allowed? That wasn't clear when I hired you and agreed to pay you a large sum of money."

"Let's just get this over with," Wren says under her breath, and turns back to her machine. She shakes her arms to remove Scarlett's phantom grip. *I'm sure I'll have bruises tomorrow.* She watches the screen load and gets her fingers ready to search *historical* plus *box*. What little of the plaque she caught a glimpse of on the building reminds her of similar ones she's seen on old houses as a kid. When she spotted a house with a plaque mounted to a pole by the sidewalk or affixed to the front of a house, her Nan would always want to stop and read about the historical significance. Nan would tell Wren how nice it was that the community recognized older buildings. In fact, Wren now remembers once going for a summer walk with Nan when their sole mission was to find and learn about as many historically-relevant buildings as they could. It surprised Wren that a very large Victorian-looking house was once a home and doctor's office for the town's first doctor. She even recalls his name, Dr. Butler. She remembers it, because as a kid she thought a doctor shouldn't have the name of another job, and it would make more sense if his name was Dr. Stethoscope.

"What were you asking me about in the hall? Something about a box?" Scarlett asks.

The search engine loads and Wren types as she answers Scarlett. "The building where Fabienne and the other girls were kept, it was a historical landmark, and it had the word 'box' embossed on the plaque." She includes Canada in the search to narrow down the results.

Scarlett crosses her legs and lets the weight of her body fall back into the plushy cushion. "Can't say I know anything about that, but it sounds like Fabienne showed you everything she could about where she was being held captive."

"I suppose." Wren leans in closer to her screen. The top searches come back for history boxes. She doesn't take the time to see exactly what they are, but assumes they are packages sent to kids for learning based on a quick glance of the accompanying photo.

"What do you see?"

"Nothing yet," Wren answers, wishing in the moment she tried harder to read the plaque. Now that she knows what to look for, she thinks that if she touched Scarlett again and Fabienne showed her the same scenario, she could focus. She swivels in her chair to face Scarlett. "I think I have an idea."

Scarlett's off in her own world, with her legs now flung over the side of the chair, her attention on her phone. "What, about a building where they made boxes?" she offers as she continues to swipe up.

"I don't think that's a real thing. A factory where they make cardboard boxes?" Wren rolls her eyes.

"Not cardboard boxes, silly." Scarlett looks to Wren over her phone. "Like jewelry boxes, or boxes for fancy cigars. I don't know, think outside of the box." She laughs at her pun.

Wren swings back to face her computer. *I guess special boxes would have to be made somewhere. And if it's historical, people would have worked in the factory, and it wouldn't be all automated and manufactured by robots overseas as I'm sure it is now.* She types in 'a historical box factory' and slams the enter key with her pinky. The results populate, but before even reading the first headline, she clicks images, positive that a full view image of the building would strike her quicker than reading. As the images load, her mind bounces to wondering if the factory was operational when the young woman were locked in the basement. *No, it couldn't be. It was probably abandoned.* The whites of her eyes grow. "Holy shit."

"What?" Scarlett asks.

Wren can't click the sepia-toned picture fast enough. The corner, the location of the streetlight on the side of the brown brick building. "It's huge."

"Let me see."

The once active and booming factory displays on the screen before them. "I know I only saw a small fragment of the building, but this is it. I swear this is it. I felt him turn a corner, and the single light source. It had to be that lamp. He parked his car right there and carried a blindfolded and bound Fabienne into the building." Wren tilts her head and continues to study the building. "That's probably how he carried in all the girls."

"Where is this place?" Scarlett's eyes dart over the image for an address.

Wren scans the image for information. There is a caption at the bottom. She reads, "JANCOR Factory first opened its doors in 1914, building wooden cabinets, but focus shifted quickly to support the war efforts, building ammunition cases. Once they no longer needed to centre their efforts on the war, the Harris Family used their manufacturing equipment to build wooden silverware cases and jewelry boxes."

"Ha! See, I told you. Jewelry boxes." Scarlett playfully taps Wren's shoulder.

Wren disregards Scarlett's commentary and continues to read. "The Box Factory, as locals called it, employed over a hundred people at the height of its success. The Factory was closed in 1980 and sold to the Strickland family. The Stricklands believed it was important to preserve its cultural significance in its contributions to Canadian manufacturing and strive to one day convert the building into an Ontario manufacturing museum." *Oh, my god. Strickland.* Wren's mouth hangs open as that name stares back at her, the connection clear in her mind.

"Oh, I know where this is," Scarlett announces. Addresses and directions are always a click away. "It's outside the city. Along Lake Ontario. Well, I'm not familiar with the town, but I've been to the pier. When we went sailing, we'd stop there sometimes for something to eat."

Wren wonders if it's still vacant. "How far?" A scenario of getting there and seeing the reality of Fabienne's final days sends a shiver down her spine—it could trigger something deeper in Scarlett. This building may very well be Scarlett's actual birthplace, she thinks.

"Just over an hour. Wanna go? You can drive." Scarlett's lips remain flat, not seeming interested or disinterested in the thought of discovering where her birth mother was held captive.

"Are you sure…"

Scarlett cuts her off. "I came to you to help find the truth, and if you say this is it, then let's do it."

Chapter 23

They climb into Scarlett's black BMW that the valet at the hotel has brought around to the front entrance. Wren notices Scarlett checking her watch every three seconds.

"Nice ride." The young valet flashes the two women a wink.

Wren thanks him as he closes the driver side door for her. *He wouldn't be looking at me like that if he saw me driving my Honda.* She buckles herself in and checks to see if Scarlett has done the same before putting the car in drive. Plus, she needs Scarlett to work her magic and make the route to the Box Factory appear on the screen. "You good?"

"Yeah." Scarlett shakes from a fog and clicks her seatbelt.

"The map." Wren continues to stare at a preoccupied, distant Scarlett.

"Sure."

Here comes the descent. The thought crosses Wren's mind to drop Scarlett off at her apartment and drive to the factory alone. Unsure of Scarlett's exact state, she's at a loss for what to do. *What's my obligation to her? I've known her for a total of, what? Sixty hours?*

"Turn left onto Queen Street. And drive straight for four

point two kilometers," the car's British navigation system instructs.

The only thing Wren can do is follow the prompts.

Scarlett sits silent in the passenger seat, glancing at her watch or the time on the screen above the map.

"I don't mind going alone," Wren says while keeping her attention on the traffic ahead. A red SUV weaves through the rows of cars without signalling. The last thing Wren needs is to be in an accident in Scarlett's car with her coming down from who knows what. She keeps extra distance between her and the car ahead.

Scarlett puts the edge of her thumbnail in her mouth and chews the peeling skin. "It's fine."

Wren decides it's in her best interest to drop the subject of Scarlett being okay. She wishes she had more knowledge on dealing with addictions. For now, she listens to the sounds of the city. Miscellaneous construction noise, honking, the thump of the bass of someone's car stereo being blasted. There is comfort in knowing she doesn't live in a big city. When she's home, she can sit in silence. Perhaps too much silence.

"You know, I'm not okay." Scarlett's one knee bounces. "I need to go to a meeting."

"A meeting?" Wren asks.

"Yes, a meeting. Please, can you just drive me there?"

This is good, Wren thinks. She knows she needs help. "Yeah, okay. Tell me where to go." The incessant checking of the time now makes sense.

Scarlett bumbles around with her phone.

"Recalculating route," the car announces.

The off-white community centre blends in with its surroundings: a row of maple trees, streetlights, and a parking lot off to the side that looks like it's shared with the baseball diamond and park in behind. Wren guesses it was built in the seventies and housed many Boy Scout, Girl Guide meetups, community garage sales, anniversary and birthday celebrations, and a safe place for people to talk about their addiction and troubles. She knows Scarlett could afford a treatment centre much bougier than a rectangle, plastic-sided building in the suburbs, but perhaps this place is safer and non-judgemental. No one would slough her off as another rich kid with a substance abuse problem, as long as she's not flashing her money around. After quick deliberation with herself, Wren agrees that this is where Scarlett needs to be.

"I'll text you when I'm done." Scarlett holds Wren's eyes in hers before she exits the car. "I hope that's okay?"

Wren keeps her eyebrows in check as Scarlett's consideration of her time surprises her. "Yeah, of course. Whatever you need." She smiles with closed lips.

"Thank you." Scarlett mirrors Wren's expression.

Wren keeps the car parked out front and makes sure Scarlett enters the building. Before she pulls away, in her rear-view mirror, a stalky middle-aged man catches her eye. His eyes are eyes she's seen before. She gasps, paralyzed with the thought that this man could be the one that got her mother pregnant thirty-six years ago, his eyes genetically passed on to her. "No," she whispers under her breath. She sinks in her seat and can't help but track this man and his salt-and-pepper mustache walking into the same door Scarlett just entered. *How could I have forgotten? How did the fact Scarlett told me she met him, here, in AA, completely vanish from my mind?* Her chest tightens, and imprints of her fingernails scar the leather-wrapped steering wheel. "Fuck. She's going to tell him. She's going to tell him I'm here and I'll be here to pick her up." Oxygen fails to inflate her lungs properly. She has to go. *He can't see me. I don't want to meet him.* The tires peel against the asphalt and the power of the engine throws Wren back into her seat.

A vibration startles Wren back to reality. Scarlett's phone lies on the passenger seat.

"Shit." A firehose of scenarios blasts her mind. *How is Scarlett going to text me to come get her? Should I drive back and run the phone into her? But he'll see me. He'll know who I am. Do I answer it? Do I go back and wait in the parking lot?* At a stop sign, she glances down. The phone stops moving. The bubble flashes with a notification that there are thirty-plus missed calls from Gabby Hernandez. Wren scans the intersection, and no one is waiting for her. The screen goes black. Scarlett has her mother's actual name in her phone instead of 'Mom', but that doesn't surprise Wren. She uses the space at the intersection to pull a U-turn and heads back toward the community centre. A rock sits heavy in the pit of her stomach and her hands tremble against the wheel.

In the parking lot, she backs in between two minivans. Even how she parks weighs on her mind. If she pulls in, there is a good chance no one will see her face, but if she backs in, she has the ability to see everyone first. Wren pops open all the hidden compartments in the hopes Scarlett keeps sunglasses close by. "Thank fuck!" she says to the empty car as she spots a red Guess eyeglass case. She pulls them from the glove box and opens the case to reveal a pair of oversized tortoise shell sunglasses, and puts them on her face, knowing they are likely the most expensive thing she'll ever get the chance to wear. In the mirror the glasses cover most of her petite oval face. She pulls the hair tie from her pony and attempts to position her dull mousy hair around her face.

A few more people trickle into the community centre, but Dave is the only one she can remember a physical description for. Wren recalls a few key pictures of her mother, like the one her grandparents kept on the mantle of them with her mom in a delicate cream gown, with a corsage and beaming smile. She always figured it was her mom's prom. It's most likely in a bin in storage with the rest of her Nan's belongings she couldn't fathom strangers pawing through at some charity shop. Because Wren was a young teen when her Nan died, the estate covered the cost of a storage locker, and once the money ran out after about eight years, Wren paid the fifty dollars a month to keep the memories secure instead of cleaning out the locker herself.

The thought of her mother is now on the surface of her brain. She has no real-life memories of her mom, but the image she saw through Hilary is still very clear. The little girl that found her was very much her mother reincarnated. The day she handed Hilary the little blue lost mitten she dropped from her stroller, she saw her mother looking in a mirror. She recognized the room was her bedroom at Nan's, and she always knew what her mother looked like. She just never knew she had died. When, where, how, a mystery. If her grandparents knew her mother had died, they never told Wren. Her mother was just someone she could never ask about. *Your mother abandoned you, that's all you need to know. Your grandpa and I love you very much, and that's what matters. Ask me what I was like when I was young and pretty.* Nan's voice is always hauntingly clear. Wren can even remember her Nan telling her those exact words at the dinner table one night when she was ten.

Wren always thought her mother was attractive. She tries to picture her next to Dave, the man who probably took her mom to prom, the man who most likely took the photo Wren stared at growing up. He seems shorter than her mom was, she thinks. But it's hard to know for sure. It makes her blood turn cold to think that this stranger makes up half of her DNA.

Her breaths steady behind the disguise of the overpriced plastic sunglasses. Although the sky is grey, it'll be dark in an hour. The thought of wearing sunglasses at night doesn't bother her if they will hide her identity until she is in the clear of Dave spotting her. Her stomach groans, and Wren knows she needs to eat. She pulls out her phone to find somewhere close. Scarlett doesn't need her phone this instant.

The last shred of daylight lingers in the sky as Scarlett searches the parking lot for her car.

Wren spots Scarlett's sad eyes looking like a kid trying to locate their lost pet, but Wren's eyes are on alert for Dave. She fidgets in her seat.

Scarlett spots Wren and walks to the car.

The second Scarlett climbs in, Wren exhales and doesn't remember how long she was holding her breath. She doesn't know what to say, so she keeps her mouth closed and her eyes on the remaining cars sprinkled throughout the lot.

"You ready to go?" Scarlett grabs her phone from the centre console. "Good, I'm glad I didn't lose this." And just like that, they are on their way. Scarlett makes their route display before them without needing to say another word.

Wren doesn't want to cut the silence with the wrong words, so she keeps her lips shut. She thought Scarlett might comment on her sunglasses, but there is not a mention. Once a few blocks away, she slides them off and awkwardly maneuvers them back into the case while keeping both eyes on the road and one hand on the wheel.

Chapter 24

No talking. No music. There is only silence on the way to find this historic building. Wren thinks that once the town knows the truth about what went on in the basement, they will want to burn this building to the ground. That's what she wants. First, they need the evidence; the police won't believe a word she has to say if there is no proof of the inhabitants held against their will almost forty years ago.

The sky has darkened to an inky blue. *Traffic is bullshit.* Wren shifts to increase blood flow to her numb butt. She thinks about asking Scarlett about all the missed calls from Gabby but decides not to ask Scarlett anything that might set her off, especially in the confined space of a car with no escape. Thoughts of her own mother bubble out her mouth. "I never hurt that little girl. And my intention was never to frighten or disturb her or her family. Curiosity just got the best of me."

Scarlett turns her head toward Wren. The car speeds up, then stops. The motion makes her insides sway uncomfortably. "What girl? What are you talking about?"

Little relief is offered with the distraction of talking. "Hilary Clarke. When you found me, you told me you knew about Hilary Clarke." Wren gives Scarlett a side glance. "Don't you remember?" The sea of brake lights flicks off like a wave. They stop on a high point of the highway and can see traffic is loosening up not far in the distance.

Scarlett turns her attention to the bumper of the car in front of them. "Oh, yeah, that. Dave told me to use that name as a last-ditch effort to get you to help me." Her hands fold together in her lap. "Do we have any water?"

Wren passes her half -drank iced tea from Subway. "We have watered-down iced tea." A few remaining cubes clink in the cup.

"Thanks." Scarlett takes the cup, opens the lid, and gulps down the remaining sugary liquid. "So why did Dave tell me to use that name? What happened with Hilary Clarke?" She returns the empty cup to the cup holder. The cool liquid momentarily calms her stomach.

Why did I even bring up her name? Wren's not sure why she even started this conversation, but here they are. The name Hilary Clarke is a name she's been trying to forget for a long time. She clears her throat. "She's someone I must stay five hundred metres away from, because I touched her hand. When I saw who she used to be, I had to touch her again. I had to see more."

"Who was she?"

"She was once my mother. The mother I never knew. The mother who ran away and left me to live with my grandparents." Wren's hands tighten on the wheel as she speeds up with the cars surrounding her.

"No shit." The corners of Scarlett's mouth turn up. "Did

you know she had died?"

"Nope."

"I guess we both have pretty messed-up mommy issues." Scarlett picks at the peeling skin next to her fingernail. "So, she found you, and this time you ran from her?"

"This time I ran towards her and she got me kicked out of Police College and I had no choice but to run from her."

"Damn. Dave didn't mention any of that."

Wren exhales. The question of whether she told Dave where Wren was is on the tip of her tongue. She swallows the question and changes the topic. "Well, at least we're moving now."

"What did you see when you touched Hilary?"

Okay, Scarlett still wants to talk about this? Wren continues. "The first time I saw her holding me as a baby looking in a mirror. And the second time I saw her running through a field of tall grass."

"Sounds interesting." Scarlett reaches for her phone.

"No, don't!" Wren knows exactly what Scarlett is thinking. And she doesn't want any connection to that girl or her mother. Nothing good can happen from finding Hilary.

Scarlett's hands freeze in the air. "Okay, fine."

"That part of my life is over. My mother is dead, and it doesn't matter 'cause I never knew her, anyway." Wren wipes the creases of her mouth with her thumb and index finger.

"Same," Scarlett chortles. "Except I am apparently a reincarnation of my birth mother and can never escape her. She fucked my life up pretty good, too."

Wren doesn't know how to respond. She's left stewing in memories she thought she would never think about again. A dull pain presses against the back of her skull. *I should have never opened my mouth.* She wishes she had her iced tea to sip on. Her hands are idle, even though she knows she needs to keep them on the wheel.

"Keep right. In one point two kilometres take the Main Street exit." The navigation breaks the taut atmosphere the two women created.

Thank God, we're almost there. Wren readjusts her hands at ten and two.

"This is it." Scarlett sizes up the building next to the car. A bright, almost full moon hangs above them. Her stomach tightens.

Wren silently exits the car and stands where she thinks Fabienne's vantage point was being carried from the car. A plaque secured to the building is exactly where she thought it would be. She approaches and trails her fingers over the tarnished bronze. It's now more weathered and covered in bird droppings.

"It looks vacant." Scarlett joins Wren beside the building.

She touches the paper-covered windows. "The windows are locked and covered from the inside."

Wren jogs to the front double doors. Locked. She pulls harder and jiggles the handle, still locked.

"Look, over here," Scarlett shouts. "A piece of the paper has fallen off. We can see in." The base of the window at the height of her hip. She bends down to peer in. "Can't see much, though, it's dark."

Wren joins Scarlett at the window, except she doesn't need to bend as much as Scarlett. A rumble pulls her attention to Scarlett. "Are you okay?"

"Honestly, I don't feel great."

Wren wonders if it's Fabienne sending a signal or Scarlett's body going through withdrawal. Wren's hand reaches out and slaps down over the back of Scarlett's hand on the window ledge.

I'm in motion. Instantly thrown into a full run. Our bare feet slap against the cold concrete floor. The hall is dimly-lit from a light behind, but there is a light ahead and a door. A single brown door with the kind of dull metal handle that stretches across the width of the door that you press to open. She's trying to escape. I use my might and run with her. I want to help. Propel her further. We reach the door, our hands extend. All our weight is ready to blast this door square off its hinges. Without warning, we tumble forward. Our face and hands plant on hard, compact dirt. "Well, aren't you a crafty one?" Roman's voice sounds from above us. He must have opened the door. Our hands sting.

We spit dirt from our mouth. A set of stairs going up is to our left. Sky. There is the blue sky.

"There is a side door. She showed me." Wren grabs Scarlett's fabric-clad wrist and pulls her around the side of the building.

"Slow down. It's too dark," Scarlett says, the syrupy liquid sloshing around in her stomach.

"There is a door around here somewhere." Wren lets go of Scarlett and focuses on pulling her phone from her pocket and turning on the flashlight. There are bits of something she's treading on. Between the sole of her sneaker and the compact dirt, it's a squishier texture. Wren aims the light down and sees cigarette butts littering the ground. She squats for a quick second and her knee cracks.

"What was that?" Scarlett asks from over her shoulder.

Wren looks closer at the discarded butts. It looks somewhat recent. She imagines a real forensic team would collect them as evidence for DNA at the scene of a crime. "What?" Her inquiry comes a few seconds late to Scarlett's question.

"I heard a noise."

"Yeah, it was my knee," Wren whispers. It crosses her mind that someone could be here and for now she's fine with lurking in the darkness. *Could they still keep women captive here?* Her heart plummets through her stomach. Near the back corner of the building, she spots an alcove, an entrance leading down. "Look." She shines her light toward the back entrance. "That must be where Fabienne tried to escape."

"Wait." Scarlett grips Wren's shoulder. "What if someone is here? I have a weird feeling about this."

"Yeah, no shit. You've been here before." Wren slows her pace. "I have a weird feeling too." She's not sure if it's because of Scarlett's intuition that someone is here or the fact they are technically trespassing on private property and fear being caught. They reach the battered concrete steps, layers of paint revealed through missing chunks of the top step.

"We're not going down there, are we?" Scarlett asks.

"Stay here, I'll go check if this is a viable way into the building." Wren turns to face Scarlett. She imagines someone a mile away could see the whites of Scarlett's haunted eyes.

Scarlett's complexation is dull, and she still doesn't feel great. She's afraid to blink.

Wren watches each step before her as she descends. The steps are pitted and uneven. Halfway down, she pauses and shines her light on the door. "Shit." She goes down a few more steps. The door has no handle. It must be an emergency exit only. It crosses her mind that it might be possible to disable the locking mechanism, and if someone was lurking around here wanting to remain unnoticed, they could have very well rigged a secret way to enter the building. She reaches the door and uses her light to scan the edges, looking for something to signal the door has been tampered with. Nothing. Splintering glass in the distance causes Wren to look back to the top of the stairs. "Scarlett," she calls out.

No reply.

Wren bounds up the stairs and quickly notices that Scarlett is nowhere to be seen. "Scarlett! Where are you?" Her voice is now louder than a whisper. The sound of another sheet of glass shattering comes from around the corner. She runs toward it.

"I found a way in."

"Scarlett, what are you doing?"

"You wanted in, right?" Scarlett wields what appears to be an old, broken piece of a two-by-four. "This is the only way. This side of the building isn't visible from the street so no one will even notice." She swirls the wood around the square pane that now contains no glass. "Just clearing out all the sharp pieces that might scratch you."

Wren inspects the hole and the pungent stench of old chemicals or glue and wood pulp smack her in the face. She's smelled this before. *This is it. One hundred percent.*

"I'll help you in. My hips are too wide to fit."

Wren's never seen her small stature as a benefit. She's always felt it held her back. It made the police physical test more difficult than someone who was taller and stronger. It made for an easy target for bullies in school. She was forever being mistaken for a child much younger growing up. She thinks back to her class in police college; no one could fit nimbly through this passage. Then she thinks they would be strong enough to bust down a locked door or use their gun to blow out the lock. Wren returns to her focus to the square entry point and double- checks for shards that could cut or snag her clothing. "I'll go unlock the front door and let you in."

Scarlett stands there blankly and vigorously shakes her head. "No, I can't go in there. I've seen it, relived it too many times." Her body is frozen in place. "Fabienne won't let me."

"Okay." Wren's seen it too and understands, and she knows she must muster the strength of three women— Scarlett, Fabienne, and herself. She spots an old crate, tests its sturdiness with her foot, and pulls it under the window as something to step on. "I'm going to go in, look for the basement, and see if I can see any signs of evidence." She mentally prepares herself for the possible sight of finding blood, pooled and crusted on the floor, dirty and worn clothing, or even finding a body, dead or alive. "Stay right here and keep watch. You have your phone?" Wren holds up her own device.

Scarlett chucks her glass-ramming baton back to the dirt along the chain-link fence where she found it. She wipes her hands on her tights and pulls her phone from the pocket of her oversized sweater.

"If you feel you're in danger, run back to the car." Wren

tosses Scarlett the fob. "Duck down and call me. And try to take note of what they look like, if you see anyone."

"Got it." Scarlett positions herself next to the crate and offers Wren her clothed forearm. "I've never felt so nauseous and relieved at the same time."

Wren can't help but smile at Scarlett's remark. "Don't be too relieved yet." She peeks inside the window to plan how to best enter the building. "I need to go feet-first. The window is about three feet from the floor." She gives the insides another quick look with the light on her phone and decides her best option is to back in feet first so she can grip the window with her hands and jump down. The musty scent of trapped glue dissipates as her nose becomes acclimatized. Wren positions herself on the window ledge and inches backwards until both knees are on the inside. The gritty cinderblock wall scrapes her jeans.

"You, okay?" Scarlett asks. Her hands are extended in case Wren needs something additional to grab.

"Yep." Wren repositions her hands on the broken frame. "Shit!"

"What?"

Wren pulls her one hand to her face and sees a thin red line appear on her palm. "I got cut." She sucks the wound and can barely taste blood. She can only taste the salt and dirt of her clammy palm. "It's not deep. I'll live."

"It's not anywhere near your heart. You'll be fine,"

Scarlett adds.

Wren twists her lips, and her stare lingers on Scarlett. "What?"

"Never mind. It's something I remember my nanny always said if I fell and scraped my knee or elbow." Scarlett waves off the comment.

Wren inspects the window again before she re-grips. *I should be good now.* She lets her legs slide down against the interior wall. Her knuckles are white from holding on with all her might. Her feet find the floor and she exhales. "I'm in."

"Good. Mind the broken glass on the floor. I'll be here to help you out." Scarlett nods.

Glass crunches under her steps. *Damn.* Wren forgot about the part of having to climb out. She makes a mental map of where the exit door was leading from the basement in relation to where she is now in case leaving through the window isn't an option. "Okay. I'll be back in a few minutes."

Chapter 25

On the floor she sees a few large machines with presses of some sort, collecting dust and boxes scattered around. She thinks the idea the Strickland family had to turn this place into a museum have long been forgotten. Or it was a ruse Duane calculated to keep attention off his true intentions to use this building to hide the missing girls.

With the light of her phone and no light from the moon or city to filter in through the covered windows, she takes stock of her surroundings before moving to where she might find access to the basement. A heavy layer of dust coats the walls, floor, and surfaces of all items left behind. Wren wiggles her nose as the dryness sets in. Her instinct is to sneeze, but she fights to keep it in. *I don't need my DNA floating around this hell.* She walks the logical path to the back of the building. She pauses and holds her light closer to the floor. There is an existing path through the dust. *Someone has walked here recently.* Her senses heighten for sounds to signal that she's not alone. She looks back to the window and sees Scarlett's silhouette fade into the paper, preventing her from seeing out, or wandering eyes from seeing in. Wren wonders what Scarlett is thinking right now. She puts herself in Scarlett's shoes. *I would be thinking about how the evidence we might find here, plus her own DNA test would implicate her parents in a crime they may or may not know they helped commit. They could go to jail. Did that thought cross Scarlett's mind? Her head is probably a mess. Your entire existence is floating in chaos.* Wren thinks back to when she met Gabby and Hank. *Gabby's concern for the wellbeing of her daughter by offering to pay me to leave is conveniently the same action a person would take if someone thought I was getting too close to the truth.*

She treads lightly and continues to think about all the pieces of the case. The text from the private number, revealing the name Duane Strickland, also remains a mystery. She knows nothing about tracing calls to decipher who sent her that text, but one person still sticks out as probable sender. *Dave. Scarlett's AA buddy and my alleged bio daddy. He would have the means to find my number; he's the one who pushed Scarlett towards me. There is a chance he knows more and for some reason hasn't come forward yet.* A chill quakes Wren's body, and she turns around to make sure no one is behind her. The factory is vacant. Not even the sound of a rat scurrying around. She thinks the scent alone is enough to keep all vermin and unwanted guests at bay.

Wren finds herself in a hall with doors open on the right and left. She peers into the first room and it's empty. Most likely an old office. The next three rooms are the same. The last open door seems to be an old lunchroom. Old wooden tables, counters, and kitchen cabinets remain. A slot against the wall is where a fridge would have been. Entering this room is Wren's last option, as there are no more doors that she passed that would suggest a stairway to the basement.

She pauses again to listen. There is something, but it sounds like a muffled car horn coming from a few blocks away. She traps her breath in her lungs. *Would Scarlett honk the horn? Could she be trying to warn me of something?* She taps her phone. *Shit.* There's no reception. Scarlett could be trying to warn her. She wipes her mouth with the back of her hand. She scans the room with her light. There is a paint-peeled navy metal door with a maintenance badge. This has to be the stairway down to the basement. The interior has offered nothing familiar so far, but why would it? Fabienne was held downstairs. She listens again and only hears the thud of her heart in her chest. She can't take a step further without checking on Scarlett.

Wren sprints lightly back to the window. She mastered the art of running using the front of her feet so as to not make a sound. This skill came in handy when she used to sneak out of her foster house and return in the dead of night. "Scarlett," she whispers. Relieved to see the outline of her figure still outside the window, Wren approaches the window, the banging of her heart rattling her chest. "Are you okay?"

Scarlett spins and pokes her head in the window. "I'm good." She covers her nose and mouth with her hand. "It smells really bad in here."

"I know. Did you honk the horn? I heard something, and I thought..."

Before Wren can finish her sentence, Scarlett shakes her

head. "No, but I heard it too. It was the beeping of someone locking their car a couple blocks away."

"Okay. Good. I found the way to the basement." Wren watches Scarlett pop away from the window and return in a couple seconds. "Let's make it a rule, only honk the horn with one long honk if I'm not answering my phone and you need to notify me of something."

Scarlett passes Wren the piece of broken two-by-four through the window. "Here. Take this just in case."

Wren takes the makeshift weapon. *I guess it's better than nothing.* It didn't occur to her to try to find something she could use as a weapon in a pinch. Her narrow shoulders droop. "What about you?"

"I have long legs. I can run pretty fast if I need to. Or I'll find something else I can use to bludgeon someone," Scarlett assures Wren.

Wren can't help feeling that having this junky piece of wood to protect her is a slight dig at her short legs, but now is not the time to dwell on this, she tells herself. "Got it. I'll be back in five."

Scarlett nods in the darkness and returns to her post.

Wren jogs back to the old lunchroom and hopes the maintenance door isn't locked. Her phone is gripped tight in one hand, the piece of wood in the other. The factory is still. Even if there were still young women trapped in the basement, she doesn't think their cries would be heard through the brick and concrete. Wren shifts the wood to her hand with the phone and clutches the items closer to her body so they don't fall. Her free hand reaches for the door handle. It opens with the same amount of strength it takes to open any metal door. "Phew." She inspects the other side of the door. It matches the door outside leading to the basement. It might be another one of those one-way opening doors. Her foot keeps the door open, and she sets the piece of wood on the ground; it keeps the door from closing. The coolness of the building is welcome as she feels sweat building under her sweater. Wren wishes she wore something more breathable, like a real wool knit sweater, not the cheap polyester one she's wearing. She loosens the fabric off her back to stop it from clinging to her skin.

The staircase down leads to a pit of black. Wren takes one step at a time, careful not to grip the railing to leave her prints. She wishes she touched Scarlett one last time. Maybe there is something else Fabienne would have shown her. Some other dreadful memory being close to this place could have unlocked a useful clue. Another door at the bottom of the stairs. She opens it and again it's too dark to see a foot in front of her face. The light cast from her phone reveals the gray walls. The same walls she's seen behind the girl's faces. She proceeds. Even if Scarlett was honking the horn, she doesn't think she could even hear it down here.

The hall splits into three ways. One way is a steel door, and with a quick consult with the blueprints she traced in her mind, she knows that that is the door to the stairs outside, the door to which Fabienne ran. *Good to know.* The other two ways both seem to lead to the dark abyss. Wren sticks left based on her logic that that way would be under the middle of the building. Kidnappers wouldn't keep people on exterior walls by choice. It's too risky for people outside to hear their cries for help. "Shit." She stumbles forward. Her foot is caught on something. Wren catches her balance. Her breath is shallow. She points her phone down. It looks like an old bedsheet wrapped around her shoe. She hops and kicks it off. The white fabric with tiny pink roses, stained brown from time, blood, and tears. *Evidence.* She's careful not to use her hands to free her tangled foot. Wren finds herself standing in a room she's seen before. Her light is too weak to illuminate the makeshift living space, but she's seen this room under harsh fluorescent lights. A bed remains in the corner. Blankets and pillows still line the wall. Wren slams her eyelids shut to hold back the tears. She can still see the images Fabienne showed her. Never has someone's past life felt so real. Never has Wren been to the actual place she's seen in a vision. What she sees always plays like a movie of the past, not a reality. When she lets go of people, she is always released back into her world. Not now. Wren's standing in Fabienne's reality. *I can't breathe.* Wren turns and collides with a wall. "Fuck." She's okay. In a dusty haze, she traces her steps. *The door to outside. It's not far.* She runs, like Fabienne that night she attempted to escape. Wren knows the way, even with the dim light of her phone. She sniffles back snot dripping from her nose. Tears streak her face. She plunges her weight into the door, and it flies open.

A cinderblock wall prevents her from tumbling to the ground, her palms shredded by its abrasive surface. Wren presses her hands together to ease the stinging. The night sky and city lights welcome her back to her reality. She climbs the stairs and catches her breath. *What was I thinking going in there?*

Wren climbs the concrete steps. Back on the compacted dirt, Wren lets the cool air inflate her lungs. She looks around to reorient herself with the building. Her eyes find someone she doesn't recognize at first in the dimness of night.

"Who the fuck are you?" the overweight, balding man asks, flicking his cigarette into the dirt.

Her voice caught in her throat. *Roman.* He's bigger and balder, but his voice has not changed. "Roman." Wren wants to look around. She wants to make sure Scarlett is okay, but she doesn't. Her instinct is to not let him know there is someone else here. Scarlett was right about no one being able to see them on the other side of the building. Surely, if Roman saw Scarlett, he wouldn't be standing here looking surprised.

"Well, that's not fair. You know my name, and I don't know yours." Roman stays in place. His lip curls to expose a few missing teeth and the ones left dangling are blackened from cigarettes and poor hygiene. "To be honest, I haven't gone by Roman in a very long time." He narrows his stare at Wren. "Who told you that name, little one?"

Wren steps back. Her heel collides with the metal post of

the railing. One foot to the left and she would have tumbled backwards down the stairs. She gulps and grips the railing behind her. *Think!* She secretly hopes that Scarlett saw the man from her nightmares and called the police, and that all she has to do is keep Roman from fleeing the scene. "Do you live here?"

"Why, you lookin' for a place to stay?" Roman's black grin stretches across his wrinkled face.

"No. I just think this building has a lot of potential. All the doors are locked..." Wren says.

Roman sniffs the air. "I smell bullshit." He takes a step closer.

"Stop. Don't come any closer to me or I'll scream." Wren projects her voice, hoping Scarlett will hear and realize they are not alone.

"I'm not going to hurt you." Roman stands in the dirt. His thick stature makes him appear to be a fat tree with no branches in the night. He reaches into his breast pocket and pulls out a cigarette and lighter. The hot orange glow burns bright in the dark. His lips pucker around the cigarette and he exhales a cloud of smoke. "You never answered my question, darlin'. Who told you my name is Roman?"

The cool air carries the smoke downwind toward Wren. She wants to cough at the stink and attempts to wave it away. *What do I say? This man made a career out of kidnapping teenage girls. I'm next.* Wren shakes the spiral of ill thoughts. The words that leave her mouth do so without warning.

"Duane Strickland." She twists the railing in her hands behind her. Her scratched flesh pulls and stings, but Wren continues to hold on for dear life.

"Ha!" Roman throws his head back. "Did you shit your pants? Cause I'm still getting wafts of bullshit." He takes another drag off his cigarette and blows smoke out of the side of his mouth.

"I saw what he did. I saw what you did. Right here in this building." Wren points to the building. She strains to make out Roman's reaction. Her strategy is now clear. Tell him the truth and confuse the hell out of him. "You must have been smart to not get caught. And to still be able to live at the scene of the crime." Wren licks her lips and lets go of the railing.

Roman stays where he is, his lips flat and his eyes lifeless. "You didn't talk to anybody. When Duane died, you were probably still in diapers."

How young does he think I am? Wren continues. "You're right, I never talked to Duane." She slowly shakes her head. "But I saw him."

"Now I know you are full of shit." More smoke billows from the man.

"I saw you, Duane, and the girls. Tell me, where is Bojana now? Where is her baby? Sold to the highest bidder?"

Wren keeps her eyes on him. "What about Sofia or Anya, where did you stash them? Where are their babies?"

Clouds pass and the moonlight reveals a brief look of confusion wash over Roman's face.

Wren continues, "Wonder how I saw?" She steps closer. "I touched a girl's hand, and I saw everything." She raises her arm and wiggles her hand at Roman. "Because you know what?"

Roman keeps his mouth shut.

"When I touch people, I can see their past life. I can see their joy, pain, and yes, even suffering." Wren takes another step closer to Roman. "Wanna take a guess at who I found?" She smirks.

"It's you? How?" Roman's eyes stare past Wren. The cigarette slips from his fingers into the dirt next to his tattered, scuffed running shoes.

"Wren." Scarlett's hand lands on Wren's shoulder. "I thought I heard your voice. What's going on? Are you okay?"

Wren spins and sees Scarlett holding a jagged triangle shard of glass. "I'm fine," she answers.

"Who are you talking to?" Scarlett looks forward and his face sets her skin on fire. "It's you!" Older, yes, but that man is unmistakable. A face who's haunted her for what feels like a lifetime. A face that's tattooed on the inside of her eyelids. A face that's been forever inescapable. Scarlett lunges forward. "I'm going to gut you like a fish!" Her glass is aimed in his direction.

Roman shields his face and stumbles back into the dirt.

"Scarlett, wait." Wren grabs her hand and holds her back with all her might. *Screaming. Fabienne is screaming. Blood everywhere. A blinding pain. Roman tosses more towels in our direction.* The scalding pain forces Wren's hand to release Scarlett. She opens her eyes, and she sees Scarlett standing over him with the glass shard pointed into his eye.

Roman on his back, raises his hands. "It can't be." He shakes his head. "I watched you die." He keeps his eyes shut.

"You watched my mother die," Scarlett spits through grit teeth.

"Scarlett. Don't. Let's call the police." Wren's blood is pumping so fast her body vibrates.

"Not yet." Scarlett keeps her eyes locked on Roman. She lifts her left leg over him so she stands straddling the man that abducted the woman that gave birth to her thirty-four years ago. Face-to-face with the man that robbed her of a normal life. "I need answers. Then I'm going to haunt his dreams for eternity."

The Scarlett that Wren knows is now high on adrenaline. All Wren can do is watch. She knows the rest of this battle isn't hers to fight.

Chapter 26

"Tell me," Scarlett screams. "Tell me why you chose her."

"It doesn't matter. Game over." Roman crosses his arms over his chest, his eyes welded shut with crusted moisture. "Just kill me."

"No. You don't get away that easily." Scarlett pulls the blade of glass away from his eye.

"Scarlett, let's call the police. They can handle Roman from here." Wren doesn't have a plan. Pieces of the truth jumble in her mind. If the cops come, they are going to question her. They are going to want to know why she is there. With a red piece of yarn in her mind, she tries to connect the dots. *Roman was working with Duane in kidnapping young women and getting them pregnant and selling the babies to the rich. Duane was arrested for other crimes and died in jail. How did I know those two men are connected? The anonymous text. The cops would ask me why someone sent his name to me.* She has no suitable answer. Saying she saw someone's past life to a cop is going to go over like a lead balloon or land her a stay in the loonie bin. Thinking about a lead balloon pulls her Nan to the front of her chaotic thoughts. Whenever her Nan heard a bad idea, she would shake her head and say, *That will work as well as a lead balloon.* It only takes a split second for her thoughts to derail.

Maybe Grandpa was right. I should pretend my abilities don't exist and never talk about them. He knew this would happen. Maybe this is what happened to Mom?

"Ahh!" Roman hollers out in pain.

Wren is brought back to reality and sees Scarlett pressing one foot into his manhood.

"You tell me now. Or I swear to God, I will keep you locked up and hire a dude to rape you until *you're* pregnant." Scarlett shows no mercy.

Wren watches, waiting for Roman to answer the question.

"Why? Why her?"

"It doesn't matter. Duane's dead. The truth will never be known. I'll take it to my grave." Roman spits and winces through the pain.

"I can tell you what happened." Wren pieces together the motive and drops to the ground at Roman's feet and peels off his shoes. They smell sour. She rips at the lace of one dirty shoe and pulls until it's free. "Duane needed a guy on the street. A guy to front his underground venture of illegal adoption to the elite." Wren takes the shoelace and binds his ankles together. "You were that guy. You were tasked with finding these young girls; girls you targeted because you thought they wouldn't be missed, immigrants you thought the cops wouldn't waste their time on." With all her might, she knots the lace and watches Roman's puffy ankle skin turn red and bubble from the pressure.

With one hand, Scarlett clamps his hands together. She sees where Wren is going with this.

Roman lays there, silent.

Wren frees the other shoelace and shuffles on her knees to his hands. "Fabienne. You found her in Montreal. Another province. No one would look for her here. You don't shit where you eat, right? Just like the others you found in Oakville and Toronto."

Scarlett stops straddling the man to give Wren better access to tie his hands, but she stays alert with her glass shank.

"Fabienne. That was her name. And you chose her for her skin. You chose her because Duane had a very wealthy mixed-race client couple who needed a baby that would look like a baby they would produce." Wren watches Roman bite his lip as she tightens the lace around his chubby wrists, ever so careful to not let her skin touch his.

"What are you? Some sort of undercover cop trying to take down old men?"

The corners of Wren's smile twist further into her cheeks. "No, I'm not a cop, but I am here to find justice for Fabienne, Bojana, Anya, Sofia, and all the other women I don't know about. And all those babies who may never know the truth."

"You mean all those babies who grew up with a silver

spoon in their mouth. Yeah, I'm sure they're real sad." Roman's lips form a straight line.

Scarlett kicks his side. "Fuck you."

Roman winces through the pain.

"You don't need to tell us what happened, because I already know." Wren keeps her eyes on Roman. She knows Scarlett has questions, but now is not the time. "I'm guessing you blew through all the money Duane paid you, or after they arrested him, the money dried up...or maybe he just promised you riches and never paid up." Wren secures the knot in the shoelace, binding his wrists.

"Why were you in Montreal?" Scarlett spits.

Scarlett's question catches Wren off-guard. She spins to face her. *What? We don't have an infinite number of questions. We need to stick to the essentials.* "What happened to the rest of the girls?" Wren trumps Scarlett's question.

"I like her question better." Roman juts his chin toward Scarlett. "The strip clubs are better in Montreal. I like watching French girls remove their clothes to music."

Scarlett kicks him harder.

Roman wiggles in the dirt.

"Answer my question, now!" Wren looms over him. A spotlight blinds her and she shields her eyes.

"Hands in the air. Everyone stay where you are," a husky voice shouts.

Scarlett chucks her makeshift weapon into the collection of debris lining the fence.

The light comes closer, and Wren's chest tightens. "We're making a citizen's arrest, officer" are the only words that form. Her breath is weak in the night air. A chill sends a shiver quaking her bones. The officers whisper something but she can't make it out.

"I'm Scarlett Hernandez and this is Wren Roussel," Scarlett announces. "And this man kidnapped my mother thirty-five years ago. He ran an illegal adoption agency for the wealthy. We have proof. My DNA is proof. Take as much of it as you need."

Wren looks at Scarlett. The truth is heavy on her heart, wondering how Scarlett is so calm. Wondering how she could blurt everything out like that so plainly when earlier today she was overcome with anger from the revelation that she has a half-sister and an uncle.

"Ma'am, state your name, please," the officer asks.

Wren cannot see who is talking though the light blinding her. Her own name is lost in the night.

"Wren. Answer the cop," Scarlett whispers. Both women still have their hands above their heads.

"Wren," she squeaks. Silence. She clears her throat. "Wren, Sir. Wren Roussel." It dawns on her that becoming a cop was never in the cards for her. Behind closed doors and in her mind, she thinks she is tough, but in a real situation, she can barely spit out her own name. Reality sets in. It's Hilary Clarke all over again. *I should have never come here.* Staring at the ground to avoid the light, she sees Roman laying in the dirt. His hands and feet are tied together. Her own actions are a blur. *Did I do that to him?* With good intentions, she finds herself on the wrong side of the law again. *Why do I even try?*

"Do you have any weapons?" the officer asks.

Wren looks at Scarlett and shakes her head.

"No," Scarlett answers.

The spotlight shifts to Roman. "Sir, are you okay?"

Roman says nothing. He only blinks.

"Sir, can you please tell me what happened."

After a long pause, he parts his lips. "I want a lawyer."

Alone, in a small room with nothing but a table and two chairs, Wren waits. She imagines Scarlett is being held separately, but in a nicer room because of who she is. Because of her adopted parents' money and clout. Wren thinks the officers are reading her file right at this moment, learning that this isn't her first time stalking someone. But she knows she wasn't stalking Hillary. She would never follow a child and make them feel uncomfortable. And she knows she never made the little girl uncomfortable. She knows Hilary was the one that found her. Hilary held all the secrets of her past. Of course, the cops would never understand, and Hilary was too young to speak. It was

Hilary's parents that were scared, and when Wren stood back and looked at the situation, she understood. Wren agreed to leave college and stay far away in exchange for the Clarkes to not press charges. She knew she did nothing wrong, but from an outsider looking in, becoming too close to a child you don't know is not allowed.

"Miss Roussel." The door opens and a female officer enters. "I'm Officer Landen. Don't worry, you're not in any trouble." The officer takes a seat and places her notebook on the table. "Eugene confessed."

Wren looks up from picking her dirty fingernails. "Eugene?"

"Once we ran his prints, he couldn't run from the truth. His real name is Eugene Duffy. Roman was one of his aliases."

Wren nods. Her stomach aches at hearing the new information. She chews the inside of her cheek and feels dumb for not figuring out his identity for herself. "What did he confess to?" she asks, curious and in need of closure.

"Abduction of minors, rape, keeping minors hostage." The cop sets her pen in the crook of her open notebook. "He's holding out on names hoping he'll catch himself some sort of deal. Forensics will arrive at the warehouse shortly. We're hoping to find some DNA matches to some in the system."

The names Fabienne, Bojana, Sofia, and Anya on the tip of her tongue. She wants to blurt, but keeps that information to herself for now. Wren knows now is not the time to have to answer how or why she knows their names.

"What we're trying to figure out, Miss Roussel, is how a wanted criminal has evaded police for four decades, but you and your friend Miss Hernandez find him living in an old factory." Officer Landen folds her hands on the table and keeps her eyes on Wren.

Wren averts her gaze, but still feels Officer Landen's eyes pierce her skin. All she can do is shake her head while she tries to form a story that will satisfy law officials. "Dumb luck, really." She pauses and waits for more words to form.

Officer Landen fills the silence. "Miss Hernandez says you're quite the amateur detective." Her lips crack her serious façade, and a smirk forms. "Are you another one of those millennials addicted to true crime podcasts?"

Wren's brows wrinkle together. "What? No. I've never listened to a single podcast in my whole life." She is telling the truth. She never got the appeal of podcasts. Wren prefers visual entertainment. She found it weird to be sitting around listening to strangers' ramble on, thinking they were some sort of expert on a topic, but really it was someone who could afford a laptop, microphone, and loved hearing the sound of their own voice. "Scarlett once told me she thought she was adopted," Wren says. The words appear with no thought. She licks her lips in anticipation of the follow-up question about how or when she met Scarlett.

Office Landen tilts her head, listening.

Wren continues. She sits up straighter. "Scarlett's parents told her she was born in Japan when her parents worked there for a year on business, but she's convinced her birth certificate was a forgery. Then she joined one of those DNA sites and confirmed her suspicions." Wren decides not to elaborate on this point, as if the police cross-reference events with Scarlett's timeline, they could easily trip her up so she changes lanes. "We got the name Duane Strickland off some business papers we found hidden in Scarlett's dad's office." That is a lie, but Wren sells it. "A quick Internet search put us on the scent of a bad guy, and we thought it could be a lead." Wren searches the eyes of the stone-faced cop, unable to read if the officer is buying what she's selling. She continues. "On a whim, I also decided to search websites of missing people. It took a while, but that's when I found Fabienne. Fabienne Delva."

Officer Landen reaches for her pen and scribbles down the name. "And who is Fabienne Delva?"

"Fabienne is or was Scarlett's biological mother."

"And how did you come to that conclusion?" Officer Landen eyes Wren.

"They look identical. Except Fabienne's complexion is darker." Wren stares back at the officer. "And when I showed Scarlett what I found, she knew. Call it intuition or whatever you want, but Scarlett knew."

"And the old factory? What put you on the scent to visit that location?" Officer Landen asks next.

Wren wets her lips. "I found online that it was a building that the Strickland family owned. Scarlett, again, had a feeling, so we took a drive to come check it out." She's suddenly aware there is no clock in the room, and they still have her phone, so Wren is at a loss for how much time has passed. Her eyelids are growing heavy. "That's when we ran into Roman—sorry, Eugene—and when he saw Scarlett, he thought Fabienne came back to find him," Wren says.

Officer Landen continues to scribble.

The door opens. "Landen." Another officer calls and makes a gesture Wren doesn't understand.

"Okay, Miss Roussel, you're free to go. Miss Hernandez is waiting for you at the front desk where you can collect your belongings." Officer Landen stands and lets Wren exit first.

Wren nods, walks past the officer, and forces a tight-lipped smile. *Is that it? It's over?* She makes her way down the corridors and spots Scarlett standing next to a counter, looking around like a lost puppy. Wren sees the sadness in her eyes, the same sadness she imagines Fabienne, Bojana, Sofia, and Anya carried with them. The thought of what those women went through squeezes her heart. She pauses and contemplates running back and telling Officer Landen the names Eugene refuses to reveal. In that split-second, the consequences of not being able to explain how she knows their names doesn't matter. *They need to know. We need to know what happened to them.*

"Wren," Scarlett calls. "Over here."

Wren turns to see Scarlett waving her over. She puffs her cheeks and exhales. *I can always send an anonymous email or call and tell them their names.* Her hand waves back at Scarlett. *I wonder what Scarlett told them.*

"You, okay?" Scarlett asks as she embraces Wren.

Wren crinkles her brow and returns the hug. It's an odd display of emotion from Scarlett, but it feels nice to be held by someone after what they have been through. "Yeah, I'm fine. Are you okay?" Wren returns the question.

"I'll be okay. It's mostly a blur." Scarlett pulls out of the hug.

"Yeah." Wren looks around the station to find her bearings. "It's crazy, Eugene confessed."

"Eugene?" Scarlett's twisted expression matches Wrens when she first heard his name.

"Roman's real name."

"What a piece of shit. I wish I had beaten him when I had the chance," Scarlett adds.

Wren leans in closer to Scarlett. "You got some real good kicks in, and you held a broken piece of glass to his eye."

"I did?"

"Yeah." Wren pulls Scarlett away from the counter. "What did you tell them in there?"

Scarlett swallows and eyes the main entrance before answering. "I told them you were the smart one, and I just followed your lead, and that Fabienne was most likely my birth mother. Oh, and don't be mad." She folds her upper lip under her front teeth.

Wren stares back and studies Scarlett's wild curly hair and wide eyes. Her heart thumps loud enough for the entire station to hear. "What did you say?" Wren asks through her teeth.

"I told them who your dad was."

Wren's chest hardens, and her eyes glaze over. Her mind turns blank. There are no words.

"I thought it could help. He's a cop. I didn't know if we were in serious trouble." Scarlett's attention draws to someone behind Wren, and she steps back.

"Wren." An unfamiliar voice speaks her name.

Wren cannot move. She doesn't need to. She knows what he looks like.

"I don't know what to say. I'm sorry. I'm a coward."

Wren slams her eyes shut. *This is a dream*, she repeats to herself. She pivots slowly in place in the direction of the voice. The ambient sounds of a police station melt away. She opens her eyes.

"I'm Dave Eccleston." He extends his hand.

Wren opens her eyes, and all she can see are his leather-gloved clad hands.

Chapter 27

It wasn't Scarlett's influence that helped us out of this mess; it was mine. It's who my estranged father is. Wren pulls the sleeves of her sweater over her hands and lets her thoughts swim helplessly in her mind, very aware that she's not wearing her gloves.

"It's okay." Dave retreats his hand.

"Do you always wear gloves?" Wren blurts, and instantly feels like a child asking a grown-up a question. She gathers that he wears gloves all the time because of who he is. *Or did he wear them tonight because he knows who she is?* She asks herself.

Dave holds his hands out before him and spreads his finger. His ten digits hold him in a daze. He flips them over, so his palms face the ceiling. "Never leave home without them."

The idea of both of her parents having this affliction never crossed her mind. *Maybe that's why Grandpa was so angry. He knew I would grow up with this curse. He knew I never had a choice.* All Wren can do is blink at Dave's covered hands.

"Forgive me if this is too forward, but can I take you out for something to eat?" Dave slides his hands into the pockets of his leather jacket. The leather squeaks with his movement.

I'm scrubbing toilets in some random foster family's home and this guy is walking around town in a leather jacket? Nothing in life is fair. I've helped take bad people off the street and all I get to go home to is a junky old car and a small, dark apartment. Why do I even try to do the right thing?

"Wren, what do you say?" Scarlett places her hand on Wren's shoulder and softly speaks in her ear. "Is it okay if Dave takes us out to get something to eat? I'll come with you."

"Okay." Wren tightens her lips and looks everywhere but at Dave. She spins to the counter to collect her phone. "Where is the car fob?" she asks the officer behind the desk.

"I asked an officer to pick up your car and bring it to the station," Dave interjects. "I hope that's okay."

Behind the desk, the officer finds the misplaced key fob and hands it to Wren. Scarlett's puffy pink keychain makes it easy to locate.

Wren clutches the key fob in her palm. Its hard plastic and chrome emblem feels cool against her skin. The tangibility of the object and seeing no vision grounds her. She rids her mind of all thoughts to prepare her for what's going to happen next. "We'll follow you." She looks at Dave's brown eyes and sees pieces of herself.

They arrive at the diner. The clock in the car tells Wren it's almost midnight. She's no longer tired, only hungry. Not just for food, but for the truth. Her whole life, she never let herself believe this moment would be possible. Her skin tingles with numbness and the events of the past five hours seem like they happened years ago.

"You okay with this?" Scarlett unbuckles her seatbelt and stares at Wren.

Wren inflates her cheeks and nods. Staring blankly at the red and blue LED open sign in the diner's window.

"Dave is a good guy. I've known him for years and he's always been supportive in AA."

Wren exits the car, wondering what Scarlett constitutes someone as being a 'good guy'.

Dave orders coffee and water for the table, and thanks their waitress, waiting for Wren to speak first.

Scarlett eyes the father and daughter but can sense it's not her moment to speak up, so she buries her face in a menu.

Wren looks small against the thick red vinyl bench seat. All the questions she ever wondered about her past remain trapped behind her lips.

"I'm sure you have a ton of questions," Dave says. His fingers interlace and rest on the table.

Wren stares back between glances at the menu.

"I was young, and so was your mother." Dave clears his throat. "You don't have to talk. I've thought about this moment for years and ran the answers to every possible question you might ask in my mind a million times."

Wren turns her attention to Dave.

"I was dumb, and I know that's not an excuse, but it's the truth. I didn't know how to handle..." He looks down at his hands and removes his gloves. "This. You know." He wiggles his fingers.

The waitress returns with coffee and water. "You guys ready to order?" the friendly young woman asks.

"We'll need another five minutes, thanks." Dave wraps his hands around the hot mug.

Wren wonders if the waitress knows how lucky she is to not be the one sitting in this booth right now. Or to not be abducted, raped, and forced to bear a child. She studies the menu to be prepared for when the waitress returns. The BLT catches her eye, and it will do. What she eats doesn't matter.

"I drank. I drank a lot. To cope with this ability. But your mother wanted more. She wanted to use this for something good. To help people." His eyes land on Scarlett for a second then return to the dark brown liquid in front of him. "I tried to be a better person, and for a while when I was with your mom, I was. But things happen, we were young and we got pregnant."

Questions spring to Wren's mind on how Dave and her mother found each other and how many people can do this. She's never met anyone that can do what she does. AJ has something, like a level of awareness and belief, but he can't see what she sees. Wren tucks the question away and listens.

"You were born, and your mother and I didn't know what to do with you. She was still living with her parents and your grandfather wanted nothing to do with me. I tried to come visit. I had a job as a line cook in a kitchen." Dave glances at the entrance to the kitchen. "I used my paycheque to buy diapers and clothes, but that wasn't good enough for your grandfather. He blamed me for getting his daughter pregnant. I fell into drinking and eventually I stopped trying." He takes a sip of his coffee. "It wasn't until one day someone grabbed my arm at a bar, and I saw a policeman in an armed robbery. He came up behind the robber and took him down. I thought I could be that hero. I may not be the biggest or strongest guy in the room—" He looks down at his body. "But I could have guts. The next day I found a meeting and got sober."

"So why didn't you come back?" Wren finally speaks.

Dave takes another sip. "I did, but your mother was gone. Your grandfather accused me of luring her away, causing her to run away from her own child, but it wasn't me. And I knew your mother probably saw something and chased it. Either way, your grandparents thought it was best for you if I wasn't in your life. They didn't believe I was stable enough to care for a little girl. They told me it would be too hard for you if I left or fell back into old habits."

Wren swallows the lump in her throat and holds back the tears as she envisions her younger self staring at the moon, wondering why her parents deserted her. She glances around the dinner for the waitress to distract herself from the truth that's been released.

The waitress returns, and everyone orders, returning the menus to the pleasant woman. "Why now?" Wren asks, slicing through the silence with her words.

Dave looks over to Scarlett. "During a meeting. Scarlett tripped over the leg of a chair, and I reached out to catch her. I don't wear my gloves to meetings, and I'm always careful to keep my hands to myself, but instincts kicked in and I grabbed her arm, so she didn't smack against the concrete floor. I saw things." The creases of his eyes arch down. "I saw a life that was in trouble. And she spoke of nightmares in meetings, and I knew they were real. Too real. I then understood her pain. I could now see it as plain as day, tattooed on her face."

Scarlett reaches out to Dave but pulls her hand back. She understands how gratitude can elate you. At this moment, her gratitude doesn't need to be said out loud. It exudes her.

"I didn't see enough to find a clue to legally investigate her past, and I couldn't touch her again. I've never been good at making it seem like an accident." Dave takes another sip. "And an older guy getting too close to a younger woman doesn't look right. As much as I wanted to help, people would never understand."

Wren fiddles with her own fingers in her lap. She remembers that when she was a kid, she would just touch people. It took a long time for her to understand how people might perceive her actions. She would never be subtle about it, and thinks if she had more foresight or actual parents who understood what she was going through, she would have had a better strategy with Hilary.

Dave continues, "Scarlett needed help, and I knew someone who could help her. I knew you moved up north, but also knew you once had a dream and maybe you could use some help, too. So I told Scarlett what you could do." He and Scarlett exchange brief grins. "She was willing to try anything."

"Did you know she is crazy?" Wren quickly turns to Scarlett. "No offence, but you did drug me."

"You drugged her?" Dave snaps to Scarlett. A darkness enters his eyes.

Scarlett absorbs their needle-like gaze. "It was the smallest dose." She pinches her finger and thumb together to demonstrate. "Call it science. I was curious to see if it would alter what she saw. I wanted her to see everything and more. I was tired of wasting time." Scarlett blows her breath out of the side of her mouth. "I went to a meeting today. You saw me there."

"Are you okay?" Dave asks Wren.

"I'm fine now. I don't trust her anymore, but I'll be okay." Wren turns her eyes back to her hands in her lap.

"Good." He turns to Scarlett. "Whatever you're still holding, you can slip it to me, no questions asked, and I can properly dispose of it."

Scarlett leans back in the booth and crosses her arms, eyeing her purse.

Dave's eyes soften as he turns back to Wren. "I'm glad you're okay. If I thought Scarlett was dangerous, I never would have sent her to you."

"I'm right here," Scarlett exclaims. "I've suffered, too, you know."

Wren straightens her spine. With all the thoughts and questions swirling in her mind from today, she's decided, "I would just like to put the whole thing behind me now." Her eyes bounce between Dave and Scarlett. "We caught the scumbag who was behind kidnapping the women for Duane. And Duane's dead. The police will do the rest."

"Wait a second." Scarlett perks. "You've just thrown a match to the house of cards that is my life. What do I do now? Hank and Gabby will probably be arrested, by birth mother is dead, and lord knows who fathered me. And I'm not sure if I even want to know."

"Scarlett, you're a full-grown woman. Most women your age already have two kids and are on their second marriage." Wren glares at Scarlett. "And you have money. You'll be fine."

"That's easy to say for someone who just found her real dad, who wants her in his life." Scarlett spits back.

"Enough." Dave raises his hands. "You've both had a long day. You're hungry and tired..."

"All right, here's your BLT." The waitress places the plate in front of Wren, removes the other two balanced plates from her large tray, and places them in front of Dave and Scarlett. Her timing is impeccable.

The three of them thank the waitress and eat their meal in silence.

"Are you girls staying somewhere here tonight?" Dave asks while setting his fork on his plate.

Wren chomps away on a cold fry. Where she was sleeping didn't even cross her mind. Planning where you're going to sleep isn't important when you're on the heels of chasing yesterday's shadows. The booth is comfy enough; she thinks if she lay down this moment, she would be asleep in seconds. Or Scarlett's car would do.

"There is a Holiday Inn up the street. It's no five-star Ritz, but it's a clean and safe place to stay. It's too late to drive back to the city tonight."

Chapter 28

Wren insists on having a separate room from Scarlett. She needs time to herself. Time to think, and process everything that's happened over the last three days. Time to process meeting her birth father. The imaginary father she had painted a portrait of in her head when she was young was nothing like the real thing. The colourful imagery of a man from the wrong side of the tracks, riding a motorcycle, wind blowing through his wavy unkept hair with a cigarette dangling from his lips. It was an image she concocted after reading *The Outsiders*. Wren once thought the man that got her mom pregnant and ran away would most likely be a no-good, unshaven greaser. And her mom probably ran away chasing after him, but that wasn't true. Nothing except for the stubble on his face, and maybe his past drinking habits matched what she thought her dad would be. He is a police officer, a man who made it his life's mission to protect people. Wren lays still on the bed in her hotel room, wishing she had more time before the next day started and reality would be waiting for her on the other side of that door. *What's next? Do I hop on a train home and go back to delivering food?* She doesn't even know if she wants a relationship with Dave. *Does he even want a relationship with me?* Wren's heavy eyelids finally close and she drifts off to sleep.

Knock knock.

Wren opens one eye and sees daylight peeking through the curtains. It's probably Scarlett wanting to go home. Wren has the key fob to her car. Maybe Scarlett wants to drive home alone and put this all behind her. She grinds the sleep from her eyes with her fists and yawns. "Be there in a second," Wren hollers. She meanders to her clothes and gets dressed.

Through the peephole, it's not Scarlett's face that's waiting for her, it's Dave's. For a split-second she contemplates not answering the door and waiting in the bathroom until he gets tired and walks away, but she remembers she already hollered that she was coming to answer the door. She slides the chain lock over and opens the door.

"Sorry, I didn't mean to wake you, but I didn't want to leave without telling you." Dave stands there with his hands in his pockets and his stubble even thicker than before. "Crime doesn't sleep." He attempts a smile.

Wren's face remains still. *What the hell is he trying to tell me?*

"Okay, well..." Dave teeters on his heels. "I know I've made a mess of things and I wish I did things a lot different, but I'd like to get to know you." He smiles, takes a card from his pocket, and hands it to Wren. "Here's my number if you ever want to talk."

Wren takes the card and reads the crisp black ink. *Staff Superintendent David A. Eccleston.* She lets the point of the corner press into her thumb. "Staff Superintendent," she says out loud without knowing.

Dave grins. "It's not what it's cracked up to be."

Wren shakes her head while staring at the card. All she wanted was to be a detective, pretty low on the totem pole compared to Staff Superintendent. This whole time she was related to someone working their way to the top. Her heart is heavy in her chest. *Does he know the Chief Instructor from the college?* Wren's jaw tightens, and she stuffs the card into her back pocket.

"I hate to leave things like this." Dave checks his watch. "I do have to be on my way soon. Will you call me, Wren?"

Wren twists her lips and looks past Dave to the few cars in the parking lot.

"I understand if you're not ready. There is absolutely no pressure. But before I leave, there is one more thing I want to tell you." Dave's eyes are soft as he stares at Wren. "I understand why you tried to get close to Hilary Clarke."

Wren's attention snaps back to Dave. Her lips part but she remains silent.

"I was so proud of you when you got into police college. You were more like me than I thought, and it was something special. You were following in the footsteps of the father you never knew."

His words tighten a rope around her heart. *How did he know of my whereabouts, and if he knew I was in shitty foster care, why wouldn't he come save me?* Wren blinks back the tears forming behind her eyes. *And could he not see who the Chief Instructor really was? What he did to hurt me?*

"When I saw your name in connection with the Clarke family, I had to see for myself. I knew there had to be something you saw. I offered to talk to the family, and little Hilary was there. I passed her a toy, and she touched my finger. And Wren, I saw you. Through your mother's eyes, I saw you. You were so small and beautiful, and she had you in the little pink dress I picked out for you." Dave wipes a lone tear from his cheek. "I heard she had run, but I didn't know she had passed. My heart broke for you. You found your mother, and no one would understand."

"She found me," Wren croaks through a scratchy throat.

"I know." Dave steps forward and wraps his arms around the woman that is his daughter. He strokes her hair and cries.

Wren's lips tremble, and she returns the hug. She welcomes the embrace, not because she finally found family, but because she found someone that finally understands. Her tears press into the leather of his jacket. "What do I do now?" she mumbles through the sobs.

"Wren, you can do anything you want. I'm here this time to help you." Dave releases Wren and holds on to her shoulders. "Your record is clean. You never brought any harm or ill will to Hilary. The Clarkes were fine with the solution of you moving away. I told them you were a good kid. They didn't want to ruin your life."

"What?" Wren wipes her face with the sleeve of her sweater.

"You don't need to hide or run from anything," Dave adds. "If I could do anything for you, it was to keep that incident off the record."

The realization that she is crying with Dave sends a jolt of energy down her spine. She still doesn't know him that well. "I have to go. My phone is ringing," Wren lies as she turns back to her room.

"I understand. I'm always a phone call away." Dave smiles at her before he turns to leave.

Wren stops her tears and turns back into the seclusion of her hotel room.

Chapter 29

"Wasn't that nice of Dave to pay for our rooms?" Scarlett sits next to Wren in her car. She lets Wren drive because she feels safe with her.

"Sure, I guess. You seem chipper." Wren keeps her eyes on the road. "Do I need to be worried?"

Scarlett turns to Wren and laughs. "No. I have nothing on me. I just feel rested, you know."

Wren cocks an eyebrow and follows the prompt of the navigation. She wishes she felt rested, but instead her limbs feel like they are filled with sand and flimsily stitched to her body. The thought of every minute passing meant she's closer to returning to her fancy hotel room and taking a nap before she has to leave. "No nightmare last night?"

Scarlett grins while watching the coming and goings of the little town whiz by. She didn't even realise that she didn't see Roman's ugly face when she shut her eyes, because the thought of him tied and tossed into the dirt is still fresh in her memory. "Actually, no. For the first time in like twenty years, I didn't see anything in my sleep." She shifts in her seat toward Wren. "You need to pull over."

"What? What's wrong." Wren tries to eye something out of place on Scarlett while keeping a watch on the road in front of her.

"Up there," she exclaims. "It's a parking lot. Turn in there." Scarlett taps her finger to the window.

Wren signals and makes the right turn into the strip mall parking lot. A couple of cars pepper the lot. Confused by Scarlett's request to stop in a mall with a cannabis shop, pet groomers, a shawarma restaurant, and some sort of tech and cheap cell phone store, her first thought is, *If Scarlett is making me stop so she can buy weed I'm going to drive away and leave her there*, but then it hits her. *She wants me to touch her.* Wren inflates her lungs and one side of her mouth twists up.

"Turn off the car and face me," Scarlett instructs.

Wren obliges. Just as curious as Scarlett, their expressions mirror one another. No words need to be said. The chat with Dave this morning had clouded her thoughts. She wants to kick herself for not thinking of touching Scarlett sooner. Roman is finally caught and Fabienne's story is no longer trapped in the past or in Scarlett's nightmares. Wren unbuckles her belt and faces Scarlett. Both of her hands extend to latch on to Scarlett's wrists.

The scent hits me first. It's warm and spicy, like someone's home cooking. The aromas of pepper, onions, and rice fill us with a familiar love. I hear singing, but I don't recognize the words. It's a woman's voice, and it's lovely. And laughter, kids' laughter, is coming closer. I can see. We're in an apartment. We're setting a table and dishes of food are placed at the table set for five. Words are spoken quickly, I don't understand, but I catch a few words and I know they are speaking French. A man and women talk in the kitchen, and I understand Fabienne call them Mom and Dad. It's before she was abducted. We all sit down around the table and hold hands. Her father says grace, and everyone smiles at one another.

"What did you see?" Scarlett's eyes are wide.

Wren pulls her hands back to her lap and emotion floods her vision. She sniffs and lets the tears flow down her cheeks. She didn't know she could cry from joy. "Fabienne was eating dinner with her family."

"Really? What was it like?"

"It was nice. Everyone was happy." Wren rubs her stained cheeks. "Her family seemed really close." Wren realizes her tears aren't only for Fabienne's happiness, but for what's missing from her life. Sitting around a table with her grandparents seems like a lifetime ago. She wonders if the memory of her eating dinner with her grandparents is a memory she will carry with her into her next life.

"Oh, I hope I see that in a dream one day." Scarlett leans back into her seat. "I could see what my grandparents looked like, and my aunt and uncle as kids."

Wren licks the salty liquid from her lips. "Why don't you reach out to them in real life?" She quickly reminds herself of the anger that surfaced in Scarlett when she told her she found relative matches on the DNA website. Wren traps her breath behind her lips, waiting for Scarlett's response.

"You found my relatives?" Scarlett leans forward.

She doesn't remember. Wren nods. "An uncle and sibling, I think." Wren envisions the boy she just saw at the table. The boy who placed his little hand in hers. She tries to imagine what he would look like now and guesses he would be in his late forties or early fifties. His dark skin is still smooth, hair dark with patches of grey. Same eyes as Fabienne and now Scarlett, eyes they all inherited from their mother.

"Really? A sibling. Like *my* brother or sister?" Scarlett points to her chest, staring deep into Wren's soul for confirmation.

The drive back to the hotel seems to fly by, while Scarlett blabs on about all the different scenarios in which her future may unravel. What if her uncle or sibling want nothing to do with her? What is going to happen with her adoptive parents? They raised her like their own and she truly doesn't want to see anything bad happen to them. Scarlett thinks it will take time, but one day she thinks she can forgive them for what they did. She even wonders if Hank and Gabby didn't know the truth, and maybe Duane Strickland kept them in the dark about the disgusting way he was obtaining his babies. "Wren," Scarlett's voice fills the car. "Will you stay with me for a bit? You know, until the dust settles. I feel like my life is a casualty of this mess. I honestly don't know what to do."

"Welcome to the club," Wren retorts. "Yeah, I can stay with you. Your life isn't the only one that feels like it's floating around like a tattered plastic bag in the wind."

Scarlett cracks a brief smile. "Are you going to see Dave again?"

Wren sloughs her shoulders.

"That's how I feel about every person in my life except you. It's almost like my life is a joke and everyone understood the punch line except me," Scarlett says and traces the blue stitching on the edge of her seat with her fingernail. "My life was made only for profit."

Wren grips the wheel with one hand and pats Scarlett's leg with the other. Many nights Wren would lay awake in bed and wonder why she was even born if all the people in her life were only going to abandon her. Nothing made sense to her after her Nan died. At least there is comfort in knowing she's not the only one who was left behind. And now finding her father added a complex layer to her rational thinking. Growing up, it was her Nan that taught her to think objectively when facing a dilemma. *If this was someone else's problem, what advice would you give them?* She can hear her Nan's words. The truth is if someone else had their estranged father walk back into their life, she wouldn't know what to tell them. Wren's thumbnail finds its way between her teeth.

"You want to stay at my place instead of the hotel?" Scarlett asks.

"Whatever works best for you," Wren answers, thinking this could be Scarlett's way of trying to conserve her riches.

After collecting her items from the hotel, Wren drives to Scarlett's apartment. "Can we park the car ourselves? The valet weirds me out."

Scarlett's reaction is blank. "You can park however you like."

Wren spots the wide corrugated steel door that leads to the underground parking and drives toward it.

Scarlett absorbs her surroundings. "It's all familiar but seems so different."

"Sobriety?" Wren blurts. Her cheeks turn red from her brashness.

"Nah. I've been sober before. Now I just know the truth." Scarlett turns to Wren. "I want to apologize for my actions. I really thought I wanted to know the answers to my question, but in reality, I wasn't ready. I'm sorry for how I treated you." She brushes back the hair from her face with her fingers. "You're a saint for still being here."

Wren finds the parking space that matches Scarlett's apartment number and backs the car into the spot, ignoring the rear-view camera that popped on the screen. She's still not used to modern car technology. "Thank you," Wren says in a quieter tone, keeping her eyes on the side mirrors to guide her safely into the spot. She turns the car off and stares at the parked cars before her. "I guess Dave was right. I needed you as much as you needed me."

Wren opens her laptop and listens to it hum and beep.

"What's the best way to transfer your payment?" Scarlett interrupts.

"Huh?" Wren looks up at Scarlett standing on the other side of the granite island.

Scarlett taps away on her phone screen. "Our agreement. What was it? Fifty-five thousand?"

Wren adjusts the angle of her laptop screen and crosses her arms under her chest. "We don't need to talk about that now." The screen comes to life and the tab she had open fills the screen. It's Scarlett's dashboard for the DNA test. Her eyes glue to the information before her and her fingers dance over the keyboard to sign in using the password she only made yesterday.

"Why does your face look like that? Like you have a secret?" Scarlett scoots over next to Wren. "What is it?"

Wren doesn't utter a word; her finger glides over the touchpad and she taps on the button that says family connections. A map loads with two markers in Canada. One is on the west coast and one, if Wren had to guess, is Montreal.

"Are those my family matches?" Scarlett turns the computer towards her. "Who's on Vancouver Island?" She bends closer and points.

Wren clicks on the icon. A box pops up with name and likely relation. "Macy Strickland. Sibling," she reads.

"Strickland?" Scarlett erects her spine. "As in Duane Strickland?" Her face twists.

Wren purses her lips, and flashes of the nightmare vision of a man standing behind Fabienne piece together. *It's him.* "I think so."

Scarlett stands completely still and her mouth hangs open. "No. I'm going to be sick."

The gravity of the moment causes Wren to slump in her seat. She knows the feeling of learning who your real dad is for the first time, and she's almost grateful her dad turned out to be a former alcoholic turned Police Staff Superintendent. Scarlett's just learned her biological father is a psychopath who hurt a lot of people. "Are you okay?" Wren slaps the laptop shut.

Scarlett bolts to the front hall, snatching her purse from the table on her way. "I'm done with this shit."

Wren presses her hand into the top of her laptop. I'm such an idiot. *Why would I click on the link to her family when she just told me she wasn't ready for the truth?*

"Wren. Let's go. It's time to fly," Scarlett shouts from the entrance.

Wren rolls her eyes; it's not the first time someone's made a flying joke to her. "Where are we going?" she asks from her seat in the kitchen. Her limbs are still heavy. All she wants to do is take a nap. *How can Scarlett not be exhausted,* she wonders. The moment has passed for Wren to recommend they take a rest. There is urgency in Scarlett's tone and Wren knows she's like a dog with a bone.

"My parents. Hank and Gabby. They might as well hear it from me that we found out the truth, because I'm sure the police are going to be contacting them soon."

Wren stands and wonders if Duane let Eugene in on the inner workings of his baby black market. If so, Eugene is going to hold out for a lot more before he squawks. "Are you sure you want to do this?" Wren asks. "Maybe it would be more of a shock if the police called them and questioned them."

The sound of Scarlett's boots click swiftly against the marble tile in Wren's direction.

"Maybe we should show them a little bit of compassion." Wren's eyes wander around the condo that the Hernandez money paid for. "This moment could change your life forever, Scarlett." The ultra-white glossy cabinets of the kitchen frame Wren's petite stature.

"I'm done with suffering. All these years of them making me believe I was crazy or imagining things when they knew my trauma. They knew the truth and refused to tell me for their own selfish reasons. Some people were never meant to have children, and Hank and Gabby Hernandez were two of them." Scarlett throws a hand on her hip and radiates certainty with her tall, lean physique.

Wren marches towards her, placing herself in the orbit of Scarlett's confidence. "Okay. Let's go."

Chapter 30

Scarlett peels into the driveway.

Wren doesn't see any harm in taking the passenger seat for the quick trip to the Hernandez estate. There is a welcome calmness in not being the one leading the charge on tackling loose ends in Scarlett's former life. The trees and bushes are barren because of the season, the sky streaked with grey clouds, and a chill tosses dead leaves about. The weather seems fitting, she thinks. If there was any joy on the inside of the walls of the Hernandez estate, it is about to be blown away with the leaves by Scarlett's truth.

Scarlett walks to the front entrance. Her casual pace doesn't match her flared mood. Her finger presses the button for the intercom.

"Why don't you try the door first?" Wren asks, remembering Scarlett's previous way of entering her family's home. Wren keeps her back pressed against the side of Scarlett's car. The black paint is cool against her touch. It is her turn to keep watch. For what, she's not sure, because it's daylight and a private residential home, but she has Scarlett's back. It crosses her mind to ask why Scarlett doesn't know the code to the house to let herself in, but Wren can surmise her own answers for why her parents keep her at a distance.

"I'm a guest in this home now, and I should behave like

one." Scarlett waits for a voice to come through the speaker and straightens herself in front of the camera.

"Miss Scarlett, hello, why didn't you text me? I would have left the door unlocked for you," Magdalene queries. Wren can sense a touch of worry in her voice.

"Hello, Magdalene. I didn't think it was appropriate to text you under the circumstances."

"What circumstances?" Magdalene's worry heightens.

Scarlett shifts her weight from one leg to the other. "Can you please let Wren and me in?"

Wren pushes her weight off the car and steps forward. "I guess that's my cue." She ushers to herself. A buzzer sounds and the door clicks. Wren scurries to follow a determined Scarlett.

"Hank, Gabby?" Scarlett shouts, and quickly turns to Wren. "Where are my manners? Old habits are hard to break, eh? I shouldn't be yelling."

Within seconds, Magdalene appears. "What's wrong?" Her hands clutch together in front of her chest. "Why aren't you calling them Mom and Dad?" The corners of her mouth bend down and the concern adds ten years to her face.

"Are they home?" Scarlett asks.

Magdalene's brows slant with discomfort. She doesn't answer Scarlett's question.

"Well, you're going to find out eventually." Scarlett rolls

her eyes. "I'm adopted."

"No." Magdalene steps back.

"Yep. They tried to keep it a secret. Are they home?" Scarlett scans all the doorways and halls she can see, not stepping further into the house, as if an alarm would pierce their ears if she did.

Magdalene shakes her head. "There must be a mistake."

Scarlett steps forward and hugs her family's maid. "I know, it's a lot to digest. Trust me. Wait until I tell you the whole story."

"Your father is in his office and your mother is out for the day at meetings." Magdalene squeezes Scarlett's hands in hers. "Are you okay?"

"I'm pretty sure my nightmares are gone, so that's something." Scarlett adds with a matter-of-fact tone. "Is it okay if we go see him?"

Magdalene bobs her head. "Child, of course, he is still your dad."

Wren keeps her lips tight as she observes this awkward exchange.

Scarlett forces a smile, biting on the words she's saving for Hank. "Thank you."

At the sight of the wooden molding and high ceiling, Wren recalls the last time she was in this house, and that Hank once was a big, strong moose. A protector of his family. *I wonder who Dave was in a past life?* He didn't seem like he was once a wise purveyor of the wilderness. Probably an average person like most people, she thinks. *No one special.*

Scarlett balls her fist and knocks on Hank's office door.

"Magdalene, I'll take my lunch in the arboretum," Hank's deep voice answers through the door.

Wren narrows her eyes. *This house has an indoor garden?*

"No, it's me. May I come in, please?" Scarlett asks.

"Sweetheart!" Hank's heavy steps smash quickly against the floor. The door swings inward. "Scarlett, darling." He wraps his arms around her. "Are you okay? Your mother and I have been worried sick. You haven't returned any of our calls."

Scarlett keeps her arms flat against her sides. Her eyes glaze over. "Yeah, you've always done your best to keep me safe," she says dryly.

Hank pulls out of his embrace of his daughter. "We love you very much. And the GPS in the BMW told me you weren't at the bottom of Lake Ontario. You know how you can get sometimes. We've gotten used to waiting out your episodes." He eyes Wren. "Your mother thought this one may be a bad influence on you, because before you met her you were doing so well."

Scarlett flings her head back and laughs. "I haven't been doing well since I was twelve years old, and all you and

Mother…" She puts air quotes around the word 'Mother' "…ever did was ship me off to special schools or doctors when all along, you knew."

Hank diverts his gaze from Scarlett and onto Wren.

Wren doesn't say a word. She doesn't have to. She watches the face of a man whose foundation is crumbling under him. Brick by brick, the life he kept secret is falling apart. A pang of emptiness hits her gut. She reminds herself to listen free of judgement. A man stands before her that wanted nothing more to father a child, to have his legacy live on, a desperate man who abused his standing in society to cut corners and get what he wanted. Being an objective bystander is harder than she thought.

"I guess you got my tip." He smiles fleetingly at Wren.

"Tip?" Scarlett steps closer to her dad.

"The text. That was you?" Wren moves out from the shadow cast by the heavy drapery. "Duane Strickland. Why?"

"Why did I send you the text with his name?" Hank swallows and dips his chin to his chest. "Because Scarlett is right. And we only superficially helped her; nothing we did lessened her nightmares. And after that day she brought you here, and she reminded me I used to tell her I would do anything to help her get better, I knew what I finally had to do. So, I texted you his name. I knew you were the one behind unearthing all these answers."

"You knew how disgusting that man is. He..." Scarlett fumes, pressing her finger into her dad's chest. "He made me call him Uncle Dewy," she adds through trembling lips.

"Scarlett, stop," Wren interrupts. She wants to reach out and pull Scarlett's hand from Hank, but she refrains. It's not the time to see what Fabienne wants to show her. "Let's hear what he knows first." She turns to Hank. "Tell us what you know. The truth, please."

Hank turns into his office and signals for his daughter and Wren to follow. "Gabby and I tried for years and years to get pregnant. No one talked about infertility in the eighties. We were embarrassed to talk about trying all the fertility drugs available. It was like living with a secret shame." Hank takes a seat on the dark green tufted leather couch. "I think Gabby struggled with it the most. All her girlfriends were getting pregnant and having babies, and she wanted one so badly. She told me once she didn't feel like a woman. She felt broken and didn't know why her body was failing her. We had everything to offer a child."

"There were legitimate adoption agencies available in the eighties," Scarlett spits. Her and Wren remain standing across from her dad.

Hank looks up with glossy, weathered eyes. "Your mother wanted a child where she could look into your eyes and see her own. She wanted her body to be your body. And it crushed me that I could never give that to her."

"And how did you get involved with Duane?" Wren rests

her hands on the back of a chair.

"I went to university with him. The dumbest smart guy I have ever met. A bunch of the guys got together for our five-year reunion. He was a weasel back then, too, boasting about his inflated business ideas to make everyone filthy rich. And thank God I didn't get tangled up in his business mess, but he shared one of his ideas with me. A new-age designer adoption agency. Where he'd pair babies with families that looked like them. I don't know how he read me, but he reeled me in good."

Scarlett's grimace leaves no mystery to what she is feeling. She opens her mouth but instantly snaps it shut.

Wren continues to listen intently.

"He offered a level of discreteness. He promised no one would know. That's why your mother and I worked in Japan for a year. And when we returned, we had a baby. No one thought anything of it." Hank removes his glasses and rubs his eye. "When Duane was arrested in the nineties, we thought we were going down with him. Gabby thought it was best if we send you to a private school in Switzerland. But no one ever came to question us. All his charges were for his other businesses."

"So you know nothing about the kidnapping and rape?" Scarlett's stare burns into her dad's skin.

"Scarlett, stop," Wren hushes.

"What?" Hank's contorted stare lands on the women

before him.

"It's true. Duane's idea of a designer adoption agency was kidnapping women, and him and his buddy Roman or Eugene, or whatever his name is, would rape these women. Young women, like under eighteen." Scarlett lets the truth finally tumble from her mouth into her dad's ears.

Wren places her arm around a trembling Scarlett.

Scarlett lets her emotions bubble to the surface. She sniffs back the snot ready to drip from her nose, her vision blurred. "Fabienne was her name. Her and her family immigrated from Haiti to Montreal. The same thin frame and complexion as Gabby." Scarlett's shoulders heave with her sobs.

"I think he was targeting women who were immigrants. Young women who wouldn't garner much attention if they went missing," Wren adds. She squeezes Scarlett tighter and rubs her back.

Hank's lips quiver and tears flow freely down his cheeks. "Scarlett. I am so sorry. We didn't know." He stands and rushes to Scarlett to hold her in his fatherly embrace.

Wren steps to the side. She exhales a deep breath.

"You found her? Fabienne, your birth mother?" Hank wipes his eyes.

"I am her." Scarlett pulls away and searches her dad's face for a reaction. "She died giving birth to me."

Hank pulls his daughter close, and they cry together.

Wren exits the room, giving Scarlett and her dad privacy. Her step is lighter in helping share Scarlett's truth, although she knows Hank will never fully understand what Scarlett meant when she told him she was her birth mother. Few people would.

Chapter 31

Scarlett tells Wren she can take her car and go back to her apartment. Scarlett wants to stay with her dad and tell her mom the truth when she gets home.

Wren understands. In the car, she drives in silence, letting the gravity of her reality set in. She doesn't blink the entire way back to Scarlett's condo. She wonders if Fabienne is finally at peace, but that justice will never match the brutal horror Fabienne and the other girls were forced to endure.

Hot water scalds her skin. Wren stands under the rain head, and she wonders how she got here. The fogginess of her thoughts signals that it is time to rest. She knows there is still more she can do, but she needs to be in a clear state of mind.

The spare room isn't hard to identify, as it's the smaller room. The room is equivalent to her room at the Plaza, pristine and untouched by a speck of dust. She imagines a cleaning person is instructed to clean this room even though it sits empty. Wren remembers what Gabby said to her, about Scarlett paying people to be her friend. The words could be complete fiction, but if Scarlett was lonely enough, she can see how paying someone to be her friend would be easier than trying to find someone genuine. If you were loaded, how would you truly know if someone liked you for you or your money? Wren's eyelids are heavy, and with her head resting on the comfiest pillow she's ever experienced, she slips off to sleep.

Visions from photographs of her own mother cast onto the inside of her eyelids as she wakes. The prom picture with her grandparents, her mom's graduation picture with long golden curls cascading down her shoulders with a big white smile and clear blue eyes and there was this one picture her Nan kept on her dresser of Heather holding a newborn Wren, uncertainty and joy hidden in her mother's eyes. *Why would she leave me?* A question she never let herself dwell on until this moment. *She must have been chasing something she saw, and it must have been something wild.* Wren's never wanted children of her own for obvious reasons, but can't help but think of a mystery compelling enough that would pull a mother away from a child. *There is a way to find out.* Her eyes snap open. *Hilary Clarke. She would be in her early twenties now. No.* She forces the idea from her mind and thinks of the haunting images Fabienne showed her. The other girls trapped with her. Their stories still need to be told. Time eludes her, but her mind is clear. If Scarlett came back, Wren didn't hear her. She climbs out from under the puffy white duvet and makes her way to the window. With the blackout curtains drawn, it is impossible to gauge what time of day it is. She pulls the curtain open and a million lights sparkle against the navy city. *How long was I asleep for?* She finds her phone on the dresser and learns that it's just after eight pm. No text from Scarlett. Wren can't decide if that's good or bad. She opens her bedroom door. "Scarlett," she calls, and waits for a response. Nothing. In the kitchen she finds herself a bottle of water in the fridge next to a container of yogurt. Scarlett doesn't strike her as someone who ventures to the grocery store very often. Most likely anything she needs or wants can be delivered.

Seated at the island, Wren takes her notebook from her purse and flips to the last page with her scribbles. She finds a pen and begins adding the events from the last twenty-four hours—everything from the address of the box factory to Roman's real name, to Duane Strickland being Scarlett's biological father. *I bet it felt like a bullet to the heart when Hank found out Duane was the man who fathered Scarlett.* She imagines Scarlett has already shared every detail with Hank and Gabby, including the details about finding a half-sister and Fabienne's little brother. Secretly Wren hopes Scarlett would ask her to join her when she first meets Fabienne's brother, but she doesn't know if Scarlett will ever be ready for that. And without Scarlett making the initial contact, it would be weird for Wren to reach out on her own. She smiles at the thought of telling Fabienne's brother how much Fabienne loved him and his sister.

Wren flips back through her notes and sees the names Bojana, Sofia, and Anya circled. She swallows the lump in her throat and rifles through her purse, looking for the card Dave gave her. *He'll understand. He'll know exactly what to do.* Her hand quivers holding the card. *This isn't about me, it's for the girls.*

Chapter 32

I'm happy you reached out." Dave sits across the table from Wren. His kind eyes dote on his newfound daughter.

Wren pulls her notebook from her purse and sets it on the table. Her stomach twists from nerves and hunger. "I have more information, and I didn't know what to do." She presses her hands into the top of her notebook, the notebook harbouring her secrets, a notebook she's never willingly shared with another living soul. "And I don't think anyone other than you would really understand."

Dave sets down his coffee, interlocks his fingers, and rests his hands on the table. "I was hoping you had more information, but it wasn't my place to pry." His lips form a tight half-grin.

"I have the names of three girls, plus Fabienne. I saw them there with my own eyes. Fabienne showed them to me. Once I heard their first names I searched missing person websites." Wren opens her notebook and flips to the page with their names scribed amongst the collected facts. "I found them all. All immigrants, I'm guessing, based on their names and accents. All still missing." Wren sniffs and pulls her notebook closer. "Fabienne Delva lived in Montreal, Anya Adamovich and Sofia Petrov were from Toronto, and Bojana Milosevic lived in Oakville."

"That's more than what the detectives have." Dave raises his brow. "Eugene is staying tight-lipped until we meet his demands."

"I'm guessing the forensics team will find at least one of the girl's DNA in the factory's basement, but without a sample to match it to, it might be tough to confirm," Wren adds.

"You'd be surprised at the DNA we have on file. The families may have provided samples when they reported their child missing." Dave attempts a fleeting smile to give Wren hope. "You did good work. Thank you."

Wren closes her book and returns it to her bag. She takes a sip of water while keeping her eyes down. Words of gratitude are foreign to her ears, and she doesn't know how to react. "Do you think they'll ever find Fabienne's remains?" Wren's eyes find Dave's.

Dave shrugs. "It's hard to say. More often than not, kidnappings from over thirty years ago rarely ever get solved. We got lucky because of your help. You should feel proud with the information we have." His hand hesitates. He wants to reach out and console Wren, but refrains.

Wren notices the action, and also the fact that he removed his black leather gloves when they sat down. She's not ready to touch him, so she continues the conversation about the case. "Will the detective be contacting Scarlett's parents?"

Dave nods. "Eventually."

"They don't know anything. I was there when Scarlett told her dad. He only knew what Duane told him: the lie that he found babies from around the world and matched them with families that had similar genetic backgrounds."

"Sounds like something Duane would say. Every word out of that man's mouth was a lie to get him what he wanted. Money. Status. He wanted the world to be jealous of his delusional life," Dave says.

"You knew him?" Wren narrows her stare.

"Sadly, yeah. I was one of the officers on his case." Dave stares down at his almost-empty mug. "He was a textbook psychopath."

"He's Scarlett's biological father," Wren blurts.

Dave puckers his lips. "What? Are you serious?" He leans in. "I'm sorry." He apologises for his hasty remarks and leans back.

"We found her half-sister on a DNA test website. Macy Strickland, lives in British Columbia."

"Yeah, that's right. He had a daughter with his girlfriend in the early nineties. I think her name was Tiffany. I doubt Tiffany even told Macy the truth about who her dad actually was. She was still pretty small when he was arrested. Tiffany had no idea what Duane was up to, but she loved him. Had a meltdown when we arrested him." Dave swirls the cold remaining coffee in his mug.

Wren's mind can't help but fall into the rabbit hole of

thinking Macy was just as lost as Scarlett. Another lonely soul who mailed away their DNA in hopes to find a connection to anyone who may know more about why she is the way she is. Wren even imagines the alert pinging Macy's phone, *New Family Match,* when Scarlett's results came in: the excitement to make her heart skip a beat, the rush of heat to flush her cheeks, her fingers shaking as she opens the app to see that she has an older half-sister. Wren forces her smile to fade as quickly as it surfaced.

"What's that smile for?" Dave inquires with a grin himself.

"Nothing." Wren looks for the waiter to see if their food is on its way as a hopeful distraction. She licks the back of her teeth. "Actually, I was thinking how Scarlett felt so alone, but she still has her mom and dad, but now she has a sister."

"What about you, too?" Dave thinks his timing is right. "You had no one; now you have me."

Wren fiddles with peeling skin around her thumbnail. She never imagined bonding with the man who is her father, or hearing the truth for the first time. It's still a lot for her to digest. "What about you?" The question leaves her lips before she has time to think about asking. "Do you have a family?"

Dave nods. "I do. A wife, her name is Michelle, and a son, Derek, he's fifteen."

His answer causes a prick of pain to pinch her heart. Forever the forgotten child that no one seems to want. Even as an adult her childhood fears leave her vulnerable.

"I've always been transparent about who you were. And there is no pressure, but you're welcome in our lives whenever or if you're ever ready. Michelle and Derek are good-hearted people." Dave looks in the distance for their meals. "Michelle told me I should have tried harder to get you back. For that I am sorry. She was right. She's usually right."

An instant family. She stares back at Dave. In all the scenarios Wren dreamed up of where her father might be, in a loving family that would welcome her, was the scene she never allowed herself to dwell on. The scene she thought would have a one-in-a-million chance of being true. The scene is only found in cheesy movie plots. "Can Derek do what we do?" she blurts.

Dave looks her in the eyes. "Thankfully, no."

The waiter appears with their food and places what they ordered in front of them. "Are you enjoying your father-daughter night?" His toothy smile beams down at them.

Dave and Wren look at each other, then back to the waiter. Both of them are waiting to hear how the other will answer. "How did you know we are father and daughter?" Wren cuts through the awkward pause. The word 'daughter' sounds foreign in her own voice.

"Oh, your eyes. You both have the same eyes. And other little things." The waiter pulls his empty tray to his chest.

Dave flashes Wren a wink, then turns to the waiter. "Like what?"

"Your posture, shape of face. It's unmistakable that you're related." He rolls on the side of his feet and raises his eyebrows. "Well, you two enjoy your meal, and I'll be back to check on you soon."

Wren curls her lips under her teeth to stop a smile. She shakes her head and pops a carrot stick into her mouth. "Have you ever met someone like us before?" Wren takes another bite of her carrot and raises an eyebrow. Right now, she only knows of three people who can or could see people's past lives, and two of them are sitting at this table. The other one is her mother, who's no longer with them.

"Your mother was the first. I think that's why we were so drawn to each other. I worked at the gas station in the neighbouring town, and your mom must have just gotten her license because when she pulled in for gas she got out and tried to pump it herself, she didn't have a clue what she was doing, and it was a full-serve station." Dave smiles at the memory. "As soon as I saw this young woman fumbling around with the pump, I ran out and grabbed it from her hands." Dave sets his fork full of lasagna down on his plate and focuses on his story. "I saw through the eyes of a woman who was washing clothes in the river. And when I let go, I'll never forget the bewildered look in her eyes, I knew. I knew she saw stuff too. Her beautiful smile was so wide, my heart burst, and it was love at first sight. She giggled and told me I lived such interesting lives."

"Lives? As in more than one?" Wren inches closer to the edge of the bench seat.

"Yep. She said all my lives rolled together like waves, and that I was an old soul, but later she told me she only ever saw multiple lives when she touched me. So, we assumed it was because we both had the ability, however I've never seen more than one past life in someone. Have you?" Dave crosses his arms and leans in.

Wren shakes her head. "I've never thought to search for people like us before."

"What about your grandfather? What did you see when you held his hand?"

Memories of her grandpa are buried deep in her mind. As she digs through them, there is no recollection of being close with the man. Wren parts her lips. "I can't remember Grandpa ever letting me get close to him."

"That makes sense." Dave nods and picks up his utensil to take a bite. "He never wanted to talk about it with your mom, and I don't think he ever touched anyone other than your grandma." He says before he slides the fork into his mouth.

"That's right. Nan was a new soul. I never saw anything when I touched her." Wren picks up the rib with the most meat.

Dave swallows. "Huh, I guess that makes sense then." He wipes his mouth with his napkin. It doubles as a shield to hide his grin.

"What's so funny? Do I have sauce on my face or something?" Wren wipes her mouth with the back of her hand.

"No, no." He returns his napkin to his lap. "I just remembered your mother telling me what she saw when she held you for the first time."

Wren chokes down the fatty piece of pork.

"The most beautiful, peaceful life you ever lived was when you were a bird. She said you had the loveliest song and lived in the sweetest garden. She said you watched people fall in love, share secrets, and be happy. In a puddle of rainwater, she saw your reflection, you were a little wren."

The name given to her at birth by a mother she never knew finally makes sense. A name she once wished she could run from now seems to suit her perfectly. "Thank you for telling me that story." The corners of Wren's mouth twitch up. A wren isn't small and weak, it is smart and chooses happiness, she thinks.

"How about you? Ever meet someone else like us?" Dave asks, and returns to eating.

Wren inhales deeply as she slowly waves her head. "No, but I have an old friend, AJ, who is my wife from my last life. He couldn't see what we see, but he knew we had a connection."

"Really? How fascinating." Dave hangs on his daughter's

every word.

"Yeah, he said he was drawn to me in a crowded airport in Italy, but he's originally from Australia. He's a bit of a nomad," Wren rambles. "A citizen of the world, he calls himself."

"Wow, that's fascinating. Really, in Italy?"

Wren picks up another rib. "Perhaps that's a story for another day." Images of that man's face. *The chief.* She feels his hands slithering over her body. Travelling halfway around the world chasing dead end after dead end just to escape. To find meaning in what she stomached. If only she could have located that stolen art. Wren shakes it off and changes the subject. "The food here isn't bad. We better eat before everything gets cold." Wren keeps her eyes on her plate. The tender meat breaks apart under her clenched bites.

"You said my mom saw your past lives in a wave?" Wren ignores her own idea to focus on her food. In that moment she instantly remembers what she experienced with Scarlett in the pool at the spa.

Dave nods through his chews.

"I experienced something like that when I touched Scarlett underwater, but it was different snippets from Fabienne's life. I should also mention Scarlett was under the influence of Adderall." Wren picks up a celery stick and takes a bite. She watches Dave's eyes widen.

"Interesting. Do you document all your experiences?"

Dave asks.

Wren taps her clean fingers on the top of her notebook in her purse. "I do."

"That's good. There is probably so much we don't know."

"Ha!" Wren lets a sharp laugh escape her lips. "Isn't that the truth."

"Maybe one day we can talk about our experiences." His eyes stay on Wren.

A pain in Wren's stomach forces her to stop eating. She's lost her appetite, and she's not sure she'll ever be ready to share her experiences with Dave.

Chapter 33

Wren and Dave linger in the vestibule of the family restaurant. The date when they will see each other again is left unsaid. "Are you going to be all right?" Dave finally asks.

"I've made it this far, haven't I?" Wren steps out of the way for a family also leaving the establishment. She's now closer to Dave. One question is on her mind. *What will happen when I touch him?*

Dave smiles. "I suppose you have." He removes his hands from his pockets, unsure if Wren would accept a hug.

Wren flashes a smile in return. Her hand finds his. No thoughts weigh the pros and cons of reaching out and touching her estranged father. No thoughts on whether she even wants to engage in physical contact with the father she just met. The old habit of touching before thinking resurfaces.

Different views of time and people or animals living their once life. A reel of images seen through my eyes with a motion similar to the waves Dave relayed of my mother's story and what I experienced in the pool. It's dizzying and difficult to focus on only one, but I try. Our hands and fingers are thick, the biggest hands I've ever seen. heaving huge grey stone bricks. The ground beneath our feet is muddy. Another view pulls my attention, vibrant foliage presses against our body, it's cool. We're close to the ground. I don't see our limbs, perhaps we're a snake or a lizard. In another, our old, weathered hands knit with off-white pulled yarn. A heavy, long skirt keeps the chill in the air off our legs. I can't tell what we're making.

Dave checks over his shoulder before he speaks. "What did you see?"

Wren's focus locks on her hand that just touched his flesh. There is much she doesn't know about herself. "So many lives." She shifts her gaze to Dave's face. "An old woman, an animal." She waves her head. "A brick layer..."

"Oh, yes, the medieval stonemason." Dave chuckles. "He was your mom's favourite. She liked his arms."

All Wren can do is stare. "What did you see?"

"Drills, military drills. Men in uniform. But you already knew that." Dave returns his hands to his jacket pocket. "Well, kiddo..."

Kiddo? Wren twists her lips at the new nickname. *It's probably what he calls Derek, too.*

"Are you staying with Scarlett?"

Wren nods. "Yeah, I guess, until I figure out what's next." She remains still, wondering how normal father and daughters say goodbye. "Will you call me if Eugene shares any information about the missing women?"

"Sure, I can do that."

"Thanks." Wren nods, spins from the awkward exchange, and pushes forward the door to the outside. A cold evening breeze hits their faces. "Thank you for dinner. Talk to you later." Once those last words leave her lips, she makes a beeline for Scarlett's car, a car she's come accustomed to driving in three short days. Or has it been four days, she questions. Time and events are a blur, especially when they braid together with visions from past lives.

"Goodnight, Wren, thanks for the info. Drive safe. I'm here if you need me," Dave calls into the night. His words carry across the crisp air into Wren's ears. She presses them into her chest and lets herself wish them to be true.

"Oh, good, you're home." Scarlett bounds to the front door. "I've been waiting for you to get back. I was going to call you, but I thought you might be with Dave, and I didn't want to interrupt. I like Dave, he's super nice, eh?"

Wren only responds with blinks, trying to piece together everything Scarlett let tumble past her lips. "Is everything okay?" A pinch of worry in her voice. Wren removes her coat and hangs it up.

Scarlett plops herself down on the chair closest to Wren and blows out an embellished breath. "Have you ever felt like you ran a marathon and you've been training for it for a very long time, then you run it and it's over, and you think, now what?"

Running a marathon would be the last physical activity Wren would choose to do, but she understands the metaphor and moves closer to Scarlett. "Well, I think I should return home. You don't need my weirdness to dampen your lifestyle." What she's concerned about is Scarlett's rollercoaster of emotions and Wren doesn't know if she has the energy to hang around. It was only this morning that Scarlett had to storm off to confront her parents, and now she is at a loss for what to do with her life.

Scarlett purses her full lips, and it makes her look like she's imitating those girls who pose with a stupid duck mouth. "Don't go yet. I need you. You've helped me more than you'll ever truly know." She extends her hand.

Wren ignores the gesture and takes a seat on the chair across from Scarlett. Now is not the time to see what Fabienne wants to show her, although a tingle in her fingertips tells her she is curious. She also ignores Scarlett's invitation to stay for longer, as she doesn't know how to answer. "So, you told your mom?"

"Yeah, they both know that I know that I was adopted." Scarlett throws her head back into the chair and her fingers fiddle with the framed trim on the decorative grey cushion. "They aren't happy about learning that Duane fathered me, but they agreed to cooperate with the police when and if they call, 'cause I told them I am the DNA evidence, and I will do whatever I need to do to help."

"I met up with Dave. I gave him the names of the other girls. Asshole Eugene hasn't told them anything yet and Dave doesn't think he ever will. But at least they have all the names now if Dave thinks it's appropriate to share," Wren adds.

"Why wouldn't he share the names right away?" Scarlett cries.

Wren tilts her head. "What's he going to say? Here are three other victims, my daughter saw them when she touched Scarlett Hernandez and saw her past life as Fabienne, one of the other girls that was taken." She shakes her head. "It sounds outrageous."

Scarlett leans her head back again. "Yeah, you're right."

"So." It's Wren's turn to blow an exaggerated breath out of the side of her mouth. "I guess I can take the train home. You don't need to waste all that time in a car..."

"No, not yet," Scarlett interrupts. "What if there is a break in the case, and we need you? And Dave lives here, and I want you with me when I meet my sister and uncle. Of course, at different times," she clarifies.

Again, Wren sifts through all of Scarlett's loaded words. *Moving? Traveling?* Her mind drowns in all the suggested changes. *This time last week I was eating ramen in the dark, hunched over my keyboard, watching a documentary about killer whales.* "What about starting with a call or FaceTime?" Wren strings some words together.

Scarlett hugs the pillow in her lap. "What? A call, like I call you?"

"Your newfound relatives," Wren clarifies, and snaps her

eyes shut.

"Oh. Yes. That makes sense, but I'm going to want to go meet them, eventually."

Wren opens one eye and keeps it on Scarlett, who's sitting there combing her cushion's tassel with innocence in her eyes. *Do I want to stay with Scarlett for a bit longer?* Wren needs to clear her mind. She wants to sleep. "Let me sleep on it. I don't know what to do, Dave is there, he wants to help, I touched his hand, we have the same gift, he may be able to..."

Scarlett interjects again. "Woah, what did you see?"

Wren explains to Scarlett what she saw, from all the different past lives, spliced with the motion of swaying water. She even includes how she's experienced something like this with Fabienne's visions before.

Scarlett's eyes are wide with interest. Her back straightens. "Yes! There is so much to learn. I want to help you. Let me help you! I know what you can do, and I believe you. See, that's why I slipped you..."

"Nope." Wren stands.

"What?" Scarlett's rigid stature deflates into the chair.

"No, this is too much to deal with right now. I'm tired. I shouldn't have rambled on about Dave," Wren says. Her shoulder blades squeeze together, and she straightens her posture. She can't control what comes out of her mouth sometimes. Even when she met AJ, she let herself babble on. She assumes she subconsciously takes comfort in people who believe in her abilities.

"Wren, you can always ramble on about whatever with me." Scarlett stares at Wren and hugs the cushion.

Chapter 34

The weight of the duvet encapsulates Wren's body. There is nothing left to do but sleep. Minutes ago, her eyelids were weak, and she felt like she could have fallen asleep standing up. Now, she lies awake. Her thoughts want to rally. *Breathe in, breathe out.* She shuts her eyes and focuses on her breaths. Flashes of Dave, Scarlett, Hank, Fabienne, and the other missing girls run rampant through her thoughts. Tomorrow's worries won't rest. *Ugh.* Wren flaps her arms against the cool surface of the blanket. Her eyes snap open and she snatches her phone off the side table. The screen illuminates the darkness surrounding her. She taps the news app and scrolls through the depressing headlines: *Poor Air Quality Going to Get Worse Before It Gets Better, Endangered Whale Washes Up on Long Island Beach.* She swipes up and opens a browser in incognito mode. Her fingers tap the letters to spell Hilary Clarke. Wren's not sure she'll even recognize the face of a grown Hilary Clarke, but she still remembers what Hilary's mother looked like all those years ago, and it's a place to start, combined with the approximate age of eighteen that she guesses Hilary would be. Businesswomen and random web pages for what looks like legal services fill her screen. She adds Ontario, Canada to her search. Links to different social media accounts appear. She's not sure if she wants to scroll through random profiles just yet, so her eyes continue to scan the first page of results. *Local Long Jumper Earns Scholarship to Arkansas University.* It was published in April of this year. *The timeline checks out.* Wren clicks the link. A long-legged, sandy blonde, Hilary Clarke stands smiling in front of a sandpit with a variety of medals dangling from her neck. *It's her.* The aqua eyes are the same aqua eyes that found her on the street that day. Her first semester would be well underway now. Wren smiles to herself. *It looks like she's doing great. Good for her.* Wren closes the browser and returns her phone to the surface next to her bed. *It seems like Mom was given a good life. She must have done something right to be reborn as Hilary. Perhaps I'll never know the demons my mother battled and maybe it's for the best.* And with that lingering thought, Wren drifts off to sleep.

The aroma of bacon fills Wren's nostrils as she wakes. It takes her a few seconds to remember where she is. *Is Scarlett cooking breakfast?* She wipes the sleep from her eyes with her finger and yawns even though she feels rested. It's time to go home. A seven-hour bus or train ride seems long, so she wants to see if she can afford a flight. She grabs her phone and taps and swipes until her bank account information is before her. The information staring back at her seems incorrect. She blinks and sits up. *There must be a mistake.* Her balance is sixty thousand more than the couple thousand she had the last time she looked at her account.

"Wake up, sleepyhead. Breakfast is ready," Scarlett shouts.

Wren scrambles from bed and hurries to dress in the

clothes she wore yesterday that she left on the dresser. "Scarlett," she says to herself.

"Good morning!" Scarlett stands behind the island holding up a glass of juice. "Want some?"

Wren holds up her phone. "Do you know anything about this?" Her eyes bounce from her device to Scarlett.

Scarlett scoops out the contents of a takeout box onto two plates. "That's your payment, silly. I couldn't remember the exact amount, so I rounded up." Her lips melt as she looks to Wren. "What? Is there something wrong? Did I promise you more?"

"How? When did you do this?" Wrens asks. She throws her free hand on her slim hip, reeling at how someone could deposit this much money into her account without her knowing. Accepting this as a payment doesn't seem appropriate. There is still much to learn and figure out about what happened to all the young women. Money seems irrelevant when these girls and their families still suffered.

Scarlett cracks a grin. "Hank has connections, but turn that frown upside down because he was happy to help you seeing how much you helped me and helped unearth this tragedy. They never would have done what they did if they knew the truth. Now I can begin to heal. I've been to enough therapy to understand..."

"It's not right," Wren cuts Scarlett off.

"You need to eat. Come. Sit." Scarlett scoots out from

behind the island and comes to Wren's side. "I ordered up a good ol' fashioned breakfast. I didn't know what you liked, so I ordered a bit of everything."

I knew she wasn't cooking. Wren's stomach gurgles as she lets herself glimpse at the arranged containers of food only a few steps away.

"See. I heard that." Scarlett dawns a knowing look. She links arms with Wren and guides her further into the kitchen.

Wren's eyes stare at their arms intertwined. She breathes relief as they are both wearing sweaters and Scarlett was careful not to let their hands touch. "I think Fabienne liked to help people, too. You probably inherited more than her looks." Wren's tight lips form a smile.

"Well, that would be something. Only the Lord knows what nastiness Duane passed down to me." Scarlett releases Wren and ushers to the drawer with cutlery.

Wren widens her eyes and stares unblinkingly at Scarlett's back. She has an idea of what devilish traits Scarlett inherited, but perhaps that's a conversation for another day, reserved for a call or text, when there is a larger distance between them. Right now, Scarlett is caring and nice, so she keeps her thoughts to herself. "This smells great. Thank you."

"Don't mention it. It's the least I could do." Scarlett passes Wren a knife and fork. "Last night I had the best sleep." She opens one box wider to inspect its contents. "Oh!" Scarlett abandons the container and bounces on her toes closer to Wren. "I didn't even tell you the best part yet!"

Wren freezes and continues to keep her eyes wide.

"I saw them!" Scarlett claps her hands.

"Saw who?"

"My family. Fabienne's family. My aunt and uncle and grandparents. We were sitting around the table eating dinner." Scarlett's face beams with excitement. "Just like what she showed you."

Wren nods and grins. "That's wonderful." She recalls seeing them gathered around the table for a family meal. One of Fabienne's cherished memories, a memory she can only imagine Fabienne playing on repeat after she was taken, wishing and hoping that one day, she would escape and be with her family again.

"My uncle. I want to go see him. Today, you and I can catch a flight to Montreal," Scarlett adds. "He's going to want to meet me. And his sister, maybe she's in the city, too. My auntie. I have an auntie." She beams.

Wren takes a seat on the stool. "Before we go hopping on planes to Quebec cities, let's send him a message or email through the DNA website. And she would be your *tante*." Wren is baffled by her random recall of the French word for 'aunt'. She must have heard it somewhere recently, she thinks.

"Yes, my *tante*!" Scarlett runs from the kitchen into the guest room.

"Hey, where are you going?" Wren spins on the stool.

Scarlett returns, holding Wren's laptop tightly against her chest. "Here." She sets it carefully down in front of Wren. "Login to my account and send him a message right now. Tell him I'm Fabienne's long-lost daughter, and that I would be interested in getting to know my long-lost family." Scarlett flaps her hand in the air. "Don't tell him any sad stuff, focus on the good, you know?"

Wren opens her machine. "Why don't you just message him?"

"Oh, no, I'm far too excited. And you're the smart one, you'll know what to say." Scarlett's eyes and toothy smile lock on Wren.

It only took one hour for Fabienne's brother, Ricardo, to respond. He is gobsmacked that his sister had a child, as she's still reported as missing; his response reads that he is more interested in knowing where his sister is now, but Scarlett is adamant to Wren to not reveal the truth yet.

"Ask him if we can meet up?" Scarlett chews on her lower lip. "Like meet him for a coffee or something." She paces around her apartment. "And ask him when."

Wren crafts the message and reads to Scarlett, "Hi, Ricardo, I was excited to receive your response. I am in fact Fabienne's daughter. The story is complex and will most likely sound like the plot of some movie, but I would love to meet you for a coffee and explain everything. You choose the time and place, and I will be there."

"Perfect, send it!" Scarlett says.

Wren does as she's told. "What about Macy? You want to contact her, too?"

Scarlett spins to face Wren. "No. Not yet. I'm not ready to talk about him. I'm not sure I'll ever want to. I know I said I wanted to meet my sister before, but I'm not sure now."

Chapter 35

Tomorrow morning, for coffee, at a place called *Café Chat Noir*." Wren doesn't attempt a French accent and knows her pronunciation sounds terrible.

Scarlett slams the fridge and snatches her phone off the counter. "Where is that? Montreal?" Her fingers frantically tap the letters. The search engine corrects her spelling and translates it into English. The image of the café's logo shows a coy black cat sipping a coffee. Her eyes scan for the address. "Yes, Montreal. I'll call the front desk to book our tickets."

"Scarlett." Wren turns away from her laptop screen. Her lips form a straight line. "Are you sure you're ready for this?"

"Yes, of course." Scarlett continues to tap her screen. "And you'll come with me, for support."

"Good morning, Miss Hernandez." A voice booms from Scarlett's phone on speaker.

"Yes, hello, good morning. I need you to book me two plane tickets to Montreal for later today. One is for myself and one for my friend..." Scarlett looks at Wren and winks. "Wren Roussel."

"Do you have a time or airline preference?" the man asks.

Wren doesn't know what to say or if she should stop this endeavour. Even though she wants to meet Ricardo, she thought she would have more time to prepare. She thought Eugene would talk and reveal where he stashed Fabienne's remains. It's a long shot, but Wren imagined returning Fabienne's remains to her family. That's definitely not going to happen in the next few hours, or however long they have to wait to board their flight.

"I can get you both on a flight tonight at seven."

"Book it. And can you also book us accommodations, please? Conjoining rooms or a room with two queen or king beds will do." Scarlett stares into her phone.

"Yes, Miss Hernandez, not a problem. I'll send tickets and confirmation to your email," the man answers.

"Great, thank you." Scarlett taps her phone and sets it down on the counter. A grin spans ear to ear. "It's happening."

Wren blinks. "Yes, it's happening." She stares down and pulls at her sweater. A smear of dirt is streaked across the bottom. She puffs her cheeks and blows out her breath. "Can I use your washer and dryer to do some laundry?" When she packed her bag four days ago, she didn't pack enough for all these excursions. She tries to remember what she was thinking when she packed. *What did I think I was doing?*

What did I think was going to happen? Wren shakes her head from her thoughts.

"No, silly, I have a laundry service. I'll show you where to put your dirty clothes and we'll call down for service." Scarlett playfully shakes her head.

"I'm more comfortable washing my own clothes."

Scarlett crosses her arms and leans on the island. "Look, we have some time to kill; why don't we go shopping and you can treat yourself to some fancy new clothes."

Wren's eyes roll. "Nothing fancy, please. A regular store is fine." She shivers at the thought of having to spend hundreds of dollars on new clothes when in her apartment there are perfectly good clothes.

"Fine, where would you like to go? Sears?"

"Scarlett, Sears closed like ten years ago." Wren rubs her ear lobe.

"Oh," Scarlett laughs. "Shows how long I've been out of it. My clothes are just always in my closet. Mother Gabby must keep me clothed."

"Let's just go to a mall." Wren does her best not to judge. Money or no money, she can't imagine living with what Scarlett or Fabienne had to endure. She pauses. *Wait, I can imagine, and it was fucking awful.*

The flight and night at the hotel fly by. Wren is a fly on the wall of Scarlett's life.

"I like the plaid sweater jacket thing you bought. Makes you look strong and woodsy," Scarlett comments. "I want to leave now and get there early." Her body vibrates.

That is the first time anyone's referenced Wren looking strong. Wren smiles to herself and grabs her purse. "Okay, I'm ready."

"Good. Uber is on its way."

"Do you know what Ricardo looks like now? I've only seen him when he was small." Wren flips her hair out from under the collar of her jacket.

Scarlett tilts her head toward Wren. "He's my biological uncle, I think I'll be able to recognize him."

Café Chat Noir's scent of freshly-ground coffee beans and cinnamon banishes the chill that arrives with Wren and Scarlett. Their eyes search the tables for eyes searching for them. "I don't think he's here yet." Wren leans and whispers to Scarlett.

The two find a quiet table where they can put their backs against the wall and watch as patrons arrive. No words are spoken as they dutifully monitor the entrance. A man in his early fifties walks in with a woman. "That could be him," Wrens says.

"No, that's not him." Scarlett answers while keeping her eyes forward. "That's Ricardo." She folds her upper lip under her front teeth.

Ricardo is a man standing about six feet tall, with grey hair at his temples, and dark eyes that match Fabienne's and Scarlett's. He spots the women he's here to meet right away. One hand cups his mouth and his other hand presses to his heart. He marches toward Scarlett and shakes his head in disbelief. "Fabienne," he whispers.

Scarlett stands to greet him. "You must be my Uncle Ricardo."

"May I hug you?" Tears well in his dark brown eyes. His arms open to pull in the niece he never knew he had.

Scarlett nods and fights back her own emotions until she can no longer keep in her tears. "I can't believe I found you again."

Wren notes Scarlett's use of the word 'again'; either Scarlett's referencing when she first saw Ricardo in her dream or Fabienne is very much with them in this reunion. She also stands and witnesses this powerful moment between family. The resemblance is undeniable.

Ricardo pulls from the embrace and places his hands on Scarlett's face. "You look just like her." He searches her eyes. "I knew she never left us. She would never do that to her family."

"Your sister was kidnapped by some terrible people many years ago," Wren adds. She wants to get the unpleasant news over with quickly.

"And you must have helped find her and bring her back to me?" Ricardo continues to hold Scarlett's face in his hands while he looks at Wren. His stare pierces Wren's skin.

What does he see? Wren nods. "Yes, I helped, but it's more like Scarlett found me." She offers a brief smile. A piece of her wants to reach out and touch Ricardo's hand to see who he once was. Something about his presence is assuring and wise.

"Thank you, young lady." Ricardo smiles. He releases Scarlett and extends his hand for Wren to shake.

Wren looks down to his hand and places her hand in his. *A body cut open greets my mind. We blink. I adjust to seeing someone's heart, lungs and insides exposed. It smells clinical. Our gloved hands enter the red and fleshy cavity.*

"What is that look for?" Ricardo narrows his eyes.

Wren pulls her hand to her chest. The vision she just saw lingers behind her eyes. Her stomach flips. "You were once a surgeon," she hushes.

"A manbo." He lifts his chin. "You talk to Iwa?" Ricardo's eyes are now slits as he studies Wren.

Wren's chin draws into her neck. "Pardon?"

Ricardo's laugh floats on the air. "Old voodoo tales from Haiti, ignore what I say." He shakes his head and returns to Scarlett. "I'm guessing Fabienne isn't joining us?" A deep worry spreads across his face.

"Correct." Scarlett steps back to the table. "Here, sit, we'll tell you everything we know."

Ricardo listens and hangs on Scarlett and Wren's every word. He doesn't bat an eye at the retelling of what Wren saw, because he believes her truth.

Wren's shoulders ease. "Fabienne was a strong and fierce woman. She tried to escape and help and fight for the other girls that were kidnapped too," she speaks. "Dreaming about her family got her through. Memories of eating with you and your family are her favourite."

Ricardo stares down at his clasped hands resting on the table. "I was young when Fabienne disappeared, but I remembered she loved food, especially Ma's cooking. She also had a part-time job at a restaurant."

Scarlett reaches across the tables and squeezes her uncle's hand. She wants to ask about his twin sister but is not sure she's ready for what the truth could be, so she decides to be in this moment with him.

"I used to think maybe Fabienne fell and hit her head and got amnesia, that's why she never came home, because she forgot where she lived. So when the technology and website offered DNA services, I knew I had to sign up on the chance Fabienne was out there looking for who she was." Ricardo squeezes Scarlett back. "And here you are. We found you." His lips quiver and he wipes away the tears rolling down his cheek.

"My mother always knew she would see you again." Scarlett smiles.

Chapter 36

It's a sweet farewell between Scarlett and Ricardo as they promise to keep in touch. As she watches them say goodbye, Wren's mind wanders back to the comment Ricardo made about voodoo. *Did he think I'm some sort of witch? Maybe I am, maybe that's what some cultures call people who do what I can do. Witches, mediums, clairvoyants.* Those are only the English words she can think of to describe what she can do. *There really is so much I don't know about myself.* Wren clasps her hands together. She makes a mental note to start writing down questions.

"Wasn't that incredible?" Scarlett leans her head against the window in the cab. Her stare washes over buildings as they pass, and she wonders if Fabienne once walked this street. She envisions her long legs carrying her elegantly down the sidewalk like it was her runway.

"It certainly was," Wren confirms.

"Wren, can you touch me?" Scarlett thrusts her arm out to Wren sitting beside her.

Wren looks to the driver to gauge his reaction. His eyes are on the road, he probably didn't even hear what Scarlett said. Wren rolls up her sleeve and latches on to Scarlett's wrist. *The world is spinning. A kid is laughing. We're both laughing. Smells like sunshine. Our arms are stretched holding on to his. His little body is floating in the air as we swing him around. His goofy grin is missing one front tooth.* Ne t'arrête pas, *he says. I recognize the word* arrêt *as stop and assume he's saying don't stop.*

"What do you see?" Scarlett's eyes are wide.

"Fabienne's playing with Ricardo in the park. Holding his hands, spinning him around. You're both laughing." Wren opens her eyes and lets go.

"I hope I see that in my dreams."

Back at the hotel, Scarlett books their flight home.

"Are you going to tell your parents about Ricardo?" Wren asks as she folds her shirt and places it in her bag.

Scarlett looks up from her phone. "I already have. We are all family now. I straight-up told them I was a package deal with any of my blood relatives."

"How did they react when you told them that?" Wren finishes packing her belongings and zips her bag.

"How could they react after learning what they were a part of? They said they would support whatever I wanted to do." Scarlett flops down on the bed and turns to Wren. "What about you? Are you going to keep Dave in your life?"

A warmness spreads across Wren's face. She wants to learn more about Dave and begin a relationship, but doesn't want to get hurt. *It's always been easier to be alone.* "Probably," she mumbles, knowing she wants to see Dave again.

"Good. It'll be good for you." Scarlett shifts her gaze to the minimalist-style light fixture hanging from the ceiling. "Are you going to tell him what happened to you in police college? He can probably help lock up that dirty creep."

The warmth under Wren's skin turns hot and spreads throughout her body. Just as she thinks she can move on, her past is always there to burn her. "I'd rather forget about that entire ordeal and get on with my life."

"He probably abused other women, too," Scarlett adds.

"And he's probably dead now, reincarnated as a useless fly forced to live in horse shit." That's what Wren wants to believe.

Scarlett laughs through her nose. "Such a wild imagination. I love it." She rolls onto her side and faces Wren. She wants to push Wren to do the right thing and come forward about what that man did to her, but knows now is not the time, so she changes the subject. "What about that guy, your friend that you were once married to?"

Wren stands there and glares back at Scarlett. "Why this sudden interest in my life?"

"You helped me, and I want to return the favour." Scarlett traces the floral pattern on the bedspread with her finger.

"It wasn't a favour. You hired me and paid me for my services. You don't owe me anything," Wren's instincts respond. She's become accustomed to her life of anonymity. It's been too long since she's let anyone get close to her. Even AJ—she's let the distance grow between them. She slumps down on the bed, envisioning returning to her dark apartment. *The universe might be giving me another option.* "Sorry. I didn't mean to snap at you."

"Trust me, I get it. I don't take it personally. Plus, you have every right to be a little angry with me. I really put you through the ringer, eh?"

Wren stares into Scarlett's eyes. "You're finished with all the shit, right? The drinking, the drugs…"

"Yes, Mom," Scarlett answers in a mocking tone. "I'm done. I'll go to meetings, I'll call my sponsor, but you know." She lays still. "I feel like a darkness that was once living in me is gone. I want to live and feel all my emotions. For the first time in my adult life, I feel I am living."

Wren lays down on her back next to her. The idea of living causes her to pause and reflect. She no longer needs to hide up north. There is nothing to run from. "AJ is a wild card. Stays nowhere longer than a month. Works odd jobs for cash to get by. He's funny and kind and was a good friend until we drifted apart. Then I moved and cut myself off from the world as punishment after the Hilary debacle and travelling to Italy and not being able to find what I was looking for. My grandpa told me to leave people alone and never touch anyone, but I was too young and stupid to listen."

"Is he cute?"

"Who?" Wren twists her neck towards Scarlett. "AJ?"

"Yeah."

Wren laughs. "Extremely attractive and smooth. That's how he gets away with jumping from country to country. He can charm the pants off anyone."

"What do you want to do next, Birrdiee?" Scarlett asks through a grin as she draws out the name Birdie.

"Get to the airport and catch our flight." Wren ignores the name Scarlett calls her.

"Then what?"

"Go back home, I guess," Wren answers. Jetting off to the Caribbean has lost its luster. It's time to stop running.

"I have a crazy idea." Scarlett wiggles with excitement.

"Scarlett, every idea that comes out of your mouth is crazy."

"Let's apply to school. You can study criminology to become a detective, and I can study psychology." Scarlett smiles with all her teeth. "We both have tons of real-world experience."

Wren lets Scarlett's idea sink into her skin. Police work doesn't seem right anymore. When she dreamed about tracking down bad guys, she didn't think about all the bad guys she wouldn't be able to catch or families she could never help find closure or find justice. "Nah, I don't want to study criminology." She pulls her phone from her pocket and taps. Ricardo's words are still fresh and curious in her mind. *Manbo,* she types into the search. *A voodoo priestess. A sacred female leader in the voodoo tradition.* She reads to herself. *Iwa* is the next word she types. *A spirit that exists within the Haitian voodoo belief.* What she reads sends a wake of electric shivers through her veins, a connection to beliefs she's never thought of before.

"What are you looking at?" Scarlett asks.

"Maybe I should study folklore or mythology or something like that." A decision that sounds hasty when said out loud, but eases years of built-up tension in her neck and shoulders. Perhaps there is truth in what common people believe to be nothing more than fables. Wren clicks her screen off, rests her phone on her chest and looks at Scarlett. Wren's let so many years pass, only allowing herself to stew in what she never accomplished. She never let herself explore different paths her life could take or the options that exist in learning what she can do.

"Oh yeah! I love that for you." Scarlett's voice is full of sincere joy, and her eyes fill with hope.

Chapter 37

Dec. 10, 2023

I't's been almost two months since our visit to the box factory and stumbling upon Roman aka Eugene Duffy, and he's finally talking. They gave him a thirty-year sentence, so he'll rot in there for the rest of his life. He claims Duane never wanted to be in the business of murder; it was only about making money. They chose immigrants, and then after the women had served their purpose, Duane put them on a plane back to their mother country and told them if they returned or told anyone about what happened, Duane threatened the girls' lives and the lives of their families living in Canada. So there is a chance Sofia and Anya are alive somewhere in Russia and Bojana in Bosnia or whatever war-torn country they sent her back to. It's difficult to think about their journey in this life. What could they have possibly done in a past life to deserve what they endured in this life? I wish Dave could have released their names so the police could try to track them down, but Eugene continues to say he never knew their names and didn't care to. And when I think back to what Fabienne showed me, I don't recall him ever calling the girls by their names. His blackened eyes said everything. But thanks to Scarlett's DNA trail and Ricardo, Fabienne's name was made public and sadly the news story focused on Duane. I wouldn't be surprised if there are talks of a Netflix special, and if there is, no one has asked for Scarlett's permission yet. She *would never agree, but if she did, I can guess that the story would have to revolve around finding the missing girls, so maybe something positive may come of a little public interest. How we know their names would be the trickiest part to explain. I don't want to get dragged into this, but that's nothing but mindless ramblings right now. Fabienne's the one who deserves to be remembered. Eugene confirmed she died giving birth, and they cremated her body, dumping her remains in Lake Ontario. The truth offered little peace to Ricardo and Scarlett, but I guess there is some sense of closure in knowing what happened instead of wondering if her bones were scattered in a field somewhere, or worse, a garbage dump. Scarlett, with Ricardo's help, is in the process of setting up a foundation in Fabienne's name to help women and girls who are victims of human trafficking. Scarlett's determination is like a freight train traveling full speed, nothing is going to stop it. Her and I are even taking university prep courses every Wednesday night. It was too late for us to apply for the winter semester, however we're applying to start in the summer. It's been a pain tracking down my high school transcripts, but at least that's done. U of T offers both programs Scarlett and I are interested in, so that is where we're applying. I moved out of my apartment and live with Scarlett in the city now. I never thought I would enjoy living in a big city, but there's more anonymity in being one person out of three million than being a stranger in a town of twenty thousand.*

"Wren, Dave's here," Scarlett shouts from the living room.

Wren closes her journal and lifts her duvet to tuck it

between her mattress and box spring. "Coming." She strides out of her room and down the hall, a lightness in her step that makes her almost float.

"You ready for dinner, kiddo?" Dave asks from the front door.

"Yep." Wren grabs her jacket from the closet. "I would have come down and met you at the car."

Dave waves off the comment. "Oh, it's fine. I wanted to come up and say hi to Scarlett." His eyebrows bounce. "And to share some good news."

Scarlett and Wren both turn to Dave and hold their breath.

"Eugene seems to recall one of the girls being named Bojana." Dave smirks. "With the timeline, we'll find her in the missing persons and show him her photo to confirm."

"Well, Wren can confirm to you right now; she confirmed it two months ago," Scarlett blurts.

Dave's lips form a hard line. "Scarlett, you understand how this must work."

Wren witnesses Dave's stern authoritative demeanour.

Scarlett slouches. "I know, it's just frustrating, you know."

"I understand." The creases of Dave's mouth twist up. "I'll let you know if we can track down Bojana's family. There is a chance someone's contact information will be on file."

"It's better than nothing." Wren slips into her black leather boots.

"Are you sure you don't want to join us for dinner, Scarlett?" Dave asks.

"Nah, you guys have fun. I have some paperwork I want to finish for the foundation." Scarlett corrects her posture.

"I'll tell Michelle and Derek that you'll join us next time."

"You should have brought them up to say hi," Scarlett says.

Dave shakes his head. "I don't talk about work stuff in front of them."

"Right, well, next time for sure," Scarlett adds, and waves.

Wren eyes her dad's bare hand. "Shall we?" She reaches out and wraps her fingers around his. *Just for a second*, she tells herself. Any reserve or hesitation she once had is now gone. *How am I going to learn if I don't experiment?* She clears her mind and focuses on the older women knitting and cleaning she's caught glimpses of before. Wren wants to learn to quiet the noise and focus on seeing one past life at a time in Dave. *Our hands are wrinkled and she's singing a tune that's faintly familiar, something about lavender blue. The cackle of the fire pops close by. A pain sparks in our knee and travels to our back. We limp to the fire, reach into the bucket, and throw a severed hand into the fire.*

Wren releases Dave's fingers. Her jaw slacks and mouth gapes.

Dave closes the apartment door and flashes a grin at Wren. "What did you see this time?"

Acknowledgements

This book would not exist without the guidance and advice from David Hamilton and members of The Ottawa Writing Workshops and David Stymeist and my classmates in the fourth year Creative Writing Workshop at Carleton University. Thank you for sharing your comments and always pushing me to improve my stories and craft. Many thanks to the superb team at Ace of Swords Publishing for also wanting to make this story the best that it could be. And my family, Andrew my husband for always lending an ear when I need to ramble on about characters and plots to work things out, my Dad for always being my first beta reader and offering honest feedback, my Mom for always being my number one cheerleader, and all my family and friends that encourage me to write and continue to take the time to read my work and always take an interest in my stories—thank you and I love you all.

Erin Forget

The Unsung Song of a Wren is Erin Forget's debut novel. She lives in Carlsbad Springs, Ontario with her husband and free-range dachshunds.

www.erinforget.ca